PRAISE FOR DAVID THOMAS MOORE

"These stories revel in both the conventions and the inventiveness of Shakespearean drama, reminding us how entertaining and subversive these plays were and can still be. Excellent stuff."
SFX Magazine on *Monstrous Little Voices*

"Moore, one of the most exciting editors in the field today, has nurtured a line-up of interesting and evocative talent for an extremely entertaining ride."
Starburst on *Not So Stories*

"A fascinating collection that talks back—not just speaks, but explicitly *talks back*—to Bram Stoker's classic 1897 novel. Moore and his stable of writers respond not just to the fictional figure and his historical counterpart, but to the cultural conversations around him as well."
Future Fire on *Dracula: Rise of the Beast*

"The stories are so beautiful and there is so much to them. I think that you could have amazing discussions about them."
Huntress of Diverse Books on *Not So Stories*

"*Not So Stories* feels as much like a collaboration
as it does a collection. These authors worked
together, drew upon each other for inspiration. They have
built something solid, something whole. It's a beautiful
idea which has taught me something new, several things
new, and raised the bar for what is possible in a science
fictional (and fantastical) anthology."
Imaginaries on *Not So Stories*

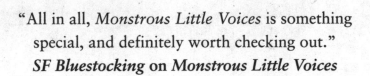

"All in all, *Monstrous Little Voices* is something
special, and definitely worth checking out."
SF Bluestocking on *Monstrous Little Voices*

"*As* a whole, an easy one to recommend.
Even if you aren't a Shakespeare fan, you'll enjoy the
stories in this collection, but fans of the Bard will
find this to be a rich feast."
Fantasy Literature on *Monstrous Little Voices*

"A good anthology should be able to surprise the
reader around a central theme, and with credit to
David Thomas Moore's editing we have five unique
stories adding to a legend where many of us thought
we'd seen everything."
Run Along the Shelves on *Dracula: Rise of the Beast*

EDITED BY
DAVID THOMAS MOORE

CREATURES

THE LEGACY OF
FRANKENSTEIN

WITH STORIES BY

**EMMA NEWMAN, PAUL MELOY, TADE THOMPSON,
ROSE BIGGIN & KAARON WARREN**

ABADDON
BOOKS

An Abaddon Books™ Publication
www.abaddonbooks.com
abaddon@rebellion.co.uk

First published in 2018 by Abaddon Books™,
Rebellion Publishing Limited,
Riverside House, Osney Mead, Oxford, OX2 0ES, UK.

10 9 8 7 6 5 4 3 2 1

Creative Director and CEO: Jason Kingsley
Chief Technical Officer: Chris Kingsley
Head of Books and Comics Publishing: Ben Smith
Editors: David Thomas Moore,
Michael Rowley and Kate Coe
Design: Sam Gretton, Oz Osborne and Maz Smith
Marketing and PR: Remy Njambi

Cover Art by Sam Gretton.

ISBN: 978-1-78108-611-7

Printed in Denmark

CONTENTS

INTRODUCTION
DAVID THOMAS MOORE

THE FIRST OF January, 1818—two hundred years ago—saw the release of one of the most important and influential works in the history of science fiction (described by Brian Aldiss, with a degree of justification, as the *first* modern science fiction book): Mary Wollstonecraft Shelley's *Frankenstein, or, The Modern Prometheus*.

Famously inspired by a challenge to produce a ghost story, *Frankenstein* nonetheless obeyed all the rules for what we consider science fiction today: grounded in the scientific discoveries of its time, it extends that work in hypothetical-yet-believable new directions, and asks what impacts such innovation would have on the people whose lives it touched. The story is driven by the will to change: the scientist seems at first more a Daedalus than a Prometheus, robbed of life and family by his hubris; but as the thief of fire he fits too (although I'm aware Shelley almost certainly intended the Roman Prometheus, who made man from clay). More than a mere homily on the dangers of science, the story is a battle-cry, a declaration of intent. Cheating death is humanity's birthright, to be snatched at the first opportunity, and Frankenstein's death the bitter retribution of a jealous God.

It's impossible to overstate *Frankenstein*'s impact on the genre. From its endless adaptations, retellings and sequels, to the centuries of debate about its themes, to successive new generations of writers adopting those themes, the spectres of Shelley's manic, inspired medical student and his tragic, soulful creation haunt every corner of our world. Their voices echo in the blandly murderous tones of Arthur C. Clarke's HAL-9000; they glitter in Roy Batty's eyes in *Bladerunner* as he contemplates his mortality; Asimov even credited his Three (eventually Four) Laws of Robotics to a fear of technology he called the "Frankenstein complex." We owe so many of the stories we tell today to that extraordinary young woman and the dream that drove her.

In the book you hold now, the scientist's discovery likewise survives the ages, brought to light by men and women searching for meaning; Prometheus returns to rob the gods again and again. From the bloodstained anatomists of Tade Thompson's "Kaseem's Way" to the bohemians of Rose Biggin's "The New Woman"; from the engineers of Paul Meloy's "Reculver" to the surgeons of Emma Newman's "Made Monstrous" and the smiling cult leader of Kaaron Warren's "Love Thee Better," Shelley's call is taken up through the years. My brilliant writers bring these times to life in furious colour: we smell the bile and rot of Tade's London and are dazzled by the lights and beauty of Rose's; our feet crunch the gravel on Paul's grey Kentish coast, and our eyes smart in the cigarette smoke of Emma's scruffy, laddish Lancashire police building. God knows Kaaron's idle, delirious sun-drenched cruise could last a week or a thousand years. And Shelley lurks in all these times, her mission timeless, her battle-cry ringing in our ears.

The first creature—Adam, he'll always be to me, though he takes up and discards names like clothes—survives the ages, too, although in some stories he's harder to find than others. Each of these stories is a tragedy, in their way, with death and sorrow attendant on every hero's (or anti-hero's, or flawed hero's, or non-hero's) endeavours, each destroyed by that jealous God; but Adam's story is a slow tragedy, too, tracking a gradual decline through the tales, well past the point where he is able to understand it. It lends the whole a melancholy that underscores the frenzied hunt for knowledge.

And both the hunt and the melancholy spring from the same source, of course, for every would-be Frankenstein is struggling, at last, with the meaninglessness of human existence, and with the isolation that brings. Every one of them is isolated: by the colour of their skin; by their sexuality; by disability and the awkwardness of puberty; by jealousy; by self-hatred. The drive to create is an externalisation of the need for human contact, for humanity itself.

In turn, of course, the creatures are also ciphers; how could they not be? The scientist's act of creation mirrors the author's own, and so the story will always have a little of the writer's soul in it. Creation, defiance, isolation and destruction are themes that can run the gamut of human experience. And so in Tade's story they serve to criticise Britain's colonial heritage, while in Rose's (herself an actor, dancer and playwright) they raise questions of art and beauty. Paul's story invokes nostalgia and innocence lost, while Emma's rages against sexism and injustice; and Kaaron's addresses the detachment of modern life, where we become so lost in the world that we are estranged from our own bodies.

Creatures, scientists, writers, all bound together by the act of creation. All monsters and all victims alike, telling their stories that we've stitched together into something whole; something— we hope—greater than the sum of its parts.

Here's our creature. We hope you like it.

David Thomas Moore
June 2018

KASEEM'S WAY

KASEEM'S WAY
TADE THOMPSON

Waterloo, London
1849

GULL FINDS KASEEM Greenshank in Lower Marsh Street while taking the air in Lambeth. The street market is lively with commerce, and the understated desperation of existence, and filth. Gull remembers when it was all marshland, before it was reclaimed, and before the Church sold the land piecemeal. The ground is still muddy, and muckrakers comb through it to see what they can find.

Gull is able to filter out the yelling and the advertising. Most would wrinkle their nose at the waste matter and dead animals, but not Gull. He does not fear that no gentleman should be found in the area, either. He comes from nothing, and nothing frightens him.

At first he thinks the child is injured, covered in so much blood, but then he considers where he is: open air market, near the butcher's stalls. Gull's next thought is that the boy is feeble-minded, and playing with entrails. He is already wondering whether to make the boy a special patient when he looks closer at what he is doing. He appears to be separating small from large intestine and measuring each with a green stick. It is a cold evening, yet the boy is wearing thin linen, no hat, short sleeves. There is a tattoo on his forearm, an ideogram unknown to Gull.

"Don't talk to 'im, guvnor; he's simple, he is," says a gruff voice from behind. Gull does not deign to either respond or look.

He pokes the child's shoulder with his cane.

The boy turns slowly. Gull notices for the first time that under all the blood and mud, the boy is dark-skinned. He is skinny, which makes his eyes seem larger than they are, and he stares.

"What are you measuring?" asks Gull.

The boy pauses, seeming to assay Gull's intent. Then he turns back to the entrails and points. "These bags of fat—"

"*Appendices epiploicae.*"

"Say the words again."

Gull does, and the boy repeats them a number of times.

"They seem to start and stop. I want to know if they start and stop at the same distance in each animal."

"Are they in every animal?"

"No. Cats, dogs, rabbits, don't have them."

"How do you know?"

"I checked."

"You checked?"

"I checked... sir?"

Gull speaks with the child about entrails some more, then enquires after his parents. The boy is called Kaz by everybody, but insists that his name is Kaseem. Gull cannot decide if he is Moorish or a half-breed of some kind. Gull notes a mild case of rickets, poor teeth, lines on the boy's fingernails, the general concavity of his belly.

"Are you hungry, Kaseem?"

This finally distracts the child from his labours. "Yes, sir."

KASEEM HAS NEVER been inside a horse carriage before. He has never had a meal that wasn't scraps and he has never bathed indoors. The clothes are still cast-offs. He does not know when he falls asleep, and the sun is in the sky when he wakes.

There are shelves full of books, galleries full of jars and paintings. The jars contain preserved organs and the paintings are of opened bodies. Human bodies.

"Do these frighten you?" Gull had come up behind him. The silence of the man's gait is unnerving.

Kaseem shakes his head.

"Splendid. First we feed you and treat your nutritional deficiencies. *Mens sana in corpore sano*, after all. Then we will teach you."

"Teach me what, sir?"

"The things that you want to know, child. The journey you started in the gutter."

KASEEM IS STANDING in a mess of blood and entrails of a horse only six hours dead. He has a kitchen knife in his right hand and has cut a cruciate cavity in the abdomen of the horse. His face is bland, without expression, and he appears intent on his task. He is fifteen.

A cough makes him turn around.

"Care to explain yourself, Kaseem?" says Gull.

"The horse died, sir. It was sick. I wanted to see its heart."

Gull shakes his head. "Well, this is altogether too messy. I need to find you somewhere to work where you won't frighten the help. Or me, for that matter."

Newgate Prison, London
13th June 1861

THE MEN DO not speak to Kaseem as they drop the body on the slab. They do not even look at him as they leave the room. Kaseem is already gowned and seated in a corner facing the door.

This dead room is probably the best in the Empire, but nobody knows about it. It has a domed, transparent ceiling to catch the sunlight, and Radha's drawings on the wall. Radha is late; by the time he comes in, Kaseem has already prepped the body. They do not greet each other. This is not unusual. Radha sets up his inks and paper, then puts on a gown to assist Kaseem. The head is engorged and black, and the eyes bulge.

"They got the drop wrong again?" says Radha. It is not really a question. Hanging is said to be a swift death, and this is true if done right. Sometimes it is not, and the prisoner strangulates, a slow, painful death in which there is no dignity at all.

Kaseem grunts. "Shall we move along? We're running out of daylight."

They work on the dissection for two hours before they hear footfalls leading up to and stopping outside the door of the dead room. The two stop and look at each other. Nobody ever visits them. Keys jangle in the lock and Gull is standing there with a leather valise.

"Sir," says Kaseem. "We were not expecting you."

"Neither was I expecting to be here. I have to be at Guy's Hospital within the hour, so I fear I must be briefer than I would like."

"Of course. What brings you here?" asks Kaseem.

"Henry Gray is dead."

"Oh."

"Yes, smallpox. The entire medical world is in an uproar. One so young and full of promise. He was thirty-four years old."

"It is sad indeed, but does that not help our work here?" asks Kaseem.

"Think on it, dear boy."

Henry Gray had written *Anatomy Descriptive and Surgical* in 1858, a book which seemed to replace all previous anatomy texts amongst medical students. Kaseem did not find Gray all that original, and Gull had set up this room in Newgate Prison for a specific project: Kaseem was to write his own anatomy text. Radha was a painter who owed Gull a debt of gratitude, and acted as illustrator for the project. Gray went from strength to strength, improving his book by elimination of errors in the American edition of 1859. Kaseem was his shadow. Gull had nurtured his natural aptitude for anatomy and taught him privately, taking him to Guy's Hospital out of hours, making texts available to him, quizzing him. Kaseem has all the medical knowledge that any doctor can have, but is not enrolled in any medical school. He considers the idea a waste of his time, at any rate: he is satisfied with the search for knowledge. He has no wish to cure maladies, to apprentice to an apothecary or to cut lumps out of people. Nor does he have patience for academic empire-building or money.

"We can still write a better book," says Kaseem.

"You are naïve. He has died young. He has attained immortality. Humans are sentimental. There will never be a better anatomy book than Gray's. There may be more intelligent texts, clearer text, etc. but this will be the standard in perpetuity. Against this will others be measured, and found wanting. No, this venture is dead."

I can write a better book than Gray's. But Kaseem does not say this, hearing the finality in Gull's voice. He has made up his mind and nothing Kaseem brings up will change it. He knows this from experience.

"Have you been outside? You look... unhealthy."

"I've been busy, sir."

"Child, you need to be alive to be busy." Gull hands the valise to Kaseem.

"What's this?"

"This is not an anatomy pursuit. This is a hunt for immortality."

Kaseem opens it; there are papers with writing in different scripts. "Another book?"

"No." Gull puts on his hat. "Actual immortality. Be careful with those. I acquired them at great expense."

THE FOG IS thick tonight, and I imagine you would have liked it.

I am abroad in London at night. The longest time I have roamed these streets was the 1813 fog. I got into the habit of travelling without concealment. I saw the Prince Regent, and he saw me. One of his outriders, on seeing me, fell into a ditch. This night it is not quite as *blacke as Acheron*, but it is sufficient to coat myself in. Odd for there to be such fog in a summer month, but I do not ponder it overlong.

There is blood on my hands: of metaphor, not haemoglobin.

Of course, you do not know about haemoglobin. I know so much more than you now, although the thought does not fill me with joy. Everything I know now, I wish you had known. All the knowledge in the future of mankind, I wish had been in your mind. This does not mean I hold any benevolent feelings towards you. I do not. My thoughts on the matter are entirely selfish. Had you known more I would have *been* more.

Walking in the fog at night is like swimming. The tendrils eddy and part when someone approaches, and, when past and walking away, close around the figure like soil covering a casket. You know about caskets, don't you? From the body snatchers who provided you with raw materials for me, to your departed Elizabeth, you and the grave are as brothers.

I come to a horse drawn wagon which has broken down from what looks like axle problems. It has gaudy lettering on the side, a freakshow. The occupants sit on the side of the road as the driver and one other person work to fix the wheel. As such things go, it is a piss-poor collection. There are no grotesques of note. They have, in captivity, an African, a pygmy, dressed in gaudy apparel for maximum fearsomeness. I have been to Africa, to the interior, to far reaches of the Sahara, to Egypt and Morocco, to the Congo basin. This is a poor example. There is a man on a cushion with vestigial arms and legs. A woman stares out of the darkness, face criss-crossed with so many scars; it looks like a net has been placed over her face, a veil of violence. In my experience, this is the work of a lover. Nobody hates like the one who loves. Her eyes do not leave me, and I must wonder if she feels kinship because of my own scars, which she cannot possibly see. They have a demoniac, caged, naked, long tangled hair stringing from some of the bars. He perhaps belongs in Bedlam. There is a 'Hindoo Goddess' which seems to my eye a number of fused twins. The girl has four legs and two arms that I can see.

"Move along, sir, unless you wish to pay for a private viewing." The barker is not quite as tall as I, but moves like he earned his keep with his fists in a former life.

I tip my hat and keep going.

I circle back and murder him by strangulation. He is not as good at fisticuffs as he thinks.

A few nights later, I find the field where they display, and I pay the fee. The scarred lady recognises me and after the tumult of the show I contrive to visit her.

"I saw you the other night," she says. "I saw you kill Stephen. Why?" There was no judgement in her voice.

"*A time to kill, and a time to heal*. It was a time to kill."

"That is no explanation, sir."

They call her Scar-Lett, the Scarred Letter of Blood. She carries a blade for this reason, American, learned her skill from a wild Plains Indian of the Tejas tribe. She looks at the back-story with derision. "I have never met a Plains Indian, and 'Tejas' is the name the Spanish call a particularly friendly tribe. I've never cut a human being, and my hair is brown."

A few nights later she says, "Excuse me, sir, but you do not sound like an Englishman."

"I was born in Ingolstadt, though my father was Genevese."

"And your mother?" she asks.

I do not answer.

KASEEM DOES NOT speak for forty hours. He knows that Radha comes and goes and perhaps speaks, but he registers these in the abstract. Screams emanate from the rest of the prison, but this is the usual background noise, subtracted from relevance automatically.

He has divided the information into letters, journal entries or reports, and process data.

He reads through all of it a third time, with his own order imposed. There are letters to a Mrs Saville from her brother, Robert Walton, from the 1700s. Then there are the Kirwin Papers, Kirwin being an Irish judge or magistrate who had investigated goings-on in Orkney Islands, also in the 1700s. The Saville letters, the Kirwin Papers, all involve one man, who generated the journal entries, reports and data.

Gull cannot be serious.

Radha presents him with a drawing of himself, bent over in study.

"My nose is not that big," says Kaseem.

"It is so. What would the doctor sahib have us do?"

Kaseem rubs his eyes, which seem coated with grit. He stops when he realises there is dust and ink on his fingers. "I think he wants us to try and reanimate a man."

"What?"

"Here's what I think happened, or what these documents would have me believe: that Walton was on a mad quest to reach the North Pole. Who even knows if that is possible? Walton's ship gets encased in ice, and they pick up a gentleman whose name has been scrubbed from the records. This man is sick—dying, in fact. Before expiring, the man claims to have brought to life a man composed of different body parts."

"So it's a fairy tale," says Radha.

"Well... no. The Kirwin Papers are trial documents. A murder trial for which the accused was acquitted, though Judge Kirwin found the claims of the man so outlandish that he sent an investigator from Dublin to Orkney Islands to satisfy himself of their veracity. That is where the journals were found. In those pages I found some evidence of scientific thinking. The unnamed man is, or was, clearly a physician, or at least anatomist of some skill."

"What happened to the man he supposedly reanimated?"

"That's where it gets murky. He writes as if this is his *second* attempt at reanimation, as if his first creation was already abroad. There is no indication as to what happened to the first. Or the second."

"Do you see anything in the technique—"

"It might as well be alchemy, or witchcraft. Or he has hidden his techniques. There is nothing of use here." Kaseem casts the papers away, and they flutter down like autumn leaves.

"But the doctor sahib thinks there is."

"Yes. Maybe. Is he testing me?"

Radha picks at the papers. "Perhaps what is important is to look at all this and systematically think of why it would not work."

"That's obvious."

"Is it?"

"Radha, I am not emotionally disposed enough or awake enough to cope with your games today."

"I'm serious. Why would reanimation not work?"

Kaseem sighs, then stands up and strides to the slab, to the body they both failed to work on. "This is your basic mammal, your *homo sapiens*. Let's say we cut this man up. Putting him back together superficially is no problem, and has been done for centuries. The muscles, the skin, these are not problematic. Going deeper, the problems compound. How do you get synovial fluid to lubricate the joints? How do you return the internal organs, the viscera, to some semblance of order, working as you would be with offal and waste? How do you remove all the coagulated blood from the vessels and replace it with fresh blood? Which brings me to the most important questions of all." He thumps on the left side of the chest, the right, and then the head. "Heart. Lungs. Brain. How do you get them to function again after death?"

Radha takes bellows from one of the hooks and inserts the nozzle into the mouth of the cadaver. He pumps, the chest rises and falls. "Have you heard of the Society for the Recovery of Persons Apparently Drowned?"

"None of those cases would have been stitched together from disparate sources."

"But people are indeed reanimated."

"Perhaps. I have not studied the reports."

"I have read of decapitated bodies retaining life for minutes after execution, during the French Revolution. Even the heads—"

"Residual electricity, nothing more."

"But what if we could maintain that electricity, or restart it?"

"Restart the brain, lungs and heart? Again, how?" He says this with less conviction, though, because an idea, a fragment of an idea—some... *conceit*—begins in Kaseem's brain, crystallising around the grit of Radha's suggestion.

You NEVER SAW the Serpentine. It coils in Hyde Park, sometimes called the Serpentine River by Londoners, when in fact it is a lake.

I swim from the western extremity all along its curve, tasting the water from the Thames as I go. Soon, I cross the Serpentine

Bridge and the same lake becomes The Long Water, and the park transmutes into Kensington Gardens. The lake curves North West and I tread water for a time. The water is cold, but we both know I have endured much worse. I spin around and swim back, passing a Humane Society boatman on the north shore. He waves from the distance, probably trying to reassure himself that I am not one of those wretches attempting suicide. Many come to the Serpentine to meet their maker, mostly by drowning, but also hanging and pistol shot to the head. The last time I saw you I was strongly contemplating suicide. I would have been dramatic, too. Self-immolation. Almost Biblical, would you not say?

I return to my clothes, wearing sword and dagger, quaint though it is. Habit is hard to break, and I have lived longer than most humans. I find it difficult to move along with their fashions. That said, I also have a revolver, a Colt. I dry my wet hair as much as possible, then coil it into my top hat. A man and a woman copulate in the shadows close by, her entreaties loud and insincere. I give a coin to the street child I asked to watch my belongings and I head for Marble Arch. Fancy; I still know it as the Tyburn Gallows and I hear the cracking necks of the condemned. I smell the shit from their lost sphincters still. The bodies of the condemned would have been yours if you had studied in London.

I haunt St George's Hospital. I watch the doctors of renown and the promising students. Not only have I shrugged off suicide as a goal, I have embraced life and health. As your creator would have it, I am to be denied that which I now seek.

What is your name?

Adam.

Why do you bind your belly with bandages?

There are things I did not say about my swims, and omissions about my suicide impulse. When I swim there are fish and other critters in my wake. They eat the nibblets of my flesh that break away into the water. Some of the braver swimmers latch on to my defect. Back then, when I thought and said I would commit suicide, I *did* build a pyre for myself. I even set it alight. I stepped into the blaze, and though it was agony, I thought it would be a brief dolorous flash, then oblivion. While my flesh peeled back, I started to think, which is the curse of this brain you gave me. It would not stop. It went over the reasons for me to die, and those reasons did not make enough sense. I stepped out of the fire with severe burns, but they healed, mostly, except for the deepest one on my trunk, which has not healed for decades, and which I must bandage assiduously. Recently, I have found it worsening, extending. It exudes pus and a powerful stench, which I must neutralise with copious amounts of perfume. It makes me seek out physicians, surgeons and apothecaries; so far, in vain.

I think I am dying. Whatever you did to breathe life into me is finally failing.

I refuse. I do not accept mortality, not with this cursed flesh. That would be an insult too far.

I refuse.

THEY NEED A dog. A live one, to start with.

This is one of the few times Kaseem leaves Newgate, and walking these distances feels strange to him. Too many people on the streets, staring at the Hindoo and the half-breed. This is prime dissecting season and Kaseem's mood is impatience bordering on anger.

"This is madness," he says.

Radha is searching the street, close to ground level. Stray dogs are not hard to find. He looks at his own two hands, held up as if in supplication. "We have no lure, no bait with which to attract this landfish."

A mangy specimen drifts by and they both whistle, cluck, and tut in vain.

"Extend the hand of friendship," says Radha.

"You extend your hand. Such extension is like to receive a bite and sharp reproof from that canine."

"What then?"

There are packs of filthy children dragging here and there, shiftless. Kaseem digs into his pockets and counts his coins. "Bait, you say?"

THE SCREWS ARE not happy to see them bringing two dogs in, but Gull's reputation—or his money—are enough to keep any objections at bay. Back in the dead room, the dogs begin to bark, creating such a racket that it disturbs Kaseem's thinking. He also detects a reticence in Radha, a slight sluggishness in carrying out tasks.

"Are you well?" he asks in irritation.

"I am not convinced this is the best course of action."

"You want us to work on humans first?"

"I do not want to kill, or cut up something that is first alive."

Kaseem blinks and puts down the test tube he is holding. "We... you and I... have cut up uncountable cadavers in this very room. Now you balk at a dumb beast?"

"That is the point, Kaz. Cadavers. They are as meat to me if they are already dead. These creatures yet live. I do not care to be the agent of their demise."

"For goodness' sake, why? They will be consumed by mange or hunger or run over by a hansom in a few days' time, regardless of what we do."

"Why are you so thirsty for animal blood?"

"I once survived on dog meat for a week in Lambeth Marsh. Pickiness is a consequence of having a choice. I mean them no harm, but I think humans come before dogs."

"If this venture were about survival as it was in your unfortunate childhood, I would not argue, but this is an undertaking of vanity, either yours or that of the doctor sahib."

Kaseem strides to the door and opens it. "Go. Sketch some of the guards. Or the prisoners. I care not which."

With one person the procedures are messy, but possible. He uses chloroform to put them asleep and takes baselines of the dogs' pulse and respiratory rates. He has no reference figures to check against, but figures what is normal for them is useful enough for his purposes. He kills them by strangulation, waits for five minutes after the vital signs cease, then attempts to revive them by steadily increasing doses of electric current. They both die. Both experience muscle contractions when current is applied, even hours after death. One of them, the younger, rouses after three shocks and opens his eyes. He seems to muster some hostility towards Kaseem, but closes the eyes and stops breathing after about three minutes. No further shocks bring the animal back to spontaneous breathing or restart the heart.

Kaseem performs a careful autopsy on both dogs, taking copious and unnecessary notes. Really, he spends the time thinking, trying to see how this information can help him.

He gets a message to Gull and does a literature search. There was Catherine Greenhill who, in 1774, fell from a height and apparently died. One Mr Squires of the Humane Society applied electricity to various parts of the girl's body. When the electrodes were applied to her chest, her pulse returned, and she lived after that. In 1775 Peter Abildgaard killed and brought back to life several hens, apparently to full function. He seemed particularly happy that one of the hens went on to lay eggs, although he does not say if any hatched to produce a normal chicken. His records are specific: electricity to the head killed the hens, to the chest restored them. Kaseem reads about Luigi Galvani, about Charles Kite's medal in 1788.

Gull sends back a note by messenger.

Look into Dr Golding Bird, of my hospital here at St Thomas. He is the sole person working with biological applications of electricity. Read his 1854 Lectures on Electricity and Galvanism.

Kaseem's subsequent experiments go much better. He applies electrodes to the chest and his revival rate rises dramatically.

"I think we should try reviving a human," he says to Radha.

"You see the problem therein? Of reviving a hanged man?"

"Enlighten me."

"How do you plan to re-attach the spinal cord?"

I AM AS at peace in hospitals as I am in the night or the fog. I therefore enter St George's without trepidation or discomfort of the soul.

There are so many deformed people that nobody notices me except for my height. This place is full of London's grotesques, and I am barely looked at. My scars are not of consequence. I move around freely, with confidence, as if I am going somewhere. I look for the dead room, there to seek what I have always sought: a surgeon, a pathologist with skill that equals your own. I thought I had found one and over the last year he examined me, examined your handiwork. I do not think he fully believed my tale, but he did believe the evidence before his eyes, and that of my heart. The heart does not lie. The dissecting room is full of students and demonstrators. There is a chalkboard with drawings on it. Light comes in from the domed ceiling, but it is fading as the day dies. I wait. The students file out and I know from months of watching them that they will find the nearest public house and drink themselves insensate, singing their songs.

> *My knowledge of medicine's rusty*
> *My knowledge of surgery's nil*
> *So I'm watching the simplest dressing*
> *And how to prescribe a pill.*

The demonstrator sees me lurking and comes over in his gown.

"May I help you, sir?" His voice is mellifluous, like he sings opera in his spare time, or he is a woman in disguise.

"I am looking for Carter."

"I'm sorry?"

"Henry Vandyke Carter. The anatomist."

The man looks blank. From under my coat I bring out my well-thumbed copy of *Anatomy, Descriptive and Surgical*. I see his eyes go wide when he twigs my gun and sword, but I have no time to reassure him. I open the title page.

"Look. *THE DRAWINGS By H.V. CARTER, M.D., LATE DEMONSTRATOR OF ANATOMY AT ST. GEORGE'S HOSPITAL.*"

"Oh, *that* Carter. He is dead."

"He is not. I have looked at all the announcements. Henry Gray is dead, but Henry Carter yet lives. Where is he?"

"I... wait a minute." He leans into the room where one of his acolytes helps clean up. "Where's Carter?"

A muffled answer comes from within.

The demonstrator turns back to me. "He's in India."

It turns out the only other person whose skill I trust has been offered a professorship in India and is gone. He works still. He has discovered a new kind of tumour, a mycetoma, from looking at what the Hindoos call Madura Foot. I think about India. I have been there. Hot. The behaviour of the English is disgraceful there. I ran into—and ran through—many East Indiamen in Calcutta. I became addicted to opium there, but also freed myself of its infernal grasp. A part of me misses India, but I went there in my prime. This body you built is betraying me at present. The fermentation under my skin will escalate under the fevered sun of Bengal.

I will not follow Carter there. I must find my destiny here.

I wait until it is fully dark, then I leave the hospital. I soon come across a black fiddler, blind, imbecilic, and from his singing accent, American. American Negroes have been in London in numbers since the Battle of Yorktown, Dunmore's Loyalists. I give him some coin. "Shut up, you slangwhangers!" the fiddler says to voices brought on by cheap alcohol. He stabs the air with his fiddle.

I curse you yet again. In the cold of the Arctic I had thought my ire for you spent. I was mistaken.

EVERY TIME KASEEM tries to revive a dog after they severed the spinal cord, it dies. Under chloroform he slices the cord, then tries to reattach it by stitching the neuromysium, ensuring that the blood supply is not lost, but it always breaks down. In his irritation, he blames Radha for not sticking around long enough to assist him. He will not assist Kaseem if it involves killing animals. They are running out of dogs. The street children are bringing fewer dogs and asking for higher amounts as recompense. This cannot continue.

Meanwhile, the human cadavers are piling up. They cannot afford to undertake two projects at the same time. Kaseem had asked the warders to stop bringing every single execution to them for the time being, but they are unruly and thick, thought processes moving through brains of treacle. And they have always been dubious about both Kaseem and Radha, mistrusting the reflected power they have from Gull or Gull's money, and the inherent foreignness of the pair. These are not sophisticated men, but old men; not in age, but in manner, each one a masterpiece of preservation, orthostats holding up the walls of Newgate, and all prisons from time immemorial.

Kaseem doodles on Radha's paper. Pulleys. Gallows. Broadly, there are two types of death by hanging: suspension and dropping. In suspension the victim is attached to a crane or pulley and lifted up by the neck until dead. The short drop method does not directly kill you, but the body weight and struggling tightens the noose and eventually the person dies of strangulation. Standard drop is a fall of about six feet, sometimes leading to a snapped neck, sometimes not. At times, the drop could be so long as to result in decapitation. Long drop involves measurement of weight, a trap door and a longer distance that guarantees a broken neck. Maybe.

At Newgate they use the long drop, which always severs the cord. Executions are not the only source of bodies for Kaseem's work. Sometimes the natural death of prisoners provides unclaimed cadavers. Struck with inspiration, Kaseem leaves the dead room and seeks out some of the guards.

"When one of the prisoners dies," he says, breathless. "Could you bring them to me immediately? Don't wait till morning, just bring him or her."

"I'll tell the lads. What's it worth?"

Despite the benefactor's power, Kaseem still has to apply bribes as social lubricant. Otherwise they spit in the food, bring cold tea, or wait until the body is rotting before bringing it to them. He hands the man a few coins.

It is a week before the first dead prison arrives. It is still warm and bleeding from the nose. A large haematoma marks where blunt force snatched quickness away from the prisoner. Abundant scar tissue from previous trauma, common, unremarkable in Newgate. No pulse, no breathing. Radha selects a pair of bellows from the variously sized ones they now have and sticks it in the man's mouth. The chest begins to rise and fall. Kaseem examines the neck, finds the vertebrae intact, nods. He applies electrodes to the chest and switches on current.

At first Kaseem feels he is under attack by Lilliputians with spears; then he realises he is receiving an electric shock, even as he and Radha are flung clear. He hits the wall and is knocked cold for a short time. Radha wakes him by pouring water in his face. He holds rubber gloves out to Kaseem. They are both bleeding and shaky, however, and that ends the work for the day. Radha goes home and Kaseem makes a bed in the dead room.

"Kaz, do you want to come and have supper with my family?" asks Radha.

"Thank you for offering, but I have to—"

"No. No, you don't." He leaves all the same.

Kaseem dresses his cuts, rolls himself in linen and tries to sleep, feeling the cold seep into him from the floor. Gull's house is open to him, but he'd rather get a head start on the day's work for tomorrow. As he falls asleep he thinks on Radha, how his partner can use two pens, held both sinistral and dextral, and write or draw simultaneously on separate sheets. In the old days, they would burn him for a witch.

LADY SCAR-LETT IS bleeding when I arrive. My intention tonight was to bid her farewell, but her injury changes my mind. This is not a good sign.

Usually, by this time, walking into the fairground is easy, since the crowds are leaving, and it is straightforward to reach her tent. This time she is nowhere near the tent. She is in the midst of a minor crowd of the freaks, but nobody seems to be able to perform the most rudimentary medical assistance. One is hunting around, looking for horse dung to smear on the wound. I know not what is more disturbing, that the boy is searching for shit on a ground full of horse-drawn carriages, or that he would add a ferment to the wound and call it helping.

"Stand aside," I say. To the boy rushing back with a handful of night soil I say, "If you come within two paces with that I will shove it up your cunt."

She smiles weakly when she sees me. "Adam."

"Let me see," I say.

"I forgot my choreography."

There is a diagonal slash across her chest, just beneath her collarbones. It is superficial, but oozes blood. It cuts across two pre-existing scars and acts like a mouth when she breathes, opening and closing. This will not heal quickly, and unless I intervene, there will be infection, maybe even gangrene.

"Does anybody have a needle and thread?"

To gaslight, in the open air of the common, I suture Scar-Lett while her senses are dulled with laudanum. Not a single soul speaks, and even the wind seems afraid to stoke my fury. My stitches are better than yours. I have taken time to perfect my technique. This was at a time when I thought I would be the one to fix myself, using a mirror and an assistant. I no longer believe this to be possible.

I take Scar-Lett to her tent. She vomits once I lay her down, and mutters something to herself. I clean it up best I can, then I lodge myself outside the opening flap. I smoke. I notice those who stare and think they are out of shot of my senses. There is a card game going on somewhere close by. A woman yells at another person in German. My patient screams once in her sleep. At about the third hour, all goes quiet. It is a clear night and I see the clouds rushing to attend the moon. I know peace.

Later, I am checking my dressing when her eyes open.

"Let me see," she says.

I hesitate.

She places a hand on my shoulder. "Show me."

I do.

In order to avoid ruining my trousers I must lie down on my side so that gravity takes the pus elsewhere. My entire trunk is darker than the rest of me, and there is a patch where the skin has sheared off, end-to-end two palm breadths. The corruption is yellow and green, and perversely, it gives off a sweetish smell of which I am ashamed. If I tense what remains of my abdominal muscles, the flow of purulence gains the stain of blood. Using wool under the bandages seems like a bad choice, because it peels away some of my skin with it. Only bravado keeps my face expressionless.

"Is it gangrene?" she asks.

"I do not know. Whatever it is, it will be the death of me."

"Don't say that."

"It's true. I can feel it. Some days, my flesh comes loose in sheets."

"Sir, is there anything I can do to help you ward this off? I have some money saved. Maybe there is an apothecary?"

"Thank you for the offer, but I am not lacking in funds. Were it that simple, I would be well by now." I cannot remember when I was last grateful or graceful to a human being. "There is one thing you may help me with."

"Name it."

"Tell me your true name."

"Laura."

She helps me replace the dressing after cleaning me. She tells me that there was nothing wrong with her choreography, that the man, the ringer they had in the audience, went off the agreed plan of movement. We kiss, but it is brief and without passion. Nonetheless, I am breathing heavily when I break it off and flee. There is no end to maledictions I have sent your way for making me like this.

On Sundays, Gull insists that Kaseem go home for at least one meal, though he does not most times. He finds his work absorbing and completing. As he walks along, he assesses each person he encounters in terms of their anatomy. He speculates on diseases. This one with a wooden nose is either a victim of a highwayman or leprosy. He sees chancres on the lips of doxies.

He sees hunchbacks, victims of Pott's disease. He does not see the riches of humanity that Gull is always going on about. Radha has called him joyless. That isn't true. He just does not show joy like others, and has a tendency to disregard emotions. Only knowledge interests him, knowledge of the body, knowledge of how to alter the body, knowledge of healing. The dinner has always been the same, Gull quizzing him about his progress, then giving him the latest medical journals, which Kaseem reads with speed and attention to detail. He tells Gull that the project is not possible, that he might as well be asked to raise a flesh Golem. Gull discusses this notion as if he knows it to be possible, as if he has seen it done, as if he has done it. Has he?

Kaseem stops to watch three-card because he wants to stare at the hands of the card-sharp. Early arthritis. Must hurt. Should find another profession.

He walks along the south bank of the Thames, thinking, watching. He sees a natural philosopher with a strange contraption sucking up foul river water and disgorging clean water from a tap. The philosopher expounds theories of purification while punters step forward to drink of the blessed font. The machine looks slap-dash, built from spare parts. There is something about it, though...the brackish water going in, the clean coming out... He turns and runs to Charing Cross, where he hails a hackney.

HE BURSTS INTO Radha's house without formality. The family is eating, and most of them look up at him like he is a lunatic. Radha looks as if it is business as usual.

"What, Kaz?"

"We need to build something."

36

Radha's eyes move to the left and right. *We shouldn't discuss such things in front of my family.*

"Not that. A machine."

"What machine?"

"I—I don't know."

"Well, that should be easy."

"I mean, it doesn't exist. Yet. I know what it has to do. We need to make it. Let's go. You need to start drawing right away."

"I need to do no such thing. First, you will greet my parents with the proper respect, you philistine. Then you will wash your hands and join us. Come. Eat. Food first, then work."

Radha looks different outside Newgate: softer, effeminate even. He seems more human, although anyone who does not smell of embalming chemicals would qualify. He sketches as Kaseem speaks. Neither of them is mechanical in their thinking, but Gull is a physiology authority. If they can get the basic concepts down, he would know someone who can build what they want, of steam or electric.

"Did Gull train you personally?" he asks.

Radha shakes his head, irritated. "No, I trained in India. Henry Carter trained me. Gull visited and stole me away."

"You knew Carter? You never said."

"You never asked. Incredible man. Gentle. Pious. Shame about his taste in women."

"What do you mean?"

"He got entangled with an unscrupulous widow. Cost him dearly, financially and emotionally. There was a big court battle and a minor scandal. He just withdrew into himself."

"The textbook spoke of him as if he was dead."

"Gray did that. Didn't want to share the glory and tried to reduce Carter's role to that of a mere illustrator." Radha stops suddenly, as if he has revealed too much. For one thing, it becomes obvious to Kaseem how much his colleague admires Carter, given the increased breathing and the colour to the cheeks. Deeper, though, is an identification with Carter. Does he see Kaseem as Gray?

He shows Kaseem the design so far. "I confess, I'm dubious. Will it work?"

"I have no idea, but if it fails, it will fail spectacularly, don't you think? If one must fail, one should always fail big."

A stream of Gujarati comes from outside and Radha responds in rapid-fire anger. The voice goes quiet.

"Sorry about that. What next?"

"Next, we experiment."

LAURA IS MORE resourceful that I expect, for she shows up at my doorstep days later.

The lady I rent from, Miss Bee, calls to me. "You have a caller, sir, a woman."

"I hope you do not mind the intrusion. I came to thank you for the other night." She is concealed, even though the day is warm. She wears long gloves, past the elbows, a high-collar dress with ruffles, and her hat gives birth to a veil. She looks like a woman in mourning. I know this look because I have used it, excepting the veil.

"How did you find me?"

"I had the dog boy follow you."

"Laura, why have you come?"

"Do you want me to leave?"

"Madam, you should answer my question, for today I am uninterested in word games; and I am lacking in patience always."

"I want to try something... on your belly."

"A cure? I've tried most."

"Not a cure. A... delay, perhaps."

"Speak plainly, Laura."

"Do you have a scalpel?"

"I do."

"This will hurt. Don't you want to take some laudanum?"

"I'm fine." The nerves you made me with are partially dead, which is why I can't feel pleasurable sensations as well as I should.

At first she squeezes at the edges of the great corruption, pus flowing freely with its evil stench and soaking into the cloth she placed in readiness. When it only runs red, she stops squeezing and starts cutting. She slices all the way to the most living, most vital tissue, which must bleed to prove vitality. I assist her by wiping the field as much as I can and pinching bleeding vessels so she can tie them up. She has no surgical training, and she stitches like a seamstress, but she is earnest and determined, and will brook no failure. I am pleased that she has done this thing. It makes me wonder if you would have done it, had you lived. It is, after all, a defect in the vessel you created. When she is done, there is a great concavity in my trunk which she packs with wool and gauze, then bandages. The pain makes me dizzy to be sure, but underneath all of that, I feel better, healthier than I have in a long time. Is this not what I try to achieve by swimming in waters and letting fish feed on me?

"What was that you were reciting?" she asks. She is sweating and I have not noticed how difficult this must be for her.

"I wasn't aware that I was reciting anything." I am surprised. "What did it sound like?"

"I wasn't paying enough attention. Something about Palestine and Beelzebub and Satan."

"Ahh, *Paradise Lost*. It is a Milton poem. One of my favourites."

> To *wage by force or guile eternal war*
> *Irreconcilable, to our grand Foe,*
> *Who now triumphs, and in the excess of joy*
> *Sole reigning holds the tyranny of Heaven.*
> *So spake the apostate angel, though in pain,*
> *Vaunting aloud, but racked with deep despair:*

"Are you, sir, racked with deep despair?" she asks.

"I am the apostate angel in pain, but not despair. In the past, perhaps."

"Allow me to be remedy to your pain, at least for a moment. You will find me meet to the task of remediation."

Never has such an elixir existed, nor will any other. I swear it. Miss Bee is most scandalised, and for days after threatens to send me out into the street. She will not, though. I pay her well, and if coin will not do it I will slice her head off.

In three days I am sufficiently recovered that I take a walk northbound on Edgware Road. I aim to see St Margaret's Church at Watling and Station Road, but I see a fire in the farmland and hear drums that I recognise. West Africans are dancing next to a fire. I have seen them before, and I go closer. They see me and are not threatened. Their customs are ancient and soothing to me. I regret that I did not learn any of the languages of that great continent. That is where I learnt astronomy.

"Is there a babalawo here?" I ask the man nearest to me. He has tribal marks on his cheeks. He sends me to the Ifa adept and I have my days read by geomancy. I will not write down what I was told.

* * *

IMPATIENT, KASEEM DOES the next bit on his own.

The apparatus is simple, a quart bell jar with three valved exits, one pumping venous blood inside, one to bubble oxygen through and a third to pump the blood out of the jar back into the body. The first attempts are hilarious. Venous blood is darker; the more oxygenated it becomes, the brighter the red. Kaseem connects a cannula to his own cephalic vein at the forearm and pumps it into the jar. As soon as he has a small puddle in the jar he begins to foot-pump oxygen. The blood initially becomes brighter, but then congeals into a mess of jelly and stops flowing, clogging up the tubing for good measure. He rebuilds out of new materials and the same thing happens. He spends a month on the clotting problem, reading up treatises, and finally settling on sodium citrate. This keeps the blood flowing and does not kill any of the dogs he injects it into. He again ties a tourniquet, connects the cannula.

The blood from the bell jar is a pleasing bright red, and Kaseem is transferring it into himself in the cephalic vein of the other side, when he blacks out. Radha wakes him up.

"Have you been using your own blood all this time?" asks Radha.

"...What...?"

Radha cuts the tourniquets before Kaseem's forearms degenerate from loss of blood supply. "You'll have to rest for a while. You look pale and I'm pretty sure you have made yourself anaemic."

The weakness and tiredness from this endeavour keeps Kaseem bedbound for two weeks, and confined to the house for three months to recover.

The first of the blood pump machines is already in the Newgate dead room when Kaseem returns. The first design flaw becomes evident in a few months. They are able to maintain a flow of oxygenated blood from and into an executed prisoner, although the pulse is an alarming one hundred beats per minute at the wrist and neck. There are no reflexes, and the body is dead, even if there is colour returned to the skin from the machine. Even without intervention, a hanged person can maintain a pulse for up to twenty minutes after execution. But the body they connect to the machine is no longer generating heat, and is cold.

"We need a heat-exchanger," says Radha just as Kaseem thinks it.

Another three months pass before the next contraption arrives. The heat is piped through a counter-current system sapped from the boiler. This pump-oxygenation-heating device works, and can keep going for five hours at a stretch.

Kaseem has an idea which he thinks will work, but he still immerses himself in the source material. Too many gaps.

My cheek had grown pale with study, and my person had become emaciated with confinement.

They had anaemia and weight loss in common. It is comforting, this corporal synchrony across centuries, but not helpful. The author is too figurative and allusive, and short on hard facts that might allow an investigator such as Kaseem the opportunity to replicate the claims.

Radha chronicles obsessively, the original project cast aside, the role of the artist-physician in this new project uncertain. Will they leave their detailed notes for posterity, so that twentieth-century reanimators may work with ease when the Hindoo and the half-breed are dust? Will this kind of work be routine by the time the reign of Victoria is done?

Kaseem writes to Gull. He will need to exert all kinds of influence to achieve what will be needed next. When he finishes the letter, he shows it to Radha first.

"So this is the Rubicon? We are to be as gods?"

"We are using the raw material of the gods. I don't know. Shut up."

"Have you thought of what will happen if we succeed?"

"What do you mean?"

"Kaz, who will this man be? Cobbled from parts, who will he be legally?"

Kaseem has no answer for this, and just shakes his head. This is a problem to be solved in the fullness of time. At present, time is definitely not full.

He seals the letter and hand-delivers it to Gull's study, then he sleeps for two days straight.

IT OCCURS TO me that I am not an Adam. I am a Cain. Or I perhaps have attributes of both. I should have liked to ask you, but you ran away from your responsibilities, did you not? You made me an Adam with intent, and then you made me a Cain by neglect. I was born or created good: *bonus homo semper tiro.* But I learned. Made an autodidact of me. I had to experiment on matters as simple as suitable aliment, raiment and voiding. You did this to me, and my hatred emanates from my nose as brimstone.

I have been in one of the London newspapers. A small paragraph, barely worth mentioning. Laura showed it to me. I am in the habit of taking her along on my nocturnal constitutionals, and it appears the nightlife has noticed us. I do not like drawing attention to myself, but Laura seems to enjoy it. She has not told me how she got her scars—the specifics, I mean—but she has let slip that she has a husband in Walsall. I am thinking of paying a visit. Destruction is the one thing I excel at, after all. Laura is my worthy apothecary. She packs my vast ulcerated belly with mould from bread and cheese, which I must confess seems to change the nature of the pus. She thinks I should get a breast plate to cover the portions without skin. She makes me dare to hope. On the warmest days, at her urging, I climb to the tallest buildings and open my sores for Apollo to fight the corruption. When I say this may as well be done in a field, she says the height brings me closer to the sun. She entertains no argument or contradiction, and her lawyering is sound. I am better. I see shelving at the edges of the rot, where before there was undermining. I no longer go swimming in the Serpentine.

The scars on Laura's body are a cartography of pain. They move like snakes when we are together and I only have to see her bare neck before I feel the effect of a Gorgon.

She tells me her show will be moving on soon.

It is my intention to follow.

Miss Bee, blind though she is, knows I am not quite like other lodgers she has had. When I give her notice she asks if I will be all right "out there." I am often at a loss as to how to respond to the little kindnesses that one encounters every day. I pledge to be careful and I pay her more than I should.

Dear Sir,

I thank you for the opportunity to take part in the project we discussed. In order for me and my most capable partner Radha to achieve success, we have determined that the following need to happen.

We need a temporary expansion of the dead room to accommodate second and third dissection tables. This is because both Radha and I will dissect simultaneously on the day in question.

Radha and Kaseem stand gowned and ready like thoroughbreds about to race. They will not have assistants, but are both experienced enough to do without. They cast furtive glances at the third table, empty, with the oxygenation contraption at the ready, hissing when the boiler discharges steam.

The clock strikes twelve and somewhere outside, four men who have emerged from the notorious Debtor's Gate take their drop.

Secondly, we will require four men to be executed on the same date at the same time. These men must be of similar body size and shape, and, because of the Anatomy Act, must not have relatives interested in their interment. That these condemned men be large in size goes without saying. The bigger they are, the easier it will be to do the fine work of joining severed blood vessels and nervous tissue.

They lay two of the men on the dead room tables, and the other two on the floor, all covered with sheets. The warders leave and lock the door behind them. Kaseem starts a stopwatch.

Radha hesitates at the sight of the four dead men, sheets tented with erections as is common with the recently deceased. One of them has ejaculated.

"There is no time to waste, brother. Begin."

"I—" says Radha.

"Cut!"

They do.

The legs and pelvis come from one source. The entire bowel, upper limbs and parts of the chest from another. The heart and lungs are removed as a unit from a third. The fourth provides the head and spinal cord. The vessels are connected to the machine and the blood flows, warm and fast. Bellows keep the lungs inflating and deflating once connected. It is hours of manic work from which there is no respite. Kaseem's arms and neck ache, and he has cut himself a number of times. The neck vertebrae of all four have been fractured, two of the faces sheared off completely by the noose. Radha literally creates a new set of cervical vertebrae for the new subject while Kaseem reattaches the spinal cord. There is no air in the dead room, and they are both soaked with their own sweat. While wiping his forehead, Kaseem notices something. He nudges Radha.

"What?"

"Look. He's sweating."

Indeed.

Working on the final sutures, they have no real idea of success or failure, but sweat is good. When they are done, there are stitches around the limbs, neck, back and torso. They use metal wire to keep the sawed chestplate of the ribcage and sternum in place for healing. There are plates holding the new vertebrae together. They coat the neck in plaster. The composite man is strapped down.

The third thing we will require is a recovery room here at Newgate, a place for our subject to rest and heal after the ordeal.

Radha and Kaseem sit on the floor, backs against the wall, staring at the breathing man on the slab. He breathes spontaneously; his heart beats spontaneously. He has not opened his eyes spontaneously, but they have found his pupils to be reactive.

"I don't like his colour," says Radha. The man has taken on a yellow hue, skin and whites of the eyes.

"This happened to the other one too. The scientist described dull yellow eyes and yellow skin. It's jaundice. I'm wondering if the liver is getting enough oxygen."

"The kidneys are, at any rate," says Radha. The bladder had filled up and they had used a tube up the man's penis to drain the urine.

"We'll need to name him." He turns to Radha. "But I have a question for you. Today you seemed uncomfortable at the prisoner's tumescence. You already know it happens, and I assume you have morning glory of your own when you wake up."

Radha opens his mouth, closes it, then opens it again. "No, I don't."

"You don't become erect?"

"No."

"You are impotent, then?"

"No, Kaz, I do not become erect because I do not have a penis."

Kaseem is shocked. "Was it cut off?"

"You imbecile. I do not have a penis because I am not a man."

Radha and I are most honoured among men to be the ones chosen for this task.

I remain your son,
Kaseem Greenshank

YOU WOULD LIKE this: I am stopped from leaving London by a newspaper article.

The bodies of four executed criminals have gone missing from Newgate Prison. They were executed on the same day. It is raising a stink and there are calls for the Anatomy Inspector to resign. Others say the resurrectionists have returned. There is then a recap of several strange goings-on in Newgate, including a black dog haunting. I know you got your bodies from charnel houses and ossuaries. Digging up the recently deceased used to be the only way for anatomists to gain skill in dissection. They paid criminals to steal corpses. Soon the criminals were creating the corpses for which they were paid, most notoriously the team of Messrs William Burke and William Hare. That was before Hare turned King's Evidence, Burke hanged at gallows and Robert Knox, the doctor they disinterred and murdered for, left Scotland in disgrace.

I've met Knox. I assayed his skill to see if he could help me. I found him mediocre. He still works in Hackney.

Now the Anatomy Act allows anatomists and surgeons to legally take the bodies of the poor. Disinterment is too costly.

But I wonder. I think of how you anatomists, you surgeons, are full of guile and are subtil beyond reason. I think I must visit the scene of the crime myself and find out why four bodies went walkabout.

IN RADHA'S JOURNAL:
   He's alive!

HE IS AS a child, this man they have brought alive.

Unknown men seal and take away the oxygenation engine. Kaseem tries to speak to them, but they understand no English. Neither Kaseem nor Radha are allowed back into the dead room, but then, it has no interest for them. This offspring of theirs takes all their time and thought. Offspring. Radha.

Distaff. They are parents, and have been pressed into that which parents do, in a perversion of the chronology.

The news is dominated by the American Civil War, but small pieces here and there bemoan the loss of four bodies from Newgate Prison. A massive comet captures the attention left over from the war, discovered in Australia, with Earth being in its tail for some days. Does this sign in the sky herald the reanimated man?

They call him Victor, as a "victory over death." He sleeps for a fortnight, although he feeds on gruel and swallows when they tube water into him. His bowels work, evidenced by the cleaning they have to keep up and the farting that punctuates the hours of the night. His heart beats strong and his breathing is regular. The yellow of his skin has gone. He opens his eyes and fixes on them. Distracted by the historicity of the moment, Kaseem looses the bonds, a mistake. Victor latches on to Kaseem's neck and squeezes. Even as the life is leaving him, Kaseem is pleased, proud even, of Victor's strength, of how well the joints are holding. Radha's efforts to remove Victor's hands are ineffective, until she uses ether.

They copulate wildly. Kaseem had thought himself uninterested in such things throughout his life, but something is unleashed when Radha reveals herself; the regard in which he holds his colleague triggers new interest.

They agree that they must teach Victor the rudiments of life. He wears clothes cobbled together. He is able to make sounds, but the memory of his life and abilities before execution are gone. It is faster than teaching a child, but slower than teaching an adult a new language. Motion is different: he seems to pick up the basics, then complexity of movement quickly, as if his muscles and joints have their own memory. They read to him from children's books and sing to him. He is no longer confused or violent and, unbound, he is calm, affectionate even. When Victor sleeps, they rut. They do not speak much, apart from involuntary sighs and encouragements, but afterwards, they hold each other in the dark without sleeping. The noise of Victor's respiration and eruptions is louder than the usual prison noises. At times Victor cries out in his sleep from a nightmare.

"Where is this going?" asks Kaseem.

Radha exhales. "If we continue like this we're bound to be blessed with an entirely different sort of victory."

"I meant with our Victor. Gull has not responded to any of my queries for guidance. I went back to the house, but he is not there, or will not see me."

"Forgive me for thinking of tenderness."

"I'm serious. Has it occurred to you that we are Newgate prisoners, after a fashion?"

"It has."

"And?"

"And we can leave whenever we want."

"What about Victor?"

"Victor... Victor, who killed his wife in a fit of rage when neighbours reported seeing her with another man? The man turned out to be her cousin, but Victor did not find out until he had driven a knife into her neck fourteen times. Or Victor the highwayman who, with an accomplice, killed an entire family he had already robbed, just because he was scared they had recognised him? Or Victor the soldier who killed his commanding officer, that Victor? Or—"

"Radha—"

"Victor will be fine, Kaz. He is not an innocent. We can leave when we choose."

They do not leave. Radha keeps an impressive record of Victor with haunting drawings, paintings and copious notes. She is doing that thing where she draws with her left hand and writes text with the other at the same time. Kaseem attempts it and gains a headache for his troubles. Victor's every bodily function is measured and documented. Within a month he makes single word pronouncements like "cold" or "hungry." He controls his waste, his appetite increases, and his scars are healing. He will never be beautiful, but he is not monstrous.

I AM LOOKING at a burial site, more wretched than a pauper's communal grave. There are various body parts all mixed together in the soil, in the process of being eaten by worms.

Let me tell you how I got here. To make sense of the Newgate disappearance, I spoke to the Anatomy Inspector of London, something you did not have in your time. He is afraid of me, but most people are, so I do not hold this as a reflection of weak character. I place a small bag of Athenian gold coins on his desk.

"Tell me everything about the missing bodies from Newgate."

To my surprise he produces a folder or ledger. He begins to speak. It seems there is a specific number of corpses that they expect from each prison and workhouse. For one the size of Newgate, the medical colleges are not getting enough bodies. This has been the case for a number of years now, but the inspector has no explanation. He does give me a document allowing me access as a proxy inspector, but this turns out to be a useless piece of paper. Through liberal bribery, I get a permit to visit Newgate from the office of the Lord Mayor of the City of London. This I leave as a second option, because visiting may alert the very people I am looking for.

I investigate Newgate itself.

Before being a prison, it was one of the gates into London. Criminals have been housed there at least since the 1200s. The current building was started in 1770 and finished in 1782. The part that interests me is the extensive remodelling in 1856. It is after this that the Inspector says the bodies dried up. The Inspector also shares rumours that the prison architecture does not conform to plans.

I stare at it from the opposite side of Newgate Street. From here I can see St Paul's Cathedral, dominating the landscape. I'm told it used to have a spire, but now it sports a cupola. Guards come and go, looking no different from prisoners themselves. Gallows are under construction and the Debtor's door is open, apparently for repairs. There is an air of incompetence about the place and I wait until dusk, then slip in. I am not impeded. I see the courtyard for debtors, the men's quadrangle and the women's quadrangle. There are abundant shadows in which to hide myself when people come around. The guards seem drunk, and there are more screams than I think there should be.

I have been to unsanitary places, and this one stands out. A foul open sewer provides a persistent miasma. Rats and insects are everywhere, en masse and in splinter groups scattered around. The authorities do not need to execute anyone from here; they will die soon enough from pestilence. Near the top of the men's quadrangle I spot an anomaly, an asymmetry. The brickwork seems different, newer perhaps. Most importantly, it shares the roof, just as one would expect a dissecting room to. My meanderings have taken time and I leave.

I do still reconnoitre around the prison and I find graves. I dig what seems to be recently disturbed soil. Having seen what I have seen, and inflicted the kind of damage I have over the years, I am unaffected by the chopped-up humans, but it is interesting. I arrange the bodies, try to put them back together. A thrill passes through me when I am finished. There are three complete men, but the parts do not match.

A fourth could have been made from parts of these three.

Which means someone is doing what you did.

From a room in Newgate Prison.

VICTOR IS AT the door, staring at it as if he is willing it to open.

For the last week he has been indicating a wish to see the world outside. Kaseem and Radha are torn. Still no word from Gull. Without instructions, Kaseem does not know whether Victor is to remain a secret inside the suite, or if they dare take him out.

"Take Victor out," says Victor. He does not exactly speak in third person, but some verbs give him trouble.

"Where's the harm?" asks Radha. Why has he not noticed how husky her voice is before now?

"The harm is he might take flight, and we will have nothing to show for our labours. Anything could happen to him out there. He might be recognised."

"It will be at night. I'm curious to see how he copes with people other than us."

Victor turns to them both. "Take Victor out."

"This course of action is pregnant with catastrophe," says Kaseem.

"Your opinion is noted. Let's find some clothes."

It goes surprisingly well. Victor does not run off or become frightened or hostile. He just stares, taking the night life of London in. He looks everywhere, at times humming to himself. Radha sketches in her common-place book, chronicling the maiden voyage. Victor is mesmerised by the gas lamps on Westminster Bridge. He stops walking at each one, then rushes to the next. Passers-by think him simple. He cannot keep his hat on, so Kaseem holds it.

When it is time to return, Victor is not troublesome. He does keep looking back all the way to Newgate.

This becomes a daily ritual.

THE FREAKSHOW IS packing up, and even before I reach her, I can see Laura and her body language. She's looking for me, waiting. When she sees me, she smiles. I don't smile back. Incidentally, I find it difficult to smile. Not just that. I cannot frown either. I usually maintain a frozen, blank aspect that is, I am told, more frightening than if my features were contorted.

"I am sorry," I say to Laura. "I am going to disappoint you." I take off my hat and my hair tumbles free.

"Why?" She cannot quite hide her dismay.

"There is something at Newgate Prison that I have to investigate."

"Something that might help you?"

"Yes. You... if you wait, I can take us both in a coach to catch up."

Laura shakes her head. "I have responsibilities. But I have something for you. Take off your coat."

It is a bronze breastplate, with leather straps to hold it in place around the sides. There is a spigot to allow the controlled escape of pus. It is not bulky and I easily wear my clothes over it.

"Go and find what you must at Newgate. Then come and find me, for I am also something you need."

That night I go back into the prison. It isn't hard; even you could have managed it. I head straight for the top level, to the distorted portion. It is guarded better than any other. There are three gaolers, and I can still smell alcohol from them. I don't know what they are guarding, but I do know that if I make noise, I will have to fight an entire prison, plus reinforcements from the peelers, potentially. I unsheath my sword.

I am a shadow, a djinn in a whirlwind. I do not cut, but hit them with fists and the hilt of my sword. I am not here to kill. Even if they were not inebriated, they would not be able to recount the adventure. I move too fast for them to register me. I enter the room they guard.

It is empty of people, but full of information. It is a dissection room if I have ever seen one. It is fitted with the most up-to-date equipment and has been maintained. On the other hand, the green copper deposits on the taps shows me they are not new, and the layer of dust over all surfaces tells me this place has not been cleaned or used in a while. There is dust on the inside of the sink. Two of the dissection tables are newer than the third. There is a lingering smell of methanol and formaldehyde. Who works here? The prison physician? I hear sounds, maybe coming from the West wall. I place my ear against it. People talking, too muffled to make any words out. This is an odd place, with a residue of evil and dead humanity. The only paper in the room is a number of exquisite paintings of anatomical structures on the wall, signed with a stylised 'R.' I tear one off the wall. It represents a cross section of the spine at T8 level. I fold it into my shirt.

The guards are still unconscious when I leave. A part of me wants to stay in the dissection room, but I feel that would be futile: nobody is using it anymore.

I steal away and stay hidden on Newgate Street. I watch. I wait.

I wait.

I wait.

I wait.

Then I see him. I don't know what I'm looking at initially, a tall man flanked by two others. But it is a hot night, and he is dressed to cover all flesh. The way he walks, the way he moves, the other two fade away from my perception. This one... this one is kin to me. Like me. I charge towards him, causing alarm in all three. He thinks me a threat and defends the other two. He is young, and strong, but he does not know how to fight. I do not want to harm him, yet he has no submission signals. I hit his companions hard enough to demonstrate my strength. He will not cower. He does not understand.

"Come with me," I say. "I am your brother."

"What is 'brother'?" he asks.

I take off my hat and show him my face in the gaslight. "I am like you."

He looks to his fallen keepers. He makes a sound of desolation, like a dog whose owner has died. An alarm rattle goes off and a bell starts clanging. Just as I feel I will have to knock him out, he moves towards me and I lead him away into the darkness, away from the noise.

You'll like this: they called him Victor. One day I will laugh at that.

"Where is he? Who was it who made you?"

"Newgate. Victor's friends."

"They are not your kind, or your friends."

"Home."

"Not home, brother. This is your home. By my side. Take off your clothes."

I look at the fine needlework that keeps Victor together. It makes me want to cry. Of course. Instead of using so many different bodies like you did, Victor's maker used but a few. Victor will pass for human. You used beautiful parts for me, but balked and ran when the whole was less than the sum of its parts. I must meet the man who has done this. I must see if he can help me.

Then Victor and Laura and I will be on our distant way, perhaps to warmer climes. Not South America. Maybe Africa, for the exile that I promised.

I am not an oath breaker, like you.

KASEEM IS SCREAMING, but not only from pain. His right forearm is broken and his left hand, with which he broke his fall, is shattered. He is screaming from fear that he will now lose his skill with the scalpel, but also that all the work, all the expense, *all* has vanished with Victor's flight. He is unsure of what exactly happened. A whirlwind? A highwayman? Several highwaymen? Kaseem has never been in so much pain. Now there are people around him, rough people who are aggravating his fractures. He cannot see Radha. Where is she? Men are arguing about Kaseem, about what to do. He passes out, and when he comes to, he is in handcuffs. His wrist feels swollen around the metal. He is in a cell, on a cold stone floor. It is daytime now, and light filters into the narrow rectangular window near the ceiling.

There is a peeler outside the cell. He notices Kaseem's open eyes and leaves without speaking. A different gentleman returns with him, plainclothes, sleeves rolled up, moustache, no hat.

"Sir, where am I?" asks Kaseem.

"Name?"

"Kaseem Greenshank, sir."

"What kind of name is that? Are you trying to deceive me?"

"No, sir."

"Are you a foreigner?"

"I am as English as you, sir. I was born in Lambeth."

"Your people?"

"I never met them. Please, sir, can you tell me what happened to my companions? Did you catch the miscreant who did this to us?"

The policeman laughs. "The girl you injured is in hospital. I know nought about any other companion."

"I did not—"

"Best not lie to me, for I am full of regrets and have not seen my wife in three nights. I wish to sort this out smartly, have a beer, and go home."

Of course. Through the questions, Kaseem gleans their working theory of what happened. They think Radha is some form of street walker, since she was in male garb, although that lacked logic: how would she attract customers while dressed as a man? They think Kaseem had gone berserk, perhaps a dispute over price, perhaps some other depravity. They think he struck her so hard that his hands broke. No explanation as to his other injuries. No mention of Victor or Newgate. Gull has not come for him, or sent word. Radha is apparently non-responsive, wherever she is being held or treated.

"Sir, I am ward to Edward Gull, the famed physician. Contact him and you will have my bona fides. All these years I have been dwelling in Newgate Prison, carrying out a special project for him."

This buys time, but it does not go how Kaseem wants it to.

*　　*　　*

LAURA IS GONE, the fairground is empty. Victor looks at me, puzzled as to why we are here, and I understand. The detritus of events remain. Lost children's toys, tiny bits of clothing, cigarette ends, food wrapping. I sit and Victor joins me. He has taken to emulating my every move, which I suppose is one way to learn. I am teaching him to read. I read to him a lot, and he is making progress. He does not like the poets, but seems to enjoy Swift and Dickens. He also eats meat. That is a departure from me, for I only eat fruits and grain. As I learn about him, I learn about myself.

I had planned to entreat Laura to stay in London, and I know she and her gang of misfits have gone to Birmingham, if they're not set upon by highwaymen. The thought of anyone drawing a weapon on her makes my blood curdle, which leaves Victor unsettled. He is better able to read non-verbal cues now, and he knows what I am capable of. I approximate a smile to put him at ease. Then I notice a greenish colouration along one of his scars. It is pus. My heart sinks.

"Let us go and find your makers," I say.

They will make us both whole again, or I will know why.

THIS HAS NOT gone as expected. Kaseem now stands before a judge. He is given to believe there are headlines about him.

Gull did not vouch for him, or even deign to respond to queries. Instead, the police make a connection between Kaseem and the disturbed plot of land near Newgate where the mutilated bodies of the prisoners are found. Not just that. Other graves are found, with the remnants of years of dissections: mostly bones, but many rotting body parts. They were meant to be incinerated and interred respectfully, albeit in pauper's graves. The judge finds the story of a dead room within Newgate to be "fantastical and insulting to the Court." Nobody agrees to investigate or even inspect the sections of the prison Kaseem mentions at first, then, without warning, he is put in rough prison cloth and taken in a Black Maria to his "so-called" dead room.

It is as if it never existed. There is no equipment in the room, none of Radha's paintings on the wall, no drain, not even a smell of bromide or any other chemical. Instead, there is a mouldering pile of old night soil in the centre. The stripped-down room looks like an abandoned part of the prison. There are even cobwebs, which boggles Kaseem's mind. Perplexed, he is dragged back to his cell while the detectives and the officers of the Court take notes.

It is postulated that Kaseem must certainly be mentally deranged and should be sent to Bedlam. He is certainly not a ressurectionist selling bodies to medical schools for profit. He obviously did this for his own sick amusement, due to whatever ruminations dwell in his fevered blackamoor brain. The judge is not convinced, though, and Kaseem almost loses consciousness when a black cap is placed on the judicial wig. He is sentenced to death by hanging. The Court kindly wishes God's mercy on his soul. Considerate.

So now he is awaiting execution, writing his "confession" in atrocious handwriting, thanks to his now-malformed hand. Prisoners across the way will not speak to him, as they think he is a toff and unhinged. He has, after all, cut up some of Her Majesty's guests. He writes anyway, recalling his childhood as best he can, running in Lambeth Marsh, fighting or fleeing gangs of feral children, no parents, living on the margins of the market off scraps, sometimes stealing, mostly running errands for casual villains—but barely registering them, because his only passion was the nature of bodies, insect or animal, it mattered not whether alive or dead. Taking creatures apart, measuring, understanding, this was his only pleasure. People thought him stupid because he never spoke. A thatcher told him one day that he was the result of a rape, and that he had been thrown away, rescued by a parson or preacher. In truth, he has nothing to discuss with them if it is not to do with survival, or street commerce. Until Gull.

He is about to begin on his time with the surgeon when he senses something, and the guard outside his cell slumps. Kaseem looks up.

There is a giant shadow there, with a drawn sword that catches what little lamplight there is. Kaseem stands, takes his candle closer, gasps. The face and skin are scarred beyond anything Kaseem has ever seen, the skin pulled tight over an irregular bone structure that offends with its asymmetry and corpse-like colour. The scars are linear, with dots on both sides, surgical scars. He wears a breastplate, carries a pistol in addition to the sword. A stovepipe hat does little to soften his appearance, and the odour from him speaks of extensive suppuration.

"Do you know who I am, Dr Greenshank?" The voice is deep, with a slight gurgle, but the consonants are crisp, and the delivery is educated.

"I do not, sir," says Kaseem. "And I am not a doctor."

The figure waves his sword like a wagging finger. "I disagree. I have seen your handiwork, Dr Greenshank. You are, or may as well be."

"Who are you?"

"I am the prototype. This is the work you attempted to duplicate."

Kaseem's mouth goes dry. "Are you here to kill me? Because it matters little: I either die here, now, or doing the Tyburn jig in a few days."

"I am here to..." He pauses and looks to his left, responding to a noise, which settles. "I am here to ask for your help. Victor is sick, I think dying."

Realisation hits Kaseem. "It was you who attacked us."

"Yes, though I regret what—"

"Radha is comatose, nobody knows if she will survive."

"I was over-enthusiastic when I saw my brother. I apologise. But understand this, if you cannot help, Victor will die. As, probably, will I." He opens his breastplate on one side and the stench in the room intensifies. His entire belly and most of his chest is... decomposing. The blighted area is moist with pus. "Gaze upon the future of your offspring, Dr Greenshank."

"I told you already, I am not a doctor. Victor is—"

A bell is sounded and shouts ring out.

I CANNOT SAY what would have been with Greenshank. His mind seems addled by his fall from grace. He is to be executed, according to the newspapers. One would expect such a person to leap at the chance of freedom. That is of no consequence now, as the guards bear down on me. There is a clamour, so I have no need to be silent. The first to reach me, I slice diagonally in Japanese fashion, shoulder to flank. The two parts of him separate. The man coming behind him slips in the gore and rather than attacking me with a truncheon, he stumbles into my raised knee, which smashes his face. Four run in a two-row formation behind him, but the narrow corridor makes them bunch together. I slice through them, ignoring their screams.

I turn a corner and surprise a guard who is still in his bedclothes. I run him through, then kick him off my sword. I am slightly turned about. I make a decision and crash through a door, but end up in the courtyard, uncertain of which one. I am surrounded by dozens of men armed with truncheons, assorted clubs and at least one shillelagh. I draw my pistol and begin firing. Two are down before the rest begin to run. I catch my bearings and sprint towards the exit. A rifle shot rings out and I feel it slam into my torso. Before I can turn, another hits, then another. The exit is only a few yards away, but the gate is now guarded. I now see the riflemen. Three of them: two kneeling, one standing. I train my pistol and shoot one of them down. I run for the exit while they collect themselves.

Torches flare into light everywhere. This is familiar to me.

Though I am diminished from my former self, I gather my reserves and leap, clearing the wall, if imperfectly. My left foot hits the top and sends my body into a spin, and I land on the other side in a heap, chest first. I hear them frantic, trying to open the gate, but I have studied the surrounding streets well, and I fade away.

London, 1862

THANKS TO HIS rising acclaim, Gull is allowed into the exhibition without paying his way. The lines extend all the way to the street, drawn by a morbid fascination with the subject matter: paintings of the deranged body-snatcher, Kaseem Greenshank. The works are signed by the mysterious 'R,' rumoured to be his assistant in his macabre endeavours, or his lover—or, according to some, the actual mastermind of the affair. The curator will not say. The fact is, in spite of the trial, most people do not know what Greenshank looked like; it could be anyone in the paintings. The captions do not speculate on his state of mind or his foreignness, but the critics have gone wild with theories. The subject of the paintings has the forearm tattoo Gull remembers from when he first plucked Kaseem from Lambeth.

Gull looks at the pieces with disinterest. He walks through the entire exhibit, though. It takes all of twenty minutes. There is one painting, the last, which shows Greenshank with a tall naked figure in shadow. Critics have speculated about this canvas, one of the largest at sixty inches by forty-five. They say the figure represents the evil nature of Greenshank and the friendliness between them shows how much he surrendered to his own dark side. Gull, knowing the truth, snorts.

Look to your own children, my husband. People are beginning to talk, saying this boy is your bastard. If you love me, and I know that you do, and considering your dedication to probity, you will pledge to sever all contact with him, today, now.

Gull, filled with regret, walks out, enters his waiting carriage, and is driven off.

RADHA NURSES THE baby. Her agent has just dropped off an envelope of takings from the exhibition, and it lies lonely on the table. Radha will not count it. She will only pick it up as an afterthought.

By the time she woke from her coma, Kaseem had been executed. Her thoughts were clouded at first, as if her brain was still recovering, awareness of the world returning in fits, revealing her grief in layers. She has not cried, but with the baby, she has been too tired to mourn.

The young one clamps gums down on her nipple and she winces. She rings the small bell and a lady comes for the child. "Letter for you, ma'am."

There is no salutation or sign off, but she knows who it is from.

Madam,

I am pleased to inform you that all is well with me. I hope that you are satisfied with how our business was concluded, and with the transfer of agreed remuneration. I can say that I am satisfied with your work. I only wish that something could have been done for Victor. I wish I knew what my creator did to make me the beneficiary of such durability. I applaud your efforts at finding out. Perhaps this shall have to remain a mystery. Knowing your obvious affection for Victor, I can assure you that his burial was respectful, and that his grave, though unmarked, will remain undisturbed.

Be assured, Madam, that among all humans, I hold only you and one other in high esteem. That said, I value my privacy, and if I must live, it will be on my own terms. I therefore repeat my previous entreaty: do not speak of our intercourse to anyone.

If you do, you will see me again, but it will not be a jolly reunion. Do not think me unaware of your pregnancy. Should I have cause to vent my wrath, it will be on two, not one.

Radha dips the edge of the letter in flame and purses her lips. As the paper blackens and curls, she drops it on the floor and stares until it is destroyed.

"Should that day come, creature, you will find that I am for you," she says. "Have at thee."

She stands, steps in the ash and grinds it out, then goes to her studio to paint, all thoughts of violence gone with the wispy smoke that the night air dissipates.

AFTERWORD

Seeing as I did not live in this time period, I had to read a whole lot of source material. First and foremost, the 1818 edition of Mary Shelley's *Frankenstein*. Others include *Frankenstein: A Cultural History* by Susan Tyler Hitchcock (2007); *The Making of Mr. Gray's Anatomy: Bodies, Books, Fortune, Fame* by Ruth Richardson (2008); *The Greatest Benefit to Mankind: A Medical History of Humanity* by Roy Porter (1999); *London Peculiars: Curiosities in a Capital City* by Peter Ashley. Special thanks to Nina Allan and Aliette de Bodard.

THE NEW WOMAN

THE NEW WOMAN
ROSE BIGGIN

THE FINAL DAYS of the nineteenth century may have appeared dormant, the hours steadily passing over the snow-covered rooftops: the remains of an exhausted century, lying dead on a slab. But throughout those last days crackled a steady current of activity that it was possible to feel—if one concentrated—in the back of the teeth. This hissing spark of life went deeper than the city's usual rat-fights in underground dens, shone brighter than its riotous cabarets, flashed stronger than its bouts of bareknuckle boxing; and it was more than the pouring of absinthe and the adjusting of hat-pins, although those things will occur, those green and sharp things. The week is going to rise up against itself, claim a strange new life of its own.

But not much of this is known, yet, on the evening of Christmas Day, eighteen ninety-nine: and, as the bells ring out from the churches, a spirit of revelry and warm laughter pushes against the ceiling and presses against the tapestry wall-hangings of a grand house in a respectable district, the house of a famous actress and philanthropist, who is currently entertaining in her dining room.

Mrs Stella Moore enjoys the status of artistic genius and eccentric national treasure: in a glittering career, long-established, she has played every romantic, tragic, and comic lead in every great play upon every prestigious stage in the world. The press and adoring public know her fondly as Mrs Stella, and she describes herself to the periodicals, fans and love-letter writers as "a keen collector of people." This year she has surpassed herself in the bohemian assemblage seated around her table, pushing their forks across their Christmas puddings. Mrs Stella finds her people in the coffee-houses, backstage of the theatres; selling their canvasses or standing bored to tears behind the counters of perfume shops, longing for anything in life but scents by the ounce. Those who sit around her table—there are five, this year—are without any other family. Mrs Stella will give them a pension; rooms, should they need (although not, quite, in Bloomsbury); and, most precious of all, an audience for their work.

Mrs Stella is holding court at the head of the table, as she always does on Christmas Day. (There was, once, a Mr Stella, but Mrs Stella never mentions him.)

She claps her hands together. The various conversations that had begun to rumble around the dining table give way to an expectant silence.

"While we finish our pudding," says Mrs Stella, "let us return to our earlier conversation, upon the relationship between art and life. Who shall start us off?"

She takes a sip of her coffee.

The china cups are white and paper-thin, decorated with filigree patterns picked out in green, highlighted with gold. The room is the height of fashionable style. The polished tables and cabinets are laid with delicate lace cloths and long-runners, topped with pieces of pottery; vases and statues imitating ancient sculptures of Greece and Rome. Tall rubber plants stand in dark green vases, their thick waxy leaves casting shadows upon the wallpaper, which bears an intricate design of winding vines. Atop the brandy cabinet are spider plants and venus flytraps.

It being Christmas, there is additional decoration: the table is clustered with gleaming candlesticks. Garlands of spruce, picked out with silver bells and red velvet ribbons, loop across the ceiling in great glittering ropes, criss-crossing the chandelier, shuddering in the air as if taking breath, demanding to be given more space. Wreaths of ivy and holly droop from the walls and ornament the table, as candles dripping pale yellow wax make the whole room flicker. Mrs Stella has given the servants the day off, and so the table has been steadily filling throughout the evening; a great goose carcass remains in the centre on a large silver plate. Its bones and torn flesh, along with a few leftover roast potatoes and slimy scraps of cabbage, glisten in the candlelight.

A French lilt across the table. "Of course, for us writers, such things as art and life, they are always of greatest interest."

Jacques-Louis Penman. His mother was a chorus girl in the least reputable theatres of Montmartre; his father a distinguished member of the English aristocracy. (He won't tell anybody *which* distinguished member of the English aristocracy, although Mrs Stella, of course, has her ideas.) Jacques-Louis makes his way through the world primarily by producing reams of waspish journalism and devastating theatrical criticism; but he has dabbled in writing a play or two of his own—under a pseudonym, naturally—and he dreams of someday composing an operatic libretto. Perhaps the gentleman to his right will dance the lead.

Edwin Turner. Principle ballerino in London's proudest opera houses. Of all of them, Edwin could choose to spend Christmas elsewhere, with any of the corps du ballet who would see him; but it is only here, at Mrs Stella's, he feels free to be himself. Edwin clasps Jacques-Louis's thigh beneath the table. "And for us, too," he says; "you could say that art *is* life, for dancers, because we dedicate our whole bodies to it."

"You mean you *ruin* them," comes another voice from the opposite end of the table. The voice is as proud and shining as a silver button. The speaker proudly cleans a monocle with a silk handkerchief. It is Oliver Allbright—wit, flaneur, occasional producer of oil paintings. His trousers are silk, his shirt is embroidered, and his velvet smoking jacket is edged with sleek fur. "The leotards make you look pretty enough," he says, "but underneath, your bodies are soon unfit for purpose, and where's the beauty in that?"

Edwin looks at Oliver, wearing an exaggerated expression of shock. He knows what Oliver is like. "We retire young, it's true," he says. "No flame can burn at its brightest forever."

Oliver examines the pearl handle of his dessert-fork. "In my opinion, it is far better," he says, "to dedicate your art to life, than to sacrifice your life to art."

Mrs Stella laughs. Jacques-Louis bangs his fist on the table. "Stop doing aphorisms! For Christ's sake, it's just saying something you don't really mean!"

There are some dull chuckles around the table, not least from Edwin, pleased by Jacques-Louis's quick defence.

Mrs Stella sits very still, her head flicking like a bird between the three of them. Oliver gazes at Jacques-Louis steadily through his monocle.

Mrs Stella wrinkles her nose and, to create a diversion,

stands and levers open the glass door of the drinks cabinet. "It seems to me," she says, pulling out a bottle of brandy, "that the boundaries between art and life are becoming ever more porous. Perhaps *that* is what our friend Oliver means. For you, of course, Oliver, your life *is* a work of art, isn't it?"

"I should hope so," mutters Jacques-Louis, "in *those* trousers."

Oliver smiles. "Just so," he says. "I greatly admire our friend Edwin's embodiment of the balletic ideal, and of course I enjoy Jacques-Louis's commitment to drama." He addresses his closing remark to the whole table. "Far better to say something you don't mean, than to mean something terribly badly but never get to say it."

Jacques-Louis throws up his hands as if to say, *there's another one!*, but the party does not take him up on it, and instead falls into silence while the brandy is poured. Mrs Stella goes around the table, tipping a heavy golden measure into everybody's glass. One of the venus flytraps moves a toothed head, grabbing at something.

"I think it is time," says Mrs Stella, resuming her seat, "to hear from our friend Christine about the newest scientific advances! I think you will find much of interest here, friends." She leaves the bottle on the table, clustered among the silver gravy jug and a pile of crumpled napkins. She winks, her eyes sparkling. "Tell them, Christine, what you were saying to me earlier."

Christine Sparks.

At first, Oliver had objected to the inclusion of a medical student in the party; he had voiced his doubts over the third cup of Earl Grey when visiting Mrs Stella a month or so prior. Surely the hard, rational approach of the sciences, he suggested, crumbling his scone to pieces in his fingers, had little to do with the higher ideals of art. And wasn't *that* what Mrs Stella wished to patronise? If she started bringing *medical students* into her parlour, where would it end?

Mrs Stella's eyes had shone as she advised Oliver to consider the practice of medicine as *the* quintessential art of the human body. And besides, she added, Christine is quite the catch.

"She is one of the finest minds in her field," she had said. "Or fields; since she has recently been pursuing astronomy and electricity in addition to medicine and chemistry. She has several prizes, a good chance of coming first in the Tripos; scholarships to continue her learning abroad." Recently, she told Oliver, as a sort of crowning fact, Christine has been studying on the Continent—and wouldn't he like to know what people are getting up to out there?

Christine pushes her dark curls away from her face. She wears a smart blue jacket with brass buttons, and a pair of trousers, wide-cut enough to resemble a skirt at first glance, but infinitely more convenient for attending lectures by bicycle. Even Oliver nodded briefly when she first arrived at the table, forced to concede that Christine possesses both aesthetic sensibilities, and the salary to exercise them.

"Tell us something wonderful, Miss Sparks," says Mrs Stella, taking up her spoon again to serve up a second helping of Christmas pudding from its silver bowl.

Christine nods, full of enthusiasm.

"If this decade becomes known for anything, as far as science is concerned," she says, "it will be for the way it treats cadavers."

"You see," murmurs Mrs Stella, cake dropping from the spoon, "in discussing art and life, we are only a shade away from contemplating death."

"The last few years have seen spectacular advances in the use of a particular substance," says Christine, "to keep a body looking much—almost exactly—as it did in life. *Formaldehyde* is a method of embalming a cadaver, uniquely, from the inside out, rather than as our present techniques attempt, from the outside in. It is still in the experimental stages."

"Where do you find the bodies to practise upon?" Edwin asks, then looks sharply towards Jacques-Louis with a pained expression, as if he has just been kicked under the table. "I want to know!" he hisses.

"They are donated to the college from those who would be part of the great journey of science even after death," says Christine, smoothly, as if speaking by rote. "They are not obtained by any malevolent means whatsoever." She clears her throat, and returns to her explanation. "It works by passing the vapours of wood spirit, in the presence of air, over copper heated to redness..."

"Speaking personally, I prefer the thought of being preserved in alcohol," says Oliver. "One should always die surrounded by what one loved in life. The old pharaohs had it right."

Christine nods; her face expresses that she has heard this sentiment often, and understands where it comes from. "Formaldehyde is much cheaper, though, than alcohol; and easier to carry in the field."

"But surely you would need too much?" Edwin twirls his hair around his hand, abstractly waving his fingers through it. "However can you carry enough?"

"You are imagining a body lying in a bathtub's worth of green liquid," says Christine. "Far less is needed. That is what I mean by embalming from the inside out. The fluid is injected directly into the body; the resulting effect is of blood passing through living veins."

"Good grief," mutters Jacques-Louis.

Mrs Stella leans forwards, her elbows resting on the table. "I just want to make sure everyone is holding up in the face of the present topic?"

Opposite Christine, someone is sitting very still, listening properly for the first time all night. They barely hear Mrs Stella speak. Mrs Stella notices this, passes over it for now.

Mrs Stella turns her sympathetic gaze towards Jacques-Louis.

Jacques-Louis looks down at his pudding. The raisins clustered densely within the heavy sponge appear to have a very particular texture, now; if pushed, he would say a distinctly *brainy* one. The wrinkled currents flicker in the light of the candle, seeming to shrink and pulse and breathe and move. The thick yellowness of the suet-custard has taken on a distinctly green pallor, and has begun to set, the skin slowly forming, trapping the sponge pudding in the centre of the bowl. He pushes it away, and the still-setting custard wobbles grotesquely. He throws his spoon onto the table with a clatter and sits back with an air of surrender.

"You may as well carry on, now," he says.

After a pause to check he means it—with no clear answer—Christine carries on.

"And the wood spirit is volatized, mixed with the forced air... anyway, how it is made is less important than the effect it has. Which is: the moment of death can be perfectly captured. The body looks just as it did. Although it does bleach slightly, since it lacks any actual blood."

A heavy silence descends over the table as the diners consider what they have been invited to imagine. Only Allbright and Mrs Stella seem to have retained their appetites enough to spoon more pudding onto their plates. Edwin and Jacques-Louis wrap their hands around their brandies and coffees as if clinging to a life raft upon the open ocean. Christine sits back, thinking about her studies; she is due to present a lecture upon the treatment of cadavers in the new year.

And the fifth guest is staring straight ahead, not seeing the candle flame before her. Her mind is racing with possibilities, a series of vivid images having come to life in her mind.

Mrs Stella leans forward, resting her chin on her hands. She directs her gaze towards her silent guest. "And how doth our sculptor?" she says. "You've hardly said a word tonight." Her manner is polite, but the words are a challenge. The others see it as clearly as if she'd thrown a glove down on the table.

The sculptor understands. She licks her lips, forces out a rushed idea. "I was thinking, Mrs Stella, about Christine's comments, and—ah—the remainder of the goose."

"You've an eye for animals, haven't you," says Mrs Stella, not knowing where the sculptor is going, whether she needs to provide friendly encouragement or a witty obstacle.

"I was wondering, if it's perfectly acceptable, as the aristocracy do, to stuff a quail inside a goose, inside a turkey, inside a swan, and so on; you could create your own, previously undiscovered festive beast by stitching several different parts of various animals together."

There is silence around the table. Jacques-Louis's mouth opens and closes to no avail; instead he settles for running his fingers idly around one of the table's holly-and-ivy adornments. Perhaps hoping a sharp spike from the leaves might draw blood across his fingers, providing a distraction from this grim company.

Christine comes to the sculptor's aid, laughing in an embarrassment. "I wouldn't want to try that," she says. "You'd create an abomination, most likely."

Mrs Stella clears her throat. "Promise me you won't attempt it," she says. There is some lightness in her tone, but an undercurrent of disapproval pulls strongly too. "What I admire about your work is its beauty. I cannot abide ugliness."

"And such a thing would be ugly indeed," puts in Oliver. He must always have a say on whether or not something might be beautiful.

"Of course!" says the sculptor, relieved to have made a contribution to the conversation, however it was received. She casts her gaze towards the ceiling, not seeing the confused looks that pass between the rest of the collective. In truth, Christine's talk led her down a different path of thought, and she threw out the animal creation as a distraction.

Mrs Stella stands and swoops around the table, gathering her guests' pudding plates and piling them up with loud pottery scrapes. "Typical of you, Fran," she says as she passes, her voice ringing across the coffee and shortbread, though she spoke softly. "Going down the morbids. I do prefer it when you see the beauty in things."

At the door she says: "When I return I will bring everybody's Christmas presents, and inform you of my plans for the new year. Perhaps a parlour game or two! I rather fancy a round of Exquisite Corpse." She leaves, and the collective breathes out as one. Christine desperately tries to catch Fran's eye, but Fran is still distracted.

Fran does see the beauty in things. Or rather, she sees beauty she herself can create. Mrs Stella's collective think of her as a sculptor, and this is true in a sense: she has made ceramic things: delicate vases, glistening sugar bowls. Mrs Stella has a plate displayed upon the sideboard even now, bearing Francesca Clayton's intricate patterns.

But Fran has been experimenting recently in making sculptures out of once-living things. Mrs Stella approves, as long as the things are beautiful. A stuffed magpie, treated by Fran, stands in Mrs Stella's front parlour, looking over her visitors with a glistening jet eye.

Next, Fran had worked for weeks on a fox she found dead beside the cobbled road, and discovered an aesthetic sense she did not know she had. She replaced the eye with a shining diamond, and woven strands of gold thread with the fox's fur, which she treated until it shone. She wove decorative knots through the fox's tail. The fever with which she worked on these animals made her barely notice that she did not, at any point, feel revulsion or disgust as she worked with the hollow carcasses, pinning silver spikes to replace bones, teasing out papery flesh into the shapes of once again living.

Fran considers herself a sculptor of dead things, these days. And Christine's description of human preservative has set her mind afire.

Mrs Stella reappears in the dining-room laden with parcels.

"Time for presents!" she cries. "And then let us sing some carols."

As THE TWENTY-FIFTH of December melts away and the next day arrives to take its place, Christine leans over in bed and gently touches Fran on the shoulder.

"What is distracting you?" she says. "You've hardly said a word since we came home, but your eyes are so alive—you seem far away."

Fran smiles and rubs her eyes. "I'm sorry," she says. "I've been distracted, that's all. Thinking over the day. I didn't mean to worry you."

Christine might not be completely convinced, but she takes it as reassurance that nothing serious is wrong. It is quite usual for either of them to become quiet when thinking over a new project, or (in Christine's case) in the approach to examinations. Her breathing soon becomes deep and regular. Fran does not manage to sleep for a long time.

ON THE TWENTY-SIXTH of December, the bohemians meet at a local cafe to gaze out at the already fading light of the early afternoon and drink away the flat greyness that accrues after any celebration. Mrs Stella does not join them; she is away, pursuing the many other demands filling her social calendar: entertaining, visiting, generally sparkling. Mrs Stella is interested in everyone, and highly desired by the public; as such, she is constantly busy. Her dance card is always overwritten: at least two partners for every waltz.

And so the group cluster around a table in the corner of the Wine & Roses, a cheap, familiar drinking den in the centre of Soho. They huddle together, nursing strong liquors. Oliver Allbright is dissolving a lump of sugar over a silver spoon into his absinthe.

"How did you get on with your family this morning, Edwin?" He means the ballet school.

Edwin smiles. "Very well, actually. I'm to play Romeo again in the new season."

"Jolly good!" Oliver taps the spoon on the side of his glass.

Jacques-Louis puts an arm across Edwin's shoulders and squeezes. "Looking forward to the new year's bash," he says. "Not least since it's bound to bring some money in. It'll be a field day for the dreadfuls. They'll want more gossip inches than even I can provide."

Oliver nods. He is no stranger to such publications, and broadly encourages their inaccurate reporting of his own activities. He turns to the others. "And have you been doing any more of your hideous anatomy preparations?"

Both Christine and Fran go to answer, which makes Oliver laugh.

A door disguised as a dusty bookshelf, hidden in the far wall, swings open: a group of people come out, giggling uncontrollably with red, watery eyes, and slapping each other on the back. They leave the door ajar, and from the back room comes a sweet-smelling, heavy fog. It is intoxicating to breathe.

"I meant Miss Sparks, of course," says Oliver, removing his monocle to wipe it with his handkerchief, "but has Miss Clayton returned to the taxidermy table?"

"And over the festive season, too!" says Jacques-Louis in not quite mock-disgust.

"Stuffing a goose, were you?" says Edwin. The table erupts into laughter.

A waiter has seen the opened door, and rushes to close it. Fran's head is already swimming with the sweet-smelling fog. And it is *this* that brings her to decide, once and for all, that she will go ahead with what she has been considering ever since the Christmas dinner.

She *will*, she thinks. She will suggest it to Christine.

AND SO IT is late on the twenty-sixth of December, the sky outside the colour of old snow, when Fran breaks her silence. The whole group has joined Oliver on green drinks, and everyone is involved in a heavy discussion—as is their wont—about the nature of art.

"I'm telling you," Oliver is saying, "this naturalism stuff... is but a blip. We shall soon tire of its exhausting, *quasi-scientific* method of analysing human behaviour—gazing down upon ourselves as if our parlours are only so many dirty petri dishes—and return to enjoying art for the sake of the sheer *pleasure* it provides."

"I hope you're right," says Edwin. "If I ever have to dance naturalistic ballet I shall pull a muscle."

"And if we writers must stick to things that have *actually* occurred," says Jacques-Louis, clutching his absinthe with an evil leer, "the gossip columns of London shall become as blank as a map of the Arctic."

Fran leans towards Christine. Her mind is still foggy with the cloud of poppy-smoke; she notices the shine on the dark blue of Christine's velvet coat.

"I can contain myself no more," she says. "I have something to propose."

Christine's eyebrow arches. "'Propose'? What about?"

"The things you said yesterday: about the preservation of a body."

"And?"

"It made my mind come alive!"

"What do you mean?"

Christine leans her head over her absinthe, clutches her fingers around the glass as if afraid Fran will put something in it—some truth serum or dangerous potion.

Fran's words gabble; if she stops now, she may never start again. "I make bodies beautiful; you know of my work on dead things," she says. "Why don't we work together?"

"Together?"

"For your medical exams. I'll make the body beautiful; I'll

treat it with my instruments the way you treat it with yours—the scalpel and the syringe and so on. And, in return, *you* preserve it as best you can; we will make it look positively eerie with life."

Christine drinks the whole of her absinthe down in one. Ignoring the shouts of congratulation from Edwin, Oliver and Jacques-Louis, who immediately set about ordering more for everyone, Christine closes her eyes and feels the flat greenness spreading through her body. It burns down her throat and into her stomach: and when she opens her eyes again, it is as if she is new-born; newly, freshly alive.

"There's something I discovered," she says to Fran, slurring the 'S'es. Fran nods, waiting. She recognises Christine's energy, which mirrors her own, and realises Christine has been wanting desperately to suggest something, too.

Christine peers into her empty glass, runs a finger around the rim and licks it. She needs every last drop of the green stuff if she is to get this out.

"We can do more than make her *look* alive," she says. "I think I've found a way we can *give* her life."

BACK IN THEIR lodgings, not a long walk from the Wine & Roses—Fran and Christine live in a cramped set of rooms, in a high building squeezed thinner by its neighbours, where mould grows on the crumbling bricks and the gas lamps flicker through the dirty windows from the street—Fran has been pestering Christine all night for more information. Every other step she tugs her sleeve, whispers, "What did you *mean*?" But Christine hasn't dared go further, beyond her first utterance. It is as if it took all her energy to announce the theme, and she has lost all energy for the details.

It was Mrs Stella's idea that Fran and Christine live together. It is perfectly natural for young ladies to share accommodation in the capital. To bring a man into the scenario would be to teeter on the edge of immorality; but two young women together, no mischief can possibly befall. In any case, Christine is often away pursuing her studies, leaving Fran to litter the tables with the hollow carcasses of flattened rodents, scatters of gemstones, gold thread and plucked feathers.

They climb the stairs with a clatter of boots on wood, and Fran pleads again as they enter the dingy parlour. Christine finally gives in.

"I made some discoveries," she says, hanging her coat on the hook, "while working—alongside the usual anatomy—on the physical properties of electricity. A delirious account of a controversy at Newgate, half a century ago; rumours of an affair on the Orkneys, years before. Things began to link together. It isn't a single method," she adds, for Fran's eyes are lighting up as she imagines turning a body on at the flick of a switch. Christine shakes her head. "I wish I had a simple recipe to show you. No; I had to compile different materials to reach my current theory. The method I have in mind, I put together myself, pulling pieces from dead or dying ideas. It's a little of everything. It's a mixture of the believed-to-be-obsolete, the known-to-be-arcane and the who-knows-how-it-works of the moment. It's a forgotten ancient alchemy in the veins; electric tendrils in the brain; a new chemistry in the heart."

"So let's try it!"

Christine's shoulders sag. She was hoping to put Fran off; as soon as she used that phrase—we can *give* her life—she lost her nerve.

But Fran is thrilled, inflamed. She takes Christine's face between her hands. "We must experiment. If it doesn't work, nothing is lost. If it does work—why, *death* will be lost!"

Christine smiles—humouring rather than humoured—and reaches up to gently take Fran's hands away. "It's a collection of scrappy theories, pulled from ancient books scattered across the continent," she says. She squeezes Fran's hands, tenderly, putting the issue, as she sees it, to bed. "It won't work."

"Think of Mrs Stella's face," says Fran, "when we tell her. And Allbright! We can make art and life one and the same thing, on a level never before accomplished."

Christine looks over the parlour table, the plates scattered about with the remnants of bread crusts and cheese crumbs. Mrs Stella's patronage added to Christine's income would stretch to employing someone to clean for them, but they prefer their living to be private. It means more things become acceptable, unremarked; like kissing the other on the back of the neck while she is reading, or lacing each other's fingers as they pass towards the door, or eating quickly in the parlour before going out, without thought to good manners. Or keeping a human body on the table in the back room.

Christine thinks. "We cannot damage the body," she says. "We must think of this as being for the greater good of science."

Fran is beaming. "With this 'formaldehyde,' we won't damage anything!" she says. "It will only become better; *more* like a work of art. That's part one. Then we apply your mysterious theories, see if they work."

"And you'll be able to cope with the process? This isn't like one of your taxidermied squirrels."

Fran's hands become fists, press to her sides amidst her

skirts. She stands to attention. "I will perform to the best of my abilities," she says.

Christine's eyes blaze with a new vitality. "Let's do it, then."

THE REASON THERE is a body in the back room, instead of where it should be—in the anatomy halls of the medical college—is mostly down to fortune. Whether good or bad fortune depends primarily upon one's perspective.

The body was not donated by a patron. It was found, days before, backstage in one of the district's many burlesque houses. One of the dancers, the owner said, had been jilted by her lover and fallen down in a faint. The others, presuming she was being her usual melodramatic self, had ignored her; it was only when she missed her cue to perform did anyone examine her closely, to discover that she would never high-kick again.

The dancer's bad fortune became Christine's good. The owner, who knew Christine through Fran—the sculptor had undertaken commissions for the establishment's decor—told Christine about it, insisting the club could not handle any public fuss. And so the body was delivered in the dead of night, providing Christine an unprecedented opportunity to get ahead in her studies.

It was initially an inconvenience for Fran, who likes to spread her taxidermy projects over that table; now, of course, she realises it is a gift.

CHRISTINE TAKES THE first shift with the body. First she needs to reapply the preservative; to replenish, as it were, the body's stores. Fran watches from the corner, her hands knitted tightly together, hardly daring to breathe.

The syringe is cold, made of tarnished silver and thick glass, and it weighs heavily in Christine's hand. She fills it with a bubbling green liquid, prepares the dosage; jetting a short burst from the pointed tip of the needle. The sickly fluid splashes her cheek and she wipes it away absently, before brushing the hair away from the body's eyes.

"There, there," she says.

She injects the formaldehyde into the chest, pushing the needle in as steadily as if she were behind the counter in The Black Cat, plunging down the brass handle of a cafetière. She injects the preservative again, into the arms, the legs, between the shoulders: turning the syringe sideways, pressing it into the temple.

The body's delicate hands seem to move imperceptibly as the chemical powers through the veins. Slowly, the body takes on the illusion of pale life.

Christine leaves on a midnight errand to the medical college, leaving Fran to take the next shift alone. This takes the majority of the night.

The instruments of taxidermy, in this era, are not dissimilar to the tools found in Christine's medical chest. Fran uses them with equal, if not greater, care.

The nails on the hands she shapes and paints; and she adds fine, barely-noticeable patterns to the soles of the feet, and colours the toenails so they glow gold. She sews rich aquamarine jewels onto the backs of the hands, and, with a rich turquoise powder— the lead-based paste she might normally use to enrich the tail of a peacock—she paints the eyelids. She adds rows of diamonds through the hair. She threads metal wire through the inside of the lips, shaping the mouth into a beguiling smile. Using a sharp device that resembles a hooked scalpel, she scrapes the teeth until they shine white, reshaping them until they sit uniform inside the pink gums. She adds a beauty spot made of jet just above the corner of the mouth, a stone she might otherwise have set into the eye of a freshly-mounted sparrow.

The sensation is curious, as she works; the arms of the body are cold, undoubtedly unliving; yet they are soft, and the formaldehyde in the veins gives the illusion of pliability. If she gets it wrong a bruise will, surely, she thinks, slowly form on the skin, mottled like dead leaves and black at the edges. She applies subtle powders of gold and bronze to the flesh. She wants the final product to appear artificially beautiful— treated, unnatural: symbolic of her art—but the effect must be subtle.

Using a needle so thin it is barely visible, she sews threads of gold into the eyelashes and eyebrows. She has some left over, and threads it delicately through the hair between the legs.

Christine re-enters the room, having snatched a quarter-hour of sleep, and they hook the body up to a collection of devices Christine has brought from the college. Fran feels her heart beating inside her chest; she is certain it must be audible across the room.

Christine presses the switch.

The electricity is silent, coursing through the body on an invisible network of arteries and nervous clusters. Once, an eyelid flickers and Fran clasps Christine's hand so tightly she is surprised Christine doesn't cry out.

Christine only shakes her head. "It is the power of the electricity," she says, "coursing through the skull, affecting the eyeball. Proof of nothing at all."

As morning light breaks and brings to the city the twenty-seventh of December, Fran and Christine stand, their breath coming deep and snagged, as if they have been running for hours, nervous sweat turning their hair to ropes. They gaze down together at the prone body. The pale light of morning is beginning to push through the windows, outlining the thin curtains with a border of grey light.

"Her pallor," says Fran, "is not what I was expecting."

"I did say bleaching would occur," says Christine.

"Yes—but this is such an extreme case. I feel as if I were looking at her through a fogged window."

"Well then, perhaps it is just as well she isn't sitting up to speak with us."

They wait a few more moments.

"It didn't work," says Christine. Her voice is as flat as the table on which the body lies. "Fool that I am. Of course it didn't."

Fran takes her hand. "She's beautiful, though," she says. "We can display her at the new year's party; nobody will think it a real body. It looks like a fine marble sculpture."

Christine shakes her head. "I'm going to get some more sleep," she says, and she goes to their bedroom, leaving Fran with the body.

Fran watches their creation for a few moments more. She focuses on one of the hands, willing it to tremble so much that, when it finally does, she believes she must have fallen asleep too, and is only dreaming. It is not until the fingers twitch all together, slowly tapping upon the table as if remembering a tune for the pianoforte, that Fran knows she is seeing something real. Her gaze moves over the body's stomach and breasts and lands with a gasp upon the body's face just as the eyes flick open.

Both parties in the room register equal amounts of shock. The silence in the room is thick, like Fran and the body are buried together under six feet of cold soil.

The shining lips move, with stiffness as they navigate their wiry frame.

Fran holds out a finger. "Stay there," she says, and within a moment the door to the back room is open and her feet are falling heavily along the floorboards.

Christine is sitting at the writing-desk in their bedroom, running her pen over an anatomic drawing, craning to use the little light that filters in through the dusty window from the street lamps. She looks up at Fran, standing breathlessly in the doorway.

"I couldn't sleep," she explains.

Fran shakes her head; she feels she will never need sleep again. "You've got to come back in."

Christine holds her gaze. "What is it?" Her pen drops ink onto the carefully-drawn diagram. The body she is drawing has a black splatter for a heart.

Fran taps on the doorframe. Impatient. "What do you *think?*"

And so the clock ticks through the early morning of the twenty-seventh of December. Fran and Christine have gone from their bedroom to the back room, to the bedroom, to the parlour, to the back room and back again into the bedroom—travelling between disbelief, horror, exhilaration; hugging, crying out; racing from one room to another. Finally they stand in the small room where the body still lies on the table, blinking and—newly, extraordinarily—slowly sitting up.

"What shall we call her?" Fran follows the curving slope of the body's shoulders down to her arms with hungry eyes. The throat trembles with the new pulse.

Christine taps her foot on the floor. "It ought to be something of magnitude," she says. "Something that signifies what we have achieved here."

The body is sitting up fully, now, her feet dangling over the edge of the table. She is looking down at her toes, wiggling them.

"One name springs to mind." A smile plays about Fran's face. "How about Eve?"

Christine's eyes widen at the audacity. "Just how many blasphemies do you propose we commit in one day?"

But Eve does seem to fit; and it is decided.

They complete the christening by clinking two high-stemmed glasses together and downing the contents. They kiss, tasting wine on each other's mouths.

CHRISTINE IS IMMEDIATELY busy; the main body of Christmas being over, she is obliged to return to her studies, and thus while it is still dark with the freshness of the twenty-seventh of December, she leaves the house, to commence once again the business of crossing the city for lectures, practical examinations, discussions. Fran, under the patronage of Mrs Stella, is able to remain at home to proceed on her sculptural work. She has a taxidermy commission. The parlour table is a tangle of hollow skin, scraps of fur, glass vials of tanning oil, the scattered gemstones that will become eyes. A full scene; a selection of mounted dormice recreating the carefree revelry of a burlesque dancehall. The door to the back room remains open, and Fran sits so she can face it, utterly unable to concentrate. The presence of Eve sits squarely across her thoughts like bars on a window.

She discovers Eve can speak when Eve comes into the parlour, standing unsteadily in the doorway. She looks at Fran for a few long moments, then asks for a picture.

"A picture?" Fran is careful.

"A pattern," says Eve. Her voice has a lilt to it—Christine

delicately aligned every vocal chord, finely tuned it like a concert violin. "I want to look like that." She raises an arm and points to one of the decorated pieces of fabric piled in a rough square on the table. (It will eventually be sewn into tiny, intricate ruffles for can-can dancing mice.)

Fran goes into the back room and paints a delicate pattern over Eve's back and shoulders, piercing it through Eve's skin with a needle. She uses black and green, outlines it with gold. A beautiful bruise.

CHRISTINE COMES HOME early; the twenty-seventh of December has been a half-day for her. A professor, still recovering from the fine port and sherry of the season, cancelled his lecture on the anatomy of the stomach.

Fran goes not greet Christine properly, but stands and immediately says:

"We shouldn't tell anyone about Eve."

Christine is pulling off her gloves. The fierce, alcoholic smell of anaesthetic hangs around her like an invisible fog. "What do you mean?"

"We should keep her a secret," says Fran. "I've changed my mind; about telling Mrs Stella. I don't think we ought to tell anyone."

Christine arches a sceptical eyebrow. "She's a medical marvel," she says. "And an artistic one. I could barely stop myself shouting out about her to the entire lecture theatre. Of course we must show her. What's gotten into you?"

Their rooms are filled with a sulky silence for the next few hours. Offended at Fran's abrupt change of heart, Christine does not tell her she has already sent an excited letter of invitation.

*   *   *

THE AFTERNOON LIGHT is waning, and the air is damp; the buildings of Soho look as if they have been seeped in pale water. The streets are lined with melting snow, most of which has long since turned to brown sludge. Sure-footed, Mrs Stella makes her way across the cobbles from a hansom cab; her umbrella hangs on her arm. Christine is peering down out of the window to watch for her arrival, and Mrs Stella has barely rapped upon the door before she breathlessly lets her in.

"I received your missive, dear," says Mrs Stella, "and came directly. This is something to do with the new year's festivities, I take it?"

Fran is sitting at the table when Christine rushes past, unwinding an old Yule wreath she found abandoned in the street. It was half trampled by horses, but still salvagable. She pulls the branches apart, separating them out; the stronger twigs will do for modelling dormice poses, and she can use the holly leaves for something. Perhaps a hairpiece for Eve. Her fingers are covered in red scratches. On hearing Mrs Stella's voice she immediately stands, and her fingers press down onto the hard wood.

"No," she mutters, but Mrs Stella is already breezing inside, raising her arms towards her. Christine follows behind, her face slightly sheepish.

"Drab old day, isn't it?" says Mrs Stella. "I was summoned," she adds, seeing the faraway glance in Fran's eyes. "I gather you have something to show me?"

Fran nods, unable to speak.

"It's through here, Mrs Stella," says Christine. The great actress adjusts her hat with a murmur of, "Marvellous," and leads the way into the parlour.

Fran marches to Christine, takes her firmly around the waist.

"I said we shouldn't," she says. "We didn't agree. What are you doing?"

"Mrs Stella needs to see her," says Christine. "It was for her benefit we went ahead with the experiment anyway."

"You didn't *tell me*," says Fran. "What if I don't *want*—"

Mrs Stella's voice ripples into the room. "My dears?"

"Coming!" calls Christine. She lowers her voice to an urgent whisper. "We *have* to show her sometime, Fran. Are we supposed to keep it a secret for ever?"

"Perhaps!"

Christine laughs and pulls Fran's arms away. "I'd rather her first sight of humanity beyond the two of us was Mrs Stella, not some ring of anonymous profs in a viewing gallery."

Fran gulps. She wants to tell Christine that neither option particularly appeals, but she is unable to swallow the hard lump filling her throat. In any case, Christine has already disappeared into the next room.

"You RECALL, MRS Stella, my conversation on Christmas Day, regarding the technologies of formaldehyde?"

"Of course! How could I forget them?" Mrs Stella is seated grandly, her gloves in one hand and her umbrella in the other. "I daresay poor Jacques-Louis is still experiencing nightmares."

"Fran and I—" Christine glances at Fran, who is standing, arms folded, in the doorway. She smiles: an olive branch extended. "We have been working on a project together. And, thanks to your inspiration, we have succeeded in something I doubt you have encountered before."

"I wouldn't be too sure about *that*, my dear," says Mrs Stella,

"I've seen some things. In eighteen-eighty-two my Rosalind toured to Leamington Spa."

"Nevertheless," Christine's eyes glisten, "I believe this will surprise you. You'll see how Fran and I made it together." At this, Fran takes the olive branch, smiling back at Christine.

Christine opens the door into the back room, beckoning Fran to follow.

Inside, Eve is standing by the window. She frowns at them as if displaced, thrown off course by the new voice.

Fran wrinkles her nose. The room smells of burnt lavender, and of overpowering basil; Christine has endeavoured to mask the chemical smell that follows Eve everywhere.

Eve nods towards the door that leads through into the parlour, clearly wondering what is happening, who is there.

"It's a good friend of ours," says Christine. "We'd be honoured to introduce you."

She holds out her hand. Eve looks down at it, unsure: and, with a flicker of her eyes Christine cannot help but notice, her gaze moves to Fran, and waits there until Fran gives the smallest of nods. Then Eve turns her gaze back to Christine, and allows her to take her hand.

Christine looks at Fran as they turn towards the door. Her look is odd, as if she is trying to place where something began.

Christine leads Eve into the room. They walk together in silence until they are by the window, where Christine leaves Eve standing alone. Christine stands besides Mrs Stella's chair; Fran remains in the doorway. She has a better view of Mrs Stella's face from there.

Mrs Stella leans forward on the wicker chair, leaning her weight into the floor, pressing onto the handle of her umbrella.

"Oh, my dears," she says, "what on earth have you done?"

Fran and Christine share a nervous glance.

"It's the new formaldehyde," says Christine, quietly. "As you see, the body looks as it did in life. Better, even."

"Quite extraordinary," she mutters. "And how do you get it to move?"

"The precise method would be difficult to explain," says Christine, as she slowly reclaims her confidence, "but it involved electricity. Needless to say, I don't believe anyone has achieved such a thing for many years—if *ever*, quite like this," she adds, with pride.

"And it… thinks, and feels, and so on?" Mrs Stella's face is held taut. "It is alive in the same sense that we are?"

"Perhaps *more* alive," says Christine, "in a sense. It did require a lot of power."

Mrs Stella frowns and looks down at her umbrella, slowly rotating it on the spot. Dirty water accrues on the floor beneath its tip. "I must confess this development worries me slightly," she says.

She looks up again and examines Eve with the keen precision of a fine art collector, examining the fall of Eve's hair, the slope of her stomach, her fingertips.

After a time none of them can measure, Mrs Stella seems to relax.

"Very well," she says. "Your enthusiasm, and, I confess, the sheer *beauty* of your creation, has convinced me. I shall suppress my doubts. I love it!" She stands. "It's darling. In fact, I've an idea. You must exhibit it at the new year's party!"

Fran leaves the doorway: she finds her voice again. "We thought that at first," she says, "but now we don't—"

"It would be an honour," says Christine.

"I've got it!" Mrs Stella is already pulling on her gloves.

"She can perform. A *tableau vivant*; that's the ticket! We'll do a beauteous display upon the stage, half undressed and completely still; in a classical attitude, so they know it isn't smut. Give her a vase to hold." She re-pins her hat into place with a sharp stab. Eve remains, standing silently, her arms by her sides. Forgotten.

Mrs Stella fluffs the feathered plume of her hat with a careless hand. "You've *made* the new year's party, my dears. It will be as your creation is: perfect. Heartiest of congratulations."

As soon as Mrs Stella is gone, Fran and Christine are at loggerheads.

"There you are, you see," says Christine, "What were you so worried about?"

"That wasn't an introduction," hisses Fran. "That was a demonstration. You didn't address one word to Eve, neither of you."

"What's gotten into you?" says Christine. "We'll present her at the party and become toast of the city! I'll be a certified doctor within weeks, I'll bet; we can move into a grand house like Mrs Stella's. What's the problem?"

Fran doesn't know. Her eyes fill with emotion: but not tears. A dry, scratching feeling, like a burn. She feels too on edge to cry. She feels as if every nerve in her body is raw.

"I don't like the way it's going," she says, "that's all."

Christine's face softens, and so does her voice. She takes Fran's hand and gently stokes it. "We've always trusted in each other before," she says.

Fran leans her face against Christine's chest. "Yes," she says. But in the red-blackness of her half-closed eyes, she sees Eve glance her way; a micro-check that everything is still all right. With a further burning feeling in the back of her eyes, Fran realises with a jolt that Eve *trusts* her, more than she trusts Christine.

CHRISTINE IS OUT again—sitting through lectures and attending demonstrations of the latest anatomical discoveries. She may be preparing for a great presentation in the new year, the reveal of Eve; Fran cannot bring herself to ask. It is the twenty-eighth of December and they have barely spoken, so enraptured have they been in their own activities. As soon as Christine leaves, Fran goes to the back room to sit with Eve, the ghost of Christine's farewell kiss still lingering on her cheek. Fran finds that she and Eve can go for hours without speaking. So can Fran and Christine, of course; but that is a silence of mutual busyness, of the contentment that arises between two people pursuing separate, but simultaneous activity. The silences between Fran and Eve are more companionable: it is the silence of two people thinking and feeling along the same lines. Unopened invitations pile up beneath the letterbox.

Mid-afternoon, Mrs Stella pays another visit. She does not ask about Eve and remains in the entranceway, refusing even Fran's offer of a cup of Lady Grey.

"I mustn't stay," says Mrs Stella. Her hat is new; its ostrich feathers threaten to scrape the ceiling. "I just wanted to pop in, see how you are. Oliver tells me you are never to be seen in the café-theatres now. He expected you to dine with him last night, spend an evening chatting throughout the applause—not that I approve of those behaviours, but there you are—but he tells me you never replied to his letter. Are you quite all right? You're not ill?"

In Fran's mind she sees Eve's tattoo, follows the delicate pattern along her shoulderblades. She has spent the morning making it bigger, spreading interlocking patterns over Eve's body. She shakes her head. "Everything is fine. It's only been a day or so, hasn't it—two days? How can Oliver say he never sees me?"

Mrs Stella holds her gaze a moment. Unconvinced. Then she blinks, and the moment snaps, and she rummages around in her carpet bag.

"I've brought you something to read, anyway. These are Jacques-Louis's old copies; sadly discontinued, of course, all of them. But he thought they might be of interest anyway. I think he wants you to get a new hobby, my dear!"

She holds aloft a thick pile of pages, brown parchment with greasy wax-covers in green, grey and garish yellow. Lurid brush-strokes outline bodies and landscapes on the front pages. Bohemian periodicals, the best in the city.

Fran takes them, deposits them heavily by the hat-stand without looking at them properly. She pushes a lock of hair out of her eyes. "To tell you the truth, Mrs Stella, I've clean lost track of what day it is."

Mrs Stella hooks her umbrella over her arm and adjusts her hat. "Oh, I shouldn't worry," she says, turning to leave. "That's perfectly normal for this time of year."

WHEN MRS STELLA is gone, Fran finds she is utterly uninterested in the gossip, doodlings and apocalyptic predictions of the magazines. She totters to the bedroom, lays on her back upon the bed and stares out of the featureless window. Her fingers play with the embroidery upon her bodice, and she pulls a thread loose, barely noticing as she does it. Her eyes wander from the blank sky across the walls of the room, and her gaze snags on a dilapidated patch in the corner of the ceiling. Here the cold and damp have combined to rot away one corner of the beams, revealing, among the splintering wood and clouded knots of the old webs of spiders, some scraps of the previous occupant's yellow wallpaper, which has become dulled with time and peels away at the edges.

Fran sighs deeply. She feels time is an exhausting tunnel she must pass through; the week is a scatter of grey days, lacking life, all badly stitched together. She rises to go into the back room, to sit longer with Eve.

A PAPERY SOUND drops through the front door, and an envelope lands heavily on all the others. This time, Fran musters the energy to open it. It is an invitation to stroll in Green Park and, not seeing why Christine should have all the fresh air, she goes.

Oliver Allbright is already there, standing by a bench, wearing green-and-yellow-check trousers, a bottle-green velvet waistcoat and a dark brown jacket with long tails. He is holding a pipe, and Fran knows better than to enquire what is in it. She takes his arm and they stroll down the path. The sky is pale and watery, the path slushed with old snow, the parklands broadly grey, peppered with patches of dull green and brown. Not many people are out in this weather. A few children play about, wearing muddied, torn scraps.

"Mrs Stella tells me you have been distracted of late," he says. "I hope it's not this absurd project with Christine I heard you talking about?"

Fran starts. "How did you know about that?"

"It is my business," says Oliver, "to hear things that are whispered urgently in the corner of an absinthe bar. I promise neither Edwin, nor Jacques-Louis, nor anyone else in the Wine & Roses heard what you were saying. Only myself. Hence, my taking the liberty of inviting you out."

Fran looks down at her feet. Her grey shoes kick lightly over old leaves that have turned to blackish slime.

"It's an artistic project," she says, "and it's overtaken my imagination. It really feels as if it has a life of its own. I can't concentrate on anything else. Apologies for my absence."

"Now that," says Oliver, "I can understand. I certainly have been lost to artistic endeavours in my time. Do you know, there's at least a few months of this year I have completely forgotten? It is all a green haze. Green and black and grey. I ask you! It's not even aesthetically pleasing. A total clash. At least you have Christine to comfort you. You'll give her my regards when you see her tonight?"

"No. She's out. Again," says Fran. "Some keynote lecture, I think, on the ethics of preservation."

"I see," says Oliver. But Fran is not quite sure *what* he sees.

They walk on a little more. A flustered nanny passes them, pushing a squeaky-wheeled pram, desperately making shushing noises into the whimpering bundle. Two boys kneel by the side of the path in a puddle of murky water, muddied to their knees, tormenting a frog.

"Will you be glad to see the year out?" says Oliver.

Fran contemplates a rotting oak leaf lying by her shoe. "A few days ago, perhaps. But now everything feels... upended, and yet the same. Let the century die, I feel I will hardly notice."

Oliver nods. "Of course, there *are* those who insist the century is not, actually, about to end. That might be why it's all the same to you. Supposedly, we ought to hold off until 1900 turns into 1901. We're a year early."

More dead leaves. Their walking breaks them up, and they merge into an indistinct wet shape. Fran shakes her head. "Does it matter?"

Oliver smiles. "Not in the least. Ninety-nine growing into a new hundred *feels* so much more satisfying, does it not? And feelings are everything. And if this year's revelry proves unsatisfactory, we can always consider it a dry run, do it over."

A breeze comes through the bare tree branches, finds its way into every buttonhole. Fran shivers. "I couldn't bear it happening again," she says. Oliver squeezes her arm.

It gets dark as they walk.

WINTER DAYS BEING what they are, it is long dark by the time Fran returns. Even as she approaches the door, something tells her that things are wrong, and her step falters; she gazes for a long moment at the tarnished door-knocker and she feels the heavy, fat presence of something waiting for her beyond the entrance. She shakes her head slightly, closing her eyes to brush off the sensation, and grasps the door handle in her gloved hand.

The rooms seem the same as when she left them, only darker with the onset of an early winter's night; from the far bedroom comes the dull yellow glow of a candle. Somebody is in, but it is not Christine; her coat, hat and boots are absent from the hat stand. Fran lets her umbrella drop to the floor, and it lands with a heavy *thunk* that makes Fran jump, sending electric prickles across the back of her neck. She finds her thoughts cycling rapidly: *Nothing to worry about. Christine must be on a late call.* Yet those very thoughts make Fran's heart beat faster: why does she feel the need to conjure reassuring thoughts?

Fran's mind races as she peels off her gloves. There is nothing inherently unusual in the candle. Eve has revealed a tendency to stay awake late, just as Fran and Christine do, stretching out the final hours of the century staring at the black square of the window, the candle's yellow glow a comfort in the dark. Eve may well have lit the flame. Yet, as Fran paces towards the bedroom, some deep dread sends a shiver up her back. Her feet make louder creaks on the floorboards than she is accustomed to, or wants.

As her hand reaches out to push open the bedroom door, a memory from a second earlier rises to the forefront of her vision. She realises that, as she passed the table, the stack of empty plates remained upon it, bearing crusts and crumbles of cheese; and that the plates have sat that way for far too long, and the bread has become dotted with dark green mould. She feels ill.

The bedroom door swings open and Fran's gaze skips first to the bed—tangled sheets, unmade—and then, in the dim light of the single candle by the window, her eyes adjust to the lumpen shape sitting in the biggest chair, facing away from her, leaning forwards, legs stretched out towards the dark, empty fireplace. She breathes a sigh of relief.

"You had me worried!" she says, and her voice bounces off the thick silence. Instantly she sees that something is very different; the body in the chair does not turn around to face her. She feels a movement to her right, and turns.

Tallow-yellow in the candlelight, her face a rictus of confusion, is Eve. She is pressed up against the wall, and her eyes blaze in the darkness, glittering more, in their confusion and fear, than the jewels on her skin.

"You said I was the only one!" she says. "I heard you!"

"What...?" says Fran. She turns back to the fireplace.

The being in the chair sits up and begins to turn around.

Fran backs against the bedroom door, her hand to her mouth. She does not scream.

It pushes itself out of the chair.

Fran's eyes take in the lumpen boots, caked with old mud, the dirty trousers, torn jerkin; fashions from an unfathomable time. The creature's arms are roped with muscle and streaked with dark, dried grazes and scars of old wounds. He takes a heavy stride up, heaving his weight from the chair, until he stands, back to the fireplace like a polite guest.

"What?" says Fran.

"He says he's like me," says Eve, from behind her. "He says we're the same."

His face is a death-mask. In the light of the candle his skin appears yellow-green, and his eyes are filmed over with a milky brown; bloodshot, but with old, dead blood. He stares at Fran. He opens his mouth again and a black tongue flickers out, licks his dry lips. His hair is like dirty straw, falling loosely across his face.

"Good evening," he says.

"You're *not* the same!" Fran presses her hands to the door, feeling the flat of the heavy wood against her sweating palms. The room smells thick, she realises, like sour milk or rotting hay. The mould on the bread. "How dare you say you're like her!"

"We are—similar, then." His voice comes from somewhere deep, beyond his throat; it rises like a bucket of sludge from an old well. When the noise reaches his throat it grates and splinters; by the time it reaches his lips, forming into words for Fran, it is a dull crackling moan, full of old pain and long-boiling anger. Every utterance, Fran sees, causes this monster a great deal of physical strife. He will not waste words.

"He came through the window," says Eve.

Fran imagines him, sitting all afternoon by her fireplace. "How did you find us?"

The monster raises his shoulders, slowly, with a popping of rotten cartilage, and lets them fall again. A shrug. "I sensed."

"And what do you want?"

"He wants us to go away together," says Eve.

Fran's head presses on the side of the wall, her eyes rolling to their whites with the effort of looking at Eve as well as trying to keep watch on the interloper. "He *what?*"

"He says the world is dangerous," says Eve. She looks down at her body, runs her fingers across herself, holds her arms there in a light hug. She has become, Fran realises, conscious of her nudity.

"Not just dangerous for me. For us both. For the *likes* of us. He said. He says people will not understand us, so I should go with him, and all the sooner."

"You want to take her *away?*" Fran can feel cold sweat down her back, dragging at the fabric against her body; it trickles down her neck, across her face.

Dark green creases form in the monster's neck as he nods.

Fran barely resists the urge to scream. "Why?"

"Safety," he says. "Companionship..." His eyes bulge at Fran; a trickle of dark brown liquid leaks out of one tear duct—too dark to be a tear, too thick to be blood. His materials cannot be categorised. "We belong together," he says. "Do you understand?"

Fran understands enough.

She races to the writing-desk beneath the window, flinging out her hand, her fingers flexing for anything she can reach. Eve cries out in anguish, causing Fran to adjust her movements by sudden instinct, as if ducking out of the way of an attack. She flings her arm out again, upends the candle, and the room is thrown into darkness.

Fran's fingers grasp something cold and sharp: Christine's brass letter-opener. She holds it out at the full stretch of her arm.

The room fills with a new odour, the ashy scratch of the extinguished candle.

The lumpen silhouette takes a heavy step closer to Fran, and Eve lets out another faint cry. Fran tightens her grip on the letter-opener. Her eyes adjust to the moonlight, which catches its edge with a golden glow, and Fran wonders what on earth she imagines she can achieve with such a narrow blade.

Nevertheless, she grips it until her knuckles go white.

As he reaches the window, it is clear the monster can see the blade too, and that he also wonders at Fran's strategy. His face splits into a wide smile, more terrible than his sterner face; his mouth surely contains more teeth than it should.

His voice takes on a new quality. Softer, like wet mud. Trying another angle. "We will eventually both require… companionship," he says.

Fran's hand shakes. "You, sir," she says, "are making *several* assumptions."

The monster throws his head back with a faint popping of vertebrae, and the tone of his voice returns to gravel-pit anger. "Try to protect her if you must," he says, "but she will see reason. I can teach you how to get by in this world; better than these people can. They will turn against you. I will not."

"We will not *turn*," says Fran. She feels Eve take some steps behind her, coming up closer behind, and her breath catches. Her heart is squeezing into the top of her chest, pressing down on her lungs and windpipe, stopping her airflow.

"I don't need you," says Eve, and for an appalling moment

Fran thinks she is talking to her. But the monster lets out a roar of frustration and leaps up onto the writing table.

Fran and Eve step back, together. Fran reaches out a hand and Eve clasps it. Eve's fingers are cold; Fran's are flattened red from her grip on the knife handle.

He is in a crouch on the table, rocking slightly on his heels. He is looking towards them, his outline not quite human; an appalling shape in the darkness. Fran has not yet taken a breath; any moment now, the table will surely collapse beneath his weight. Some pale light reaches the window from the gas lamps that line the street, illuminating his greasy hair and picking out the gray-green of the ghastly skin on his shoulders and arms. Through the gaps in his ragged shirt, she catches a glimpse of bronze, battered and verdigrised.

The monster's head moves a fraction and, even though she cannot make out any of his features, Fran knows he is speaking directly to her. "Just wait," he says. "If you do not turn, *she* will." And, with a smooth elegance she would not have expected, in a single movement he has opened the window, swung himself out across the casement, and let go, flinging both hands out with splayed fingers. For a moment he is fully framed by the window, his hair streaming behind him, as he sails silently through the night, cutting the air like a blade. He disappears to land, silently, in the street.

Fran and Eve remain in the darkness of the bedroom for some time. Fran places her hands over her knees, leaning over with the effort to get her breath, taking it in deep, heavy, gasping sobs, while the remaining adrenalin pounds through her mind and spins itself out between her shoulders. Quicker to compose herself, Eve steadies and relights the candle. Its new light shines on her skin and its gemstones, showing the curve of her stomach, clinging to her breasts and thighs. Her arms are covered in gooseflesh and she rubs her hands over them, crossing her arms over herself.

She steps towards Fran. Fran stands and takes Eve's hands in hers.

"I promise," says Fran.

Eve's face is entirely open, trusting. Before Fran realises what she is doing, she has bent her face towards Eve and touched Eve's mouth with her own.

Eve's lips are soft, with a fullness revealing the hard copper wires that shape them. Their kiss becomes harder, and Fran raises her arms to clasp Eve around the shoulders. Eve's hands, in turn, take Fran around the waist, and her white, straight teeth gently bite Fran's tongue. It sends a pulse of electricity across Fran's body, spinning the adrenalin of fear into a new kind of rush. She looks deeply into Eve's eyes. They shine like emeralds.

They move to the bed. Eve's body shudders as Fran's hands explore it. Her caresses draw on her experience pleasuring Christine and herself, of course; but partly they express the admiration of an expert craftswoman surveying her handiwork. Fran knows Eve's body well. She strokes her fingers lightly down Eve's stomach, teases across her golden hair, and down her thighs. Eve's breathing becomes heavy and thick. Fran feels the movement of Eve's chest with wonder, matches her quick breathing as they kiss again.

Eve pushes herself up and holds the back of Fran's neck. Fran shudders as Eve's moist lips tenderly press down onto her neck, over her shoulders: Eve's gentle tongue reaches Fran's breasts, and Fran leans her head to the ceiling and arches her back against the bed. Her eyes catch, once again, the yellow wallpaper in the corner near the ceiling; the beams seem to have rotted even further since she last looked. In the flickering of the lone candle the decay seems almost to move.

Her attention leaves the wall as Eve stops kissing her and leaves the bed. She goes to the corner where Christine's medical bag sits, squatting heavily on a wooden stool. Eve reaches inside and pulls out a large, silver wand-like instrument, and for a moment Fran fears some divine retribution, a kind of electric revenge.

But, of course, she realises what it is.

It is a relatively new medical technique. The vibrations are intended to bring about an ease of anxiety, massaging the tenseness from hard-working shoulders.

Eve brings the tool back into the bed, and her legs intertwine with Fran's. Eve places a hand upon the small of Fran's back, and with the other, switches on the device.

Bright sparks of electricity zip through the inside of the machine. Fran's eyes widen.

"What are you going to do?" she whispers.

Eve places Fran's arms above her head, holding her wrists together. As a joke, Fran wiggles, pretends to struggle, pressing her weight into the tangled sheets of the bed. She finds she cannot move. Even a light touch from Eve is able to pin her, totally, to the bed. For a moment Fran feels a spike of fear, a thrill of the unknown; in an instant, it is unclear who has more power. Eve notices and lets go.

"Are you all right?" she asks.

"You're very strong," says Fran, rubbing her wrist.

Eve looks down at her arms, considering. "I don't *feel* strong," she says. "He—before you arrived. He told me I would be able to withstand most anything. That the world is dangerous because of what I can withstand. Perhaps that's what he meant. That I'm stronger than... than I ought to be."

"That's interesting to know," mutters Fran. A faint thought passes over her mind, like a wispy cloud crossing the moon: Christine would like to know that.

"I'll have to be gentle," says Eve, and she moves the vibrator closer to Fran, gently places it upon Fran's skin.

Fran arches her back again as the pleasure rises. Her first orgasm is swift, building rapidly and peaking with electric efficiency. It happens quickly, opens her appetite rather than fulfilling it, and she is left gasping for breath and renewed with energy.

The vibrator glows, a living silvery-blue. Fran is hungry. She rises, propping her body on her elbows, feeling shaky and delicious.

"Give it to me," she says, and she pulls Eve onto the bed and straddles her, taking the silver wand into her own hands. They take it in turns, building and slowing, rising and falling, gasping for joy and losing their breath.

NIGHT FALLING, THE twenty-eighth of December. Mrs Stella, seated at her writing-desk, her pen flying across the paper.

She is following up invitations to the new year's party. The high importance of the event is repeated; reiterated. She writes to those who initially sent their apologies, as well as those who have already confirmed their attendance.

She writes that she has a magnificent surprise in store for the guests; a piece of entertainment never before seen in this city. She acknowledges the feelings of hopelessness or despair the addressed may be feeling as the century dies, but explains that her planned event is surely to bring it back to life, just for a moment, before it leaves forever. She signs off with love and the fondest of wishes, and, finally, again, just the once more, repeats how much, and how earnestly, she hopes the addressed will be in attendance. If they have already informed her that they must keep to other plans, she begs them to reconsider. She remains, sir, madame, your most gracious, obedient, and humble, servant.

When a thin green-and-white cup is placed beside her, she barely looks up from her work. The tea grows cold as she begins the next letter.

IN THE MIDDLE of the night, the darkest part of witching hour; the twenty-eighth of December has passed into the twenty-ninth, and Fran wakes in the pitch-black bed. The covers are tangled over her legs, and the pillow has a fold in it; her neck is pained, stretched at an awkward angle. She feels the weight of Eve beside her, the cold heaviness of her arm resting across Fran's chest. She strokes Eve's arm lightly; it feels smooth, like living marble.

She's wide awake.

"Eve?" she says.

Eve does not reply in words, but her other hand begins to gently stroke Fran's hair.

"I feel extraordinary," says Fran. A red hot fire is burning between her legs, smouldering low in her stomach. She feels wet, awake, all over. "I feel as though a thirst has opened up in me that can never be quenched," she says. "All I can think is: I want to do this again, and again, and again, and again."

"So why don't we?" murmurs Eve, and she leans over to

113

pick something up. In the quiet dark of the bedroom there is a metallic switch, followed by a gentle, insistent hum.

CHRISTINE IS GROWING tired of Fran's distracted state. On the thirtieth of December—early in the afternoon—she cracks, and says so.

She is in the bedroom, unpacking her satchel of papers scribbled with diagrams and formulae. "You haven't touched those dormice," she says, striking a match and putting it to the candle. "Am I the only one pursuing any work?"

Fran shakes her head. The room smells of dying lilies, with an undercurrent of ozone. Eve's scent. "I *am* working," she says. "I can't be blamed if you're never here to see me!"

Christine comes towards her, offers a brief kiss of apology, and rummages through her bag, motioning that she has something exciting to share. Fran wonders that Christine can't smell Eve on the bedsheets, or on Fran's tongue; but Christine is visibly exhausted. She pulls out a bottle from her bag and brandishes it aloft.

"It's a medicinal bitter," she says. "I got given it today. A scholar invented it to combat malaria, but turns out it tastes *incredible* with gin. Go and get the bottle."

The drink they make is dry like black pepper, with a tang of bitter orange that burns the back of the throat. The quinine in the bitter gives Fran the distinct feeling she is taking medicine, but it isn't unpleasant. She looks at Christine as they clink their glasses. They don't kiss again, and after the first sip Christine goes immediately back to her papers.

Fran feels she is watching her work from behind a pane of glass.

*   *   *

EDWIN TURNER LOOKS out over the city from the high windows of the dance school, temporarily distracted from the swishing of tulle and the wheeling of limbs.

"What you looking at?" asks a young woman in pale pink who has just pirouetted into his vicinity. She stretches out a leg on the barre, pretending to deal with a sudden attack of cramp, cocking her head to gaze keenly at Edwin. Her sash is an odd shade of green, which jars with the pink in a way he wasn't expecting. He feels a strange pulsing at the back of his mind; the beginnings of a headache.

"Just the city," he says. "Doesn't it make you feel dizzy?"

She looks out, following his gaze. "What, the view? Same as always isn't it?"

"The *date*," says Edwin. "The end of the century."

"Speaking of which." She points something out. "That's where *I'm* going tomorrow night," she says, "no matter what the rehearsal schedule is. Reckon I can sneak in. Madame says it's where the best party will be, in the whole city. Won't stop going on about her invitation, smug old sow. Wish she'd take me with her."

Edwin thinks it would be cruel to admit that he is also invited. Instead he smiles sadly and nods, and together they look out towards the district where, even from here, a crackling green light can be seen sweeping over the houses and the church spires.

THE DULL WINTER weather being what it is, the hands of the great clock tower have only just drifted past the hour of noon on the thirty-first of December, and already the day has begun to grow dark. Christine performs some cursory work, revising from a lecture on the structure of bones, and after an equally cursory meal—some old beef, cutting off those parts which are going green at the edges—Fran and Christine dress for the party. Fran is borrowing Christine's medical coat and brown leather bag. She adds a stethoscope, hanging it heavily around her neck.

"Very professional, my dear Doctor Jekyll," says Christine, with a wink. She—as Hyde, in a shabby blouse and long skirt they've slashed with a knife—back-combs her hair, deposits some twigs in it, and paints manic shapes around her eyes. They grin at each other, pleased with the effect. Before they leave, they look again at Eve's mask, slightly adjust the angle. Eve wears a black dress trimmed with black lace and subtle beads of jet (the dress is usually reserved for mourning); her Venetian mask is painted with abstract shapes in green and yellow, shot through with dramatic black intersecting lines.

And so, arms linked, with Eve in the middle, the three leave their lodgings and make their way on foot through the freezing streets of Soho, occasionally stopping to stamp their feet on the floor to warm them. Once Fran does this in the wrong spot, upending a loose piece of pavement; Christine laughs at the muddy splashes it leaves over her skirts, as well as soaking Fran's shoes. By some luck of angle, or quirk of timing, Eve remains untouched by any smudges of dirt and mud, and does not seem bothered by the cold in spite of her bared shoulders. Eventually, the three join the crowds milling about and greeting each other—a mix of formal coats in black, with eccentric masks and headdresses. They are all heading towards the most notorious dancehall in the city, drawn by its famous green glow.

The great blades of the windmill, as they sweep around and

around, add a sense of urgency, of inevitability, to the crowds passing along the sludgy street. They enter the mill with the sense they may simply be chewed up and spat out again; it seems appropriate to Fran that this is a place where a whole century will pass by in seconds. The blades themselves are picked out in glass globes that send an eerie green light across the street.

The Moulin Vert has only recently opened, but its reputation towers over Soho. Mrs Stella would host a new year's gathering nowhere else.

The three stop a moment outside the main doors, a steady stream of people passing inside. Fran and Christine exchange excited looks, then turn to Eve. She raises a hand to adjust her mask, leaning back a little; intimidated by the great sweeping blades with their green shine. Fran squeezes her arm.

"You'll be all right," she says. And they go in.

Inside the Moulin Vert is a glittering cavalcade of large mirrors, sparkling crystal and polished wood. The spicy, earthy colours of the walls and furniture shine elegantly in carefully arranged light. Great chandeliers pour from the ceiling, elegant waterfalls of diamond, picking out the dancers and glinting off the champagne bottles. Round tables decorated with potted ferns cluster at the edges of the great hall and surround the dancehall's centrepiece—and the true key to the Moulin Vert's success—its large, open, *public* dancefloor. A glistening platform of polished oak, it is already filled with people. Above it are the upper galleries, where it is possible to sit and drink and watch the dancing from a happy multiplicity of angles. People fan themselves, jostle for best position, lean over the dark green rails to stare.

There is a stage at one end, shrouded in a velvet curtain in dark green edged with gold; but the centre of attention is only rarely to be found there. The public dancefloor, and the people upon it, are what's really on display.

Fran immediately loses sense of herself among the crowds, as their route to the dancefloor must navigate tables, sprawling chairs and secret alcoves, all of which seem already full to bursting. They pass groups of cheering drinkers, their tables filled with wine bottles and liquor glasses, their hairpieces lopsided with great feathers that dance through the air. Gleaming beads line the puffed sleeves of ballgowns; the tasteful light from the chandeliers winks bronze upon costumes of velvet, silk and fur, in black and grey and dark green—the air is filled with roaring cheers, the clink of glasses, the clatter of dice.

"There!" cries Christine, pointing. A particularly golden aura flashes from the centre of the dancefloor. The three navigate their way towards Mrs Stella.

Mrs Stella's costume comprises strips of golden silk, dripping with gold beads and pearls. In one hand, instead of a corsage, she carries a disembodied head made of foam. Several strands of red ribbon trail from its spongey neck. Its eyes are painted white, as if the pupils have rolled up out of sight. It swings absurdly as Mrs Stella raises her hands in greeting.

"I'm Salome!" she cries. "I would dance for you, my dears, but I shan't be held responsible for the consequences."

She adopts a pose from her performance in the role, a half dance with delicate arms and lurid suggestions of falling cloth. Just as suddenly, she drops her arms. "I'm so glad you could come. And to you," she adds, curtseying to Eve.

Eve says nothing. She remains standing, still and silent. She is holding herself tight, almost shivering, as if she were caught in a cold breeze. Fran supposes she is overwhelmed with the bustle of the event; imagines it will pass.

"What a party!" Fran says to Mrs Stella, to get the conversation going again.

"Oh yes! And I must speak to you about the entertainment, later—the *tableau vivant*. I haven't forgotten. Now, I think she should—Oh! Hello!"

A black cloak swoops into the throng, held by a crooked arm over the wearer's face.

Mrs Stella shrieks with delight. "What have we here?" she says.

The arm is lowered to reveal the grey-painted face of Oliver Allbright.

"Count Dracula, at your service," he says. It is unusual to see Oliver in black. His suit is as sharp as a knife, the high collar wrapped with a blood-red cravat fastened with a crystal pin. He spreads his arms dramatically, to reveal his red-lined cloak. The puckered silk recalls the inside of a coffin.

Eve is trembling beneath the soft touch of Fran's arm.

"You look *divine*, Oliver. And have you brought the young man you've been telling me about?" All mention of the tableau has stopped—Mrs Stella's eyes flash a brief a warning to Fran and Christine. It is clearly to remain a secret until the moment of unveiling. Mrs Stella places her hand affectionately on Oliver's shoulder. "I had hoped to meet that fine gentleman tonight—a poet, wasn't he?"

"Oh, *him*," says Oliver. "He shan't be coming."

Mrs Stella's face collapses. "What happened?"

Christine leans forwards, craning her neck to hear the gossip. Fran checks Eve, who is still quiet.

"I had no choice but to end it," says Oliver. "I discovered a fatal incompatibility of opinion."

"Which was?" A smile plays around Mrs Stella's mouth, matching Oliver's expression. They have both coloured their lips with smudged red paint; their smiles do not resemble the sharing of a friendly in-joke so much as the bloody ecstasy of Dionysian revellers.

Oliver performs an exaggerated sigh.

"I am an atheist," he says, "and, tragically, so was he. You can't possibly agree with your lover on something so important; it leaves you without anything to talk about."

Christine and Mrs Stella throw their heads back and laugh; Eve does not move. Fran feels caught between them.

"Outrageous! Mr Allbright, you are a *one*," says Mrs Stella, wiping her eyes.

Oliver nods. "But I have met a wonderful *new* person," he says, "who may be along later. She is quite lovely; studying fine art. I hope to bring her to your next dinner, in fact."

"That would be wonderful," says Mrs Stella, and Oliver bows and departs with a swirl of cape. She turns back to Fran, Eve and Christine, her eyes wide with insincere contrition.

"*So* sorry about that interruption—now, where were we? Oh! Whatever's wrong, Fran?"

On finding Christine's gaze upon her, and Eve's too, Fran suddenly realises she is frowning, and that her jaw is clenched. She tries to release the pressure; she can feel her teeth grinding with the effort. "If I may speak honestly, I feel Allbright ignored Eve just now."

"Well of course; he won't address a young woman in a mask he hasn't been introduced to. You could have made the effort yourself."

Fran is unconvinced, but a thought occurs: if Oliver had lavished Eve with attentions, she wouldn't have liked that either.

But there is no time to think on it further; for they are assailed once again by a pair of party guests, clinging to each other as if for dear life, with the aniseed stickiness of absinthe already upon them.

"You two look the perfect picture," says Mrs Stella. Her role as hostess is her favourite to play; she is practically glowing. Fran smiles in recognition, but Christine frowns.

"Who are you supposed to be?" she says.

"Who do you think I am?" says Jacques-Louis. Beneath a tweed cape he wears a dark red smoking jacket, grey trousers and a pair of slippers. On top of his head is a tweed deerstalker, pulled down to a rakish angle. He holds up a bulbous magnifying glass on a long brass handle, and peers at the others through it. "I'm Sherlock Holmes, the city's greatest detective," he says, and through the glass one enormous eye closes and opens in a grotesquely lopsided wink.

"And I'm Irene Adler," says Edwin, tossing his feathered scarf anew around his neck. He wears a costume borrowed from a member of the corps of swans at the ballet school. He grabs Jacques-Louis's arm and kicks up a leg as if trying to climb up to steal the deerstalker hat. "I'm outsmarting him at every turn."

They merge together back into the dance floor.

Mrs Stella is visibly overjoyed. She claps her hands, sending her golden beads rattling across her costume. "The libraries must be empty, for all the devils are here!" she cries. Fran and Christine look at each other, and then, together, at Eve. Eve is, by now, visibly shaking.

Christine makes a decision. Fran is grateful for it. "We're going to sit for a moment," she tells Mrs Stella. Their host nods, and spins around to greet another dear friend she has just that moment spotted, while Fran and Christine cling tightly to Eve and lead her away from the dancefloor, in a futile search for a less crowded corner. (Mrs Stella's voice comes after them:

"Darling! Such delicate lace on your bodice: who—? Ah! You're the very *spit* of Edna Pontellier, dear! Mind you steer clear of the water feature...")

They make their way along the walls of the great hall, and eventually push through a door to emerge into the landscaped pleasure gardens. The air is cold and sharp out here, but the music is quieter—muffled by the ornate doors—and they manage to find an empty table. The trees send long shadows over the grass.

"Are you all right?" says Fran, looking with concern at Eve. "What's the matter?"

"I'm not comfortable here," says Eve.

Christine jolts back in her chair, and Fran realises she is hearing Eve's voice for the first time. Christine's eyebrows knit together. Analysing.

An attempted diagnosis: "It's too cold for you?"

"She means *here*," hisses Fran. "The whole place. She doesn't want to be the entertainment at this godforsaken party. And I don't want her to either."

Christine relaxes, as if that is nothing that cannot be dealt with. Fran feels a quirk of irritation in her stomach. "Well—tough!" says Christine. "It's all been arranged. Wouldn't surprise me if half the people here have come especially to see her."

A passing group of revellers, half of them in white robes and wigs, and delicate pearl-coloured masks, and the other half in brown, angular make-up with strips of thick, mottled fur bulging through their waistcoats—a group costume, Morlocks and Eloi—squeeze by their table, reaching out to grab each other apparently at random, twirling and laughing. One offers Christine a cigar as they pass, and she takes it, drawing in deeply and blowing the smoke out into the air.

Eve puts a hand beneath her mask to wipe her eyes. Her head bows, then rises again; the slightest of nods. An acquiescence.

"I can't believe you're ganging up on me like this," says Christine.

Fran holds Eve's other hand beneath the table. It is difficult to know whose fingers are colder.

THE MOULIN VERT is growing more raucous. Mrs Stella darts to and fro, trying to be in every corner of the party at once: she vaguely snatches at Fran's arm, reiterates that she wants the performance by Eve to commence soon—but then she is gone again. She also wants to pour more champagne; to show people around the pleasure gardens; to sign autographs; to admire the flowers; to dance with everybody in the room. The hours pass.

Christine and Fran stand in the middle of the dancefloor, jostled by bodies, shouting at the top of their lungs.

"You said she would be safe here!" cries Fran.

"She's not supposed to go wandering off!" says Christine. "If she takes it upon herself—"

Fran bites her lip, looks around the dancefloor at the blur of stockings, raised skirts and half-masks, distorted faces. She feels herself coming apart, separating into lots of little pieces.

"It's like he said," she murmurs.

"What?" Christine leans back as a pair of madly waltzing revellers in animal masks spin about them, nearly knocking their wine over her tatty Hyde blouse. "In fact; never mind. I don't need to know. I've got to tell you something," she says. "About next year."

Fran's gaze snaps back to Christine. "What?"

"Things are different," says Christine. "Since it happened, I mean. Eve. Things are strange and broken between us and it's too much for me."

Fran's mouth moves. Nothing comes out.

"I don't even need the scientific glory of it any more. It is only making me miserable." Christine scrapes her hand through her back-combed hair, releasing twigs and dead leaves that drift down to the floor. The effect makes her look even more distracted, frightened even; a doctor haunted by their own creation.

"I've been offered a new scholarship," says Christine. "The train leaves in the morning. From thence, a ferry, and maybe even a balloon. I'll be gone. You and... *her* can hide away together and be happy. Do whatever you want." She turns on her heel, and heads towards a group of people who appear to be attempting a human pyramid, just as it topples.

Fran puts her hands out to stop her, but Christine has already disappeared into the throng. Fran spins about, trying to discover the quickest exit, or catch a glimpse of Eve's graceful walk. But she recognises nothing. The world has turned into a smudge of dim colour, and she can feel her own energy leaking out to join it; her edges are blurred, she is unsure where her panicked grief starts and stops. With a deep, difficult breath she lets Christine go: but she must continue to look for Eve.

A FEW SECONDS until midnight.

Fran cries out with a noise that sounds like a high-pitched whine, and, her heart thumping against the bone cave of her chest, she races through the Moulin Vert and out into the street, the vision blurring through her salt tears.

"No!" she cries. The retreating figure of Eve does not turn, does not answer. Cold stars look down over the city.

And the bell tolls: and one drunken actor in a green suit raises his glass to begin cheering for the new year; and two dancers cling together on the balcony, oblivious to the chaos down below as their legs wind together; and three, three empty absinthe glasses roll from the table as Allbright's head lands unconscious in his hands, spilling drops of green liquid over shattered fragments of glass; and four horses, pulling carriages, rear up on their hind legs to avoid the woman in the road, her gaze blank as if unseeing, as she walks through the streets and away; and five, five is the number of people Mrs Stella is trying to dance with at the same time when the clock strikes, her hair flying as she twirls her veils around her body, her head thrown back in the reverie of the dance, the disembodied head long lost in the corner of the dancehall and forgotten; and six musicians continue to play brightly from the band upon the dancehall stage, sending energetic rhythms across the bouncing, crowded dancefloor; and seven, seven pipes of opium send out billows of fat smoke into the air above the pleasure gardens; and eight layers of fabric create an effective dancehall skirt, thrown up into the air and tossed about as dancers high-kick on, knocking champagne glasses out of the hands of the patrons, to roars of joy and the thundering of applause; and nine cries of "get out of the way!" and "watch it now!" follow Fran as she sprints away from the Moulin Vert, her breath coming as clouds of steam that rise into the indifferent air, shaded green by the windmill's great blades; and ten, ten gas lamps stand along the street, hissing and spitting, sending pools of pallor across the snow, melting to sludge, as Fran runs along the street, losing a shoe in a cold puddle and tripping, tearing the skin over her arms as she falls; and eleven streets away by now, moving fast as a spider, goes Eve, heading out of the city, and beyond, to a coastal town, to steal passage out of the country on a rusty vessel churning green smoke behind it; and, as the final toll of the bell fades into silence, Fran's hearing is filled with a dull roar, which she recognises as the onrush of despair: and she lies in the gutter, helpless and trembling, looking up at the stars, but between her tears and the fireworks bursting over the city it is impossible to see them.

RECULVER

RECULVER

PAUL MELOY

I WAS A boy when I watched the grey planes run the coast.

Unmarked they were, long bombers with their strenuous noise, their fierce English engines, propeller blades frozen in their speed. The black ball payload dropping from the bomb bay, following the belly of the plane for seconds before the bomber banked hard and left it behind, straining up into the cold seafront sky, an open hand that had cast its stone.

THE DRUMMING ENGINES of the incoming bombers, skies over Kent black with a Biblical plague of enemy aircraft, cities burning, collapsing, blown apart in flesh and cinders, the retreating drone giving way to the doodlebugs' sudden silence; the rain of incendiaries, iron kegs of fire, obliterating entire streets; butterfly bombs twirling down, murderous jack-in-the-boxes designed to kill curious children; it was a time of the sky, of things falling upon us, as though the very air above England had become the threshold to a second, hellish Estate, where the Fallen threw their ordnance at us.

*   *   *

AND IT WAS a time of myths, and of creatures of myth. Angelic men raised up for the work of defiance. I realise now, knowing their names, knowing their stories, apprehending their timeless, orthogonal minds, that they were placed here with perfect historical synchronicity. Only God could have shaped them, and I understand now the passage that reads, *I knew you before I formed you in your mother's womb.*

I LIMPED DOWN to the beach past the rolls of barbed wire thrown upon the dunes, through the sawhorses nailed with their Wartime civic warning signs. The steely declarations of the Ministry of Defence, a very English deterrent. The spinning bomb had gone, bounding into the distant waters of the North Sea to sink and be forgotten; no hydrostatic fuses to detonate these duds.

I think of them now, lying in the shelving sands, caked with weed and molluscs, empty husks, un-bombs, prototypes, asleep and maybe dreaming of the dams they could have sundered.

I COULD SEE the man standing on the beach. He, too, had watched the plane and now looked down at a clipboard, the stiff breeze trying to lift the pages that he held down with the nib of his pen. He was making notes.

The gray sea rushed clattering up the shingle, sounding more like metal in a rotating machine than it did water. The man did not seem to notice as it spumed over the toes of his boots.

I stood at the bottom of the shallow dune and watched him. I had seen him here before, studying the planes, making his notes, his spectacles glinting in the flat coastal light, grey-haired and serious. Once I had seen him and thought him a madman. A bomb run had ended in failure, the bomb shattering on impact with the water. The man had thrown down his clipboard, stripped to his underwear, and waded into the freezing sea to salvage some fragment of the bomb. I had kept my distance, hiding in the grass at the side of the road, and covered my mouth with my hand to smother my laughter. He was not an old man yet, but older than my father. My father was in North Africa, fighting under Montgomery, that colossus of war. He was on the big guns. Stukas raining in like gulls around a tip. *Boom, boom, boom,* my dad's cannons went, blowing them out of the sky. He had fought in Italy, too. He had seen Vesuvius erupt. Dad said millionaires would have given their fortunes to see what he had seen.

But millionaires didn't fight in wars.

THE MAN LOOKED up from his clipboard and appeared to be waiting, watching the sky to the East. I heard the plane before I saw it, thundering low, nosing out of the mist that had gathered beyond the twin towers of St Mary's and stretched out across the water in a silvery band.

The man followed the progress, his clipboard pressed flat against his chest and his pen held tight in his hand, his head turning as the plane flew past, sixty feet above the water, so skilfully piloted. I could see the ballgunner curled tight like a tadpole in his turret.

The bomb bay doors fell open and the bomb dropped, spinning backwards. The plane rose, banked and turned inland, heading for a Kent airfield somewhere. The bomb hit the water and sprang off, away from the surface, flying in a white eruption of spray, for hundreds of yards until gravity pulled it back to the water. It hit, bounced again and was gone, the distance travelled shorter, the trajectory lower. A third strike and it was wobbling, yawing. It pitched and it cut into the water and was gone, tumbling for a moment and then sinking beneath the waves.

Even from where I stood, the wind at my back, I heard the man say, "Bugger!"

And then he saw me.

I FROZE, MY bad leg aching, wanting to turn and run back through the wire and barricades, back to Reculver, and hide in the town. But I could not run, and never had. Instead, I waved. It was a strange thing to do, I recall, to wave at a stranger like that, but I did not want him to think me a spy, or a threat. He looked surprised but not alarmed, or angry. And then he smiled and started walking towards me. I stepped onto the beach, and stumbled. The man waved his clipboard at me, flap, flap. "Don't move," he said, but it wasn't a command, nothing soldierly about it, not like the town copper catching you up to no good. He sounded kind, well-bred, not wanting me to risk my leg on the shingle at the base of the dunes. "I'll come to you," he said.

He did, and there on that otherwise deserted beach in May of 1943, I met Barnes Wallis.

"POLIO," HE SAID. "Is it just your leg?"

"Yes," I replied.

The man appraised me, seeing a small, weedy boy with a

pigeon chest and pale complexion. He smiled. "Do you go to school?"

I did, but I avoided it when I could, because I was bullied when I went, called names, and got into fights. Yes, I fought. Bad leg and scrawny chest, I fought. My dad told me to, so I did, clobbering them no matter how big they were, enjoying the look of shock on their faces, and the childish tears that sluiced away the certainty of their spite. There were boys at that school who would never call me *cripple* again.

That was why I was there that day, skirting the beach and watching for the planes, wondering at their mission. There were rumours, but the town was closed off, shops boarded against looting, and people moved away by the Army. School was in Herne Bay, not far up the coast, and we were staying with my aunt. But I loved the town, my desolate Reculver, and I roamed the empty streets like a stray dog. I trod the ruins of St. Mary's and watched the Lancasters come, sighting them between the tall towers, imagining I was a gunner, too, fighting alongside my father, blowing Nazi fighters out of the hot African sky.

"In Herne Bay," I said.

"Are there any teachers you like?"

I thought about that. There was Mrs. Bennett, but she did not teach me now; she taught the first years. But she remembered me, and had always been kind and asked after me when she encountered me between lessons. She was still pretty, and she had a daughter, Ann, who was prettier; Ann Bennett, whom all the boys loved a little because she was good-natured, and serene and, at sixteen, with her long nylon-stockinged legs, her wide, gray-green eyes and platinum blonde curls, was the guileless instigator of our first crushes, lusts and troublemaking dreams. Ann Bennett, the prettiest girl in Herne Bay.

I didn't get a chance to tell the man about her, though.

Another plane was coming.

WE WATCHED IT together. A speck, a toy, a plane, an unyielding British bomber, routing the air with its broad propellers. Low, lower, sixty feet and the bomb bay dropping open like a mouth shouting a sudden base command, and the bomb dropped, top-spin silence, skimming, skimming, the plane lifting away on screaming engines, pulling its crew to mist-shrouded safety, flak-free, unstitched by tracers, imagining the runs to come along the darksnake length of the river Eder.

WE STOOD FOR a while, not talking, the man making notes on his clipboard. When I look back, my memory clear and sharp as the long cold blade of the inrushing tide, I remain enthralled by the moment, rendered an encounter with a wondrous, benign beast sent to liberate a benighted land. These mythical men, these illuminated beings, so far removed from the monsters sent to blister our skies. But there on that beach, I did not know the future, or this man's place in it.

I did not get a chance to tell Wallis about Ann Bennett, but I shall tell of her now. That I stood alongside a legend of human history, a man tasked with creating perfect, mathematical destruction in order to save more lives than he would take— to give me, and boys like me, a future free from tyranny; that I stood there, and shook his hand, and promised him utmost secrecy for the Effort of War, and had done nothing to stop the tragedy that came that May, or would make no amends for it, makes me tremble with fear for my soul.

But enough of my soul and its destination. I can do no more; I cannot save myself. I place it in the hands of the One who promised salvation for those who confess.

So, a confession.

ANN BENNETT WORKED in one of the munitions factories in Canterbury. I imagine her sitting at a long bench assembling components; her blonde hair tied back with a headscarf, surrounded by other girls like her, but none so pretty, none so bright and joyful a character, all doing their bit for the War. I imagine the gossip, the high shrieks of laughter, sharing cheap cigarettes outside in the yard and drinking hot, pale industrial tea. I picture them piling out, on clacking heels, wrapped in coats and shawls, chatting, joking, waiting for the buses that will take them home in the dark at the end of their shift.

Ann would go home to her mother and her younger brothers, past gaslit shops and unlit alleyways, to the cottage they rented, and settle into the routine of helping to prepare the evening meal. She would unknot the headscarf and brush her hair. She would lift up the wooden worktop that covered the sink and pour a kettle of hot water, to wash her face and hands. She would be tired but content, and her cheeks would be flushed from the heat of the water.

She would save the water and clean vegetables using the scrubbing brush beneath the sink, and cut thick slices of bread with a blunt wooden-handled knife.

Her mother would be sitting by the fire, her brothers in a tin bath, splashing, their hair golden in the flickering flames. The wireless would be on, tuned to a station playing big band music, or perhaps waiting for the latest propaganda broadcast from

Lord Haw-Haw: '*Germany calling, Germany calling,*' in his high-born English accent, and they would stifle laughter and make fun of his treacherous, preposterous, inadvertent comedy.

THERE WAS A young man who, like me, had been the victim of polio as a child. His name was Geoffrey Dodd. He had a withered right arm, which he kept pinned inside his shirt, but aside from that he was more robust than I would ever be. His gait was sure and his body strong, not rendered scrawny by having to hobble like me. He was eighteen and had missed the draft because of his arm. Notwithstanding the obvious handicap, he still suffered the sidelong glances and whispers of resentment from those whose husbands, fathers, sons and brothers were at war. He could not be labelled a coward; I didn't want to believe anyone would be that cruel. Who knew how long this war would last? One day I would be of age to fight and be denied the privilege because of my leg. Would I be accused of cowardice? The thought revolted me. Even now I wanted to blow Nazis out of the air, gun them down in tatters, put a knife in their dirty kraut throats.

Geoffrey was assigned work in the same factory as Ann. He was one of very few young men who laboured there, working amongst the perfume and chatter of all those girls. There were a couple of conchies there, but they worked the administration block, pushing paper to avoid the predictable attitude of the girls on the factory floor, who all had fathers and brothers on battlefronts across Europe and Africa, and who could not be trusted not to slip something nasty into their tea.

Despite his wasted arm, Geoffrey was a popular lad with all the girls. He joked with them that it was because of the lack of competition, but in truth he was handsome, charming and funny, and these attributes have always been the consolation of men not embittered by their misfortunes.

And so it was of little surprise (although there was quite a bit of offhand head-tossing and mild, good-natured sulking), when Geoffrey and Ann began leaving the factory together, walking to the bus stop and sitting close, as far to the back of the bus as they could get amongst the jostle and crowding of the workers.

They walked home together after alighting in Herne Bay, and after some weeks of courting would hold hands when the streets were retiring with darkness and silence. Geoffrey would see Ann home, stand smiling as she let herself into the cottage, promise to see her tomorrow at the factory (they did not walk together in the morning light at first, wary of too much rumour and gossip), and then Geoffrey would wander home with a blameless swagger.

I imagine most of this, of course, but the path of relationships and the early stirrings of love were predictable in those dark, self-conscious days of our childhoods and youth. There were conventions and rules instilled and closely-guarded, perhaps rightly so, that no longer apply today. It's not a great fiction to describe the beginnings of Geoffrey and Ann's association in this tender way.

I did, however, see them together just once.

I'D BEEN IN a fight. The other boy had bested me but not without suffering a punch to the side of the head that had rocked him on his feet. My arms were bruised from where he had twisted them as he knelt with all his weight on the small of my back. His name was Daniel Briggs, and I think the shock of the blow prevented him from causing me greater injury that morning in the playground, surrounded by a crowd of braying boys and trembling, excited girls.

It had been Mrs. Bennett who had pulled him away, scolding and smacking, shaking him with the horrified fury engendered, I think, by both compassion and the kind of appalled pity that often made people over-react in my presence. Daniel skulked away, his shoulders rolling with equal parts shame and a compensating attempt at unruffled insolence.

I got up and hobbled away. My leg hurt like a bastard, a deep, sickening ache from hip to ankle. I could hear Mrs. Bennett calling after me but I ignored her, sniffing hard and jutting my jaw, teeth clenched to stem the tears that wanted to come, tears for the pain more than the humiliation, because I was long past that. I wanted to be past the pain, though, because sometimes it was so rotten that I wanted to wrench my whole leg from its socket and cast it into the bloody sea.

It was a clear day and the streets of Reculver were cool and silent. There were no planes bombing the coast as yet. That was a few months away, as was my impressionable meeting with Barnes Wallis. The Ministry of Defence had been here, though, putting up barricades and signs and clearing everyone out. We were used to their company, enigmatic men in their jeeps with determined looks in their eyes and a dutiful economy of movement.

I roamed the streets imagining I was the last man alive. Coppers patrolled in regular stints to keep an eye on things, but there was little danger of looting here. It was a small town and there was nothing much to steal. I knew their routines and knew how to keep out of their way.

I managed to walk the worst of the ache out of my leg, but my arms still smarted where Daniel Briggs had jammed them up my back. I flexed my fingers and swung my arms in circles to ease the throbbing muscles.

There was a small meadow at the north end of town, a patch of wild flowers and high grass not much bigger than a football field, and beyond it a set of swings on a bank of earth high enough to look over the meadow and keep an eye out for any prowling copper. I liked to sit and swing for a bit, thinking about the War, and what my dad was doing. We got letters, frequent and short, written in his hasty, unschooled hand, telling us he was well, and that the Germans were getting a pasting. His early letters were heavily redacted, information deemed too sensitive edited out by an anonymous administrator, the heavy, scowling black blocks laddering the pages, but dad had not been educated in official secrets then, like whereabouts and numbers and names. Now his letters were more circumspect, as were our replies, but a great comfort nonetheless.

I was thinking about Dad when something caught my attention. There was movement out of the corner of my eye. I stopped swinging, dragging my heels in the ancient groove of dirt beneath the swing. I let go of the chains and sat forward. I looked straight out across the meadow.

Someone was coming across the meadow. They were keeping low and there was furtiveness to their movement. My heart leapt. I hadn't seen them coming, I'd been lost in thought. They must have crept from around the row of cottages at the end of the road leading up to the bottom of the meadow. I jumped down from the swing and ducked down so I wasn't visible above the long grass. Bloody coppers. If they caught me I'd be in trouble this time. We all knew something was going on in Reculver and it was understood that we were to keep away. I'd get more than a clip; my mother would be informed and that would mean a proper clout and no more skipping school. I was annoyed with myself, because I'd let my guard down, sitting there swinging like an imbecile and daydreaming of things I had no influence over.

Despite my alarm and the pressing need to get away, I paused. My anger with myself had been diminished by a more enervating dismay. I dropped my head and clenched my jaw. I wouldn't be here if it wasn't for Daniel Briggs. I wouldn't be crouching in the dirt on the outskirts of a deserted town if it weren't for all the bullies that had ever crossed me. I wouldn't be here if it wasn't for my damned leg and the polio that had caused it. I felt a part of nothing, a piece of dry, sea-scoured wood blown up on the beach, a beetle clambering in panic along the stony rim of the meadow, a tremulous blue petal on a forget-me-not in the earth between my knees.

I heard something that snatched the thoughts away. I was suddenly clear-headed, and I looked up, blinking, the curtain of meadow grass inches from my face. I had heard a laugh, the high, sweet laugh of a girl, and now my heart was beating fast again, not with fear but with a strange excitement.

I heard another voice, that of a man. He was speaking in a quiet, gentle way, though I could not make out the words yet, just his tone. The girl laughed again and the grass moved yards away from me and to my right. I got to my feet, keeping low. My leg was aching again but I ignored it; I would be safer hiding in the same long grass they were using to conceal themselves. I stepped off the rough ground and slid into the meadow.

So now we were all hidden in the grass. Three people, all of whom should probably be somewhere else, doing more productive things, hiding from the world for a moment, from authority, work, the War. I heard the man speak again, still soft, but more urgent. They had stopped a few yards from where I was squatting and I heard the grass rustle and swish, and the girl sighed, and I could only imagine they were flattening a patch in which to lie.

I edged forward, the pain in my leg all but forgotten. I felt a different ache, radiating from my chest to the pit of my stomach. As I drew nearer, the meadow grass thinned, became filmy. Dirt crumbled beneath my knees, between my fingers. A crow bombed overhead, shouting: *Raaaaak! Raaaaak!* The girl laughed again. I drew a deep breath and nosed forward another slow foot. I could see them now.

She was lying on her back. I could see the minuscule soft specks of grass seed clinging to her stockings. The man was kneeling over her, kissing her mouth. The girl reached up, almost absently, and began to undo the buttons on his shirt. The man sat up, ending the kiss, and the girl moaned, her fingers stroking his cheek as he used his left hand to finish unbuttoning his shirt. He shrugged the shirt from his broad shoulders, and his right arm dropped to his side, thin and wasted.

He kissed the girl again and his left hand slid between her thighs, moving the hem of her dress into a bunch at her waist. His hand kept moving, inward, upward, and the girl pulled him down against her, one hand pressed to the back of his neck, the other reaching for his belt.

I sat back against my calves in a daze, a thin veil of grass and the couples' complete absorption in each other hiding me as efficiently as if I had not been there at all, and, God forgive me, I watched.

I watched Geoffrey Dodd make love to Ann Bennett, probably for the first time because she cried when it ended, and held onto the strong young man who had taken her there, in that meadow, on a sweet mattress of grass, with arms that were bare and trembling, while a black augury of crows exclaimed in the blue air above them.

When it was over, I slipped away. I never forgot how beautiful Ann had looked, or how gentle Geoffrey had been with her, for the rest of my life.

I WENT BACK to school. I kept my head down and tried to enjoy the feeling of relief resulting from not being caught roaming the silent streets of Reculver. But I could not summon it. My nights were restless with dreams and waking fantasies. If my leg woke me, tiresome and dismal, I would lie recumbent and peer up into a darkness that became a meadow under moonlight, hiding silvery bodies entwined. Daylight brought no relief; my walk to school, which took me past Ann's cottage, was a slog heavy with the hope of a glimpse of her that never came.

And then, one morning, I saw her.

The door to her cottage was open and I could hear from inside the uproar of a family at odds. I stopped a few yards away from their step, double-minded as whether to carry on or linger. Curiosity got the better of me and I stopped near the kerb, ready to march on in feigned ignorance should someone emerge.

Ann was crying, that much I could make out; sobbing beneath the coarse, hectoring, scolding, almost unintelligible voice of a man. I heard something smash, then a scream that may have been Ann's, and another voice—I recognised Mrs. Bennett—shouting, "*Bastard!*"

I decided to head off, discretion being the better part of valour, but as I drew past their open door I was nearly knocked off my feet as Ann fled the house, a coat thrown across her shoulders, her lovely face red and blotchy with distress. She saw me, and her face crumpled. She raised a hand to me absently as she took off up the street and past the alleyways; she was gone around the corner towards the bus stop before I could pick up my pace again.

I saw a shape lunge from the shadows within the open cottage door and recoiled. It was Ann's father, Shaun Bennett, in a grey vest and army trousers, bare-footed, sweating and drunk despite the hour.

He saw me but either chose to ignore me or had summoned only the energy and drunken determination sufficient to scream after his daughter: "*I'm home five minutes and find out my daughter's a whore!*"

He appeared spent now, and slumped against the doorpost, the filthy nails of his left hand clawing the wood. He slid back into the shadows and I could hear more crying, from both the little ones and from Mrs. Bennett. Something fell to the ground and shattered.

I found that I was shaking. What was Shaun Bennett doing home?

I carried on to school. Mrs. Bennett did not come in for the rest of the week, and when she returned the following Monday, there were fading bruises on her cheek and beneath her left eye.

My MOTHER HAD been a seamstress before the War, and now for extra pennies, she mended and patched garments for our neighbours, sitting by the fire long into the evening, sewing and darning, ruining her eyesight in the weak orange light from the flames. People did not just bring my mother items to mend; they brought her information, too. My mother was no gossip, but she listened, and found out what she needed to about the Herne Bay and the lives people led there.

I told her about Shaun Bennett that evening when I came home from school.

My mother did not look up from her sewing. She was working on a pretty green dress, taking up the hem so it could do for another summer, passed down to someone's daughter. The needle glinted orange in the firelight as it shuttled in and through, in and through.

My mother did not pause or look up from her sewing, although the movement of her fingers slowed a little as her concentration became more focused.

"That man," she said, and for a moment it was all I thought she was going to say on the matter, the weight of her disapproval captured amply within those two words. But then she did stop her work and folded her hands in her lap upon the folds of the dress, and looked at me.

"He's back from the front," she said. "And won't be going back, I hear." As she spoke, she plucked at the dress in her lap and I knew from whom she had heard the information: Mrs Bambrick, with her three growing daughters and keen nose for chatter.

"Why not?" I asked, thinking of my father still battling in the strafing white kiln of North Africa.

"Shellshock, he's saying. Maybe it is, but he's back down the pub quick enough, just like before the War."

She resumed her sewing and we spoke no more about Shaun Bennett and his contribution to the War. Maybe he was a hero, battle-weary and exhausted, traumatised by the endless shelling and terror, the numbing imminence of fatality and the sight of his fellow men cut to ribbons. But we all knew Shaun Bennett, and heroism seemed a distant, unseemly fiction. The man was a brute and a coward, not befitting even the lowly status of Private in The Queen's Own Royal West Kent Regiment, the ranks of which had suffered terrible losses abroad.

I took myself to bed and lay there on top of my blankets staring at the low beams that shored my ceiling like lines struck from a letter home. I couldn't sleep, so I let myself drift down the fast-flowing stream of fantasy that had swollen around my experience in the meadow, an erotic drama that was neither soothing nor noble, and I was as much ashamed as aroused by it.

I turned and lay on my stomach, my eyes closed, feeling sleep come at last. Ann is looking at me through the fronds of grass, I cannot move. She sits, her skirt still gathered around her waist. Where Geoffrey has been, what I could never erase from my thoughts, is still exposed and gleaming from him, but he is gone. He was never there. Ann is waiting for me. Ann holds out her arms and smiles. I stand and come through the grass into the dell she has made with the shape of her body.

I am dreaming now, and the treachery of it is that it will not play out. The scruples we learn and which lay down deep pathways in our brains censor what our waking desires would have us do, knight's-move our dreams in ways we would not go in our daylight imaginings. We trade vividness for subconscious policing, self-defeat and frustration.

As I kneel between her legs something enters the meadow. It is a presence felt rather than heard, a dark thing. I cannot smell anything of Ann, despite my proximity to what I so want; I can smell a low, brown rot, a sluice of decay. The sky is twilit, cold, and Ann is gone. I am alone in the shape left from her, which is closing in, narrowing, as though her legs had closed before she had faded, not to envelop me but to fix me there, upon my knees, exposed to what is coming.

It is her father. It is not her father. It is a monster.

The meadow grass is moving behind me as the thing slogs across the earth. It is powerful. I strain to stand, to fight, to *wake*.

I am empty of every feeling except fear. The shape of Ann has gone, a leap sideways, and I am now squatting in a shallow pit dug from the earth. The grass is higher, dense with thick, segmented stalks. I am kneeling in a bell of cold metal. It shines with an internal pestilence. I can believe metal rots: putrid iron, rust, the stench of it, the bloody carcass-stink of the butcher's block. Guilt roams the meadow, out there, searching, long-armed; the blood congealed in its massive fists, swinging black, long-nailed fingers.

It is behind me. I cannot turn my head. The muscles of my neck, my shoulders are wooden with terror. Something flexes, a twist of reflection in the blighted metal depression, and a soiled hand takes hold of the back of my neck.

I am awake and out of bed. I am tearing at the thin curtains that cover the window, not sure where I am, who I am, still forming my consciousness out of the small death of sleep. I stand for a long time at the sill, looking through my pale reflection, out into the night, wondering who I *really* am.

AFTER SCHOOL FOR the rest of the week, I wandered the streets of Reculver. I lobbed pebbles into the sea. I collected sticks of driftwood, cool, light and gray, like bones of a prehistoric bird, and made a pile of them on the shore, tried to set them alight with a half-full box of Lucifers I'd found in a bin, but the wood, and the matches, were too damp. I climbed fences and dropped down into the yards behind boarded shops and looked for treasure. I felt daring and chancy. I found a rusty box of tacks, and a claw hammer with a handle split along its length and held together with twine, in a teetering shed at the back of the grocer's shop. I took them, and spent an hour hammering the tacks into a tree trunk at the top of the meadow near the swing. Rust coloured the tips of my fingers a dull orange. I rubbed the pads of my fingers beneath my nose, smelled the dead metal. I sat on the swing and rocked in a shallow, moody arc. The chains that rattled and buckled as I swung made my palms smell, too, but of a fresher, slicker species of iron, cold and resilient and polished with the oils from the palms of a hundred other children. I looked out across the meadow. I waited.

MY FATHER WAS a pipe-layer before the War. He dug trenches in roads and fields and put down lengths of concrete stormdrain pipe. His hands were gray and dusty from the clay soil of North Kent and he peeled crescent rinds of it from beneath his nails into the sink when he washed his hands.

The clay stained the lines on his palms, and the webs of skin between his fingers, and the nets of wrinkles on his knuckles. It did something to the texture of his skin, as though his clay-encased hands had been fired in a kiln and made hard as pots. He was not a big man, but he was strong from his work, and his temperament was kind, his outlook courteous—up to a point— and he attempted to lead a life on good terms with his fellows.

But I saw him take on Shaun Bennett once, and once was enough.

It was a Sunday and we had been to church. It was the year

before the War, before we got involved and our men were called to fight, but there was tension and a readiness starting to form, a sense of inevitability that had everyone on edge. The churches were full again.

There was a fete outside on the green that afternoon, and my father said we could go, and he gave me a handful of pennies to spend at the stalls. I took off and he and my mother walked, holding hands, at a more dignified pace until they came to a stall selling jams and chutneys, which were a treat but one my mother occasionally approved, as often our meals were bread and cheese and little else. And these were homemade by Mrs. Bennett, and her preserves were, in everyone's opinion, the very best. Her stall was a bench covered with a floral cloth and there were still a few jars left, lids screwed down over waxed paper circles.

I paid a penny and threw a wooden hoop to win some liquorice, but the hoop missed its mark and clattered against the base of the peg. I took another penny from my pocket but did not get a chance to spend it because I could see Ann Bennett running up the lane and she looked to have been crying.

She ran to her mother. I could see her shaking her head and pointing back along the lane. My father looked calm but alert and he drew my mother aside and spoke to her. My mother frowned but did as he had asked, leaving his side and coming over to where I was standing by the hoopla stall.

"What is it, mum?" I asked.

"It's Shaun Bennett," she said. "He's in a rage about something. He's given Ann a clout and now he's coming for his wife."

As my mother said this, we heard the man himself coming roaring and cursing up the lane. People gathered their children, and the activities ceased. There was a hush.

Shaun appeared at the gate that opened onto the green. He

looked a dreadful sight. His thinning hair was lank with grease and smeared to his low, sullen brow in a fan. His eyes were bloodshot and narrow, and they darted about, trying to focus on his wife and daughter. His vest was filthy, the front drenched with a dark wet stain of cheap brown ale. He wore long johns and from where I stood I could see the yellow stain of urine that had spread, dried, spread again. He had pulled on unlaced boots in his fury and haste to catch hold of his daughter. That, more than his drunkenness, had slowed him enough for Ann to make her escape.

"Oh, look at him," my mother said. "What a disgusting creature."

Shaun Bennett stumbled onto the green and cast around, arms swinging at his side, fists clenched. For a moment he looked perplexed, lost and pathetic, and I hoped he would realise his spectacle and turn and do the dignified thing and go home. But I watched his expression change when he saw his wife and daughter standing transfixed with fear and shame behind their stall. The look on his face went through a swift modulation, the limited repertoire of the psychopath, expressed in an instant: loathing, cunning, vile ingratiation, coercion.

Shaun's face settled into an expression of sly reasonableness. He trod across the grass and stood looking over the stall at his ladies. He opened his arms in an oily gesture of magnanimity. He was unsteady and had to shuffle his loose-booted feet to keep from falling. He blinked and must have seen the looks of revulsion on Ann's and his wife's faces, the undisguised shame, for at that moment he roared:

"*I want my dinner! Where's my fucking dinner?*"

He reached out and I thought for a moment he was trying to steady himself against the edge of the stall, but he grasped the cloth in both fists and wrenched it from the table. The few remaining jars flew from the tabletop and hit Mrs. Bennett in the chest. She cried out, wincing at the pain and shock, and Ann reached for her, to take her in her arms. Shaun stood swaying, the floral cloth clenched in his hands.

"My dinner," he said, with a belligerent pout. He feinted a lunge across the table and Ann and her mother shrieked.

"Shaun," my father said, his tone mild, unthreatening.

Shaun Bennett straightened up and turned his head. His expression was now one of wonder; that someone had dared to break into this drama and draw his focus away from dealing with his unruly women.

Shaun Bennett grinned and returned his attention to his wife and daughter. He balled up the cloth, wiped his face with it, blew his nose on it, and tossed it over the stall, where it fluttered to the ground at their feet. Ann had been gradually leading her mother backwards, taking discreet steps away from her intoxicated father. There were a few feet now between them. Shaun noticed and found a new determination. He straightened his back and took a single swaggering step around the stall. He was going to drag these women home by the hair if he had to, and they'd not defy him again.

"*Shaun!*"

"*What,* you cu—"

My father stepped forward and hit Shaun Bennett in the mouth with one of the hardest punches I've ever seen thrown to this day of telling. He swung that clay fist like a bludgeon, and in the silence that followed the combined gasp of all who had witnessed it, Shaun Bennett was left writhing on his back beneath the stall, clutching a dislocated jaw bereft of all molars on the left side.

My father went home that day with the three remaining jars of pickle left on Mrs Bennett's stall, and they didn't cost him a penny.

I WAITED, BUT they did not come. Nor did I really expect them to. I gazed into the grass, towards the spot where I had watched them make love. The wooden seat of the swing was hard and cold beneath my backside, tightening the muscles in my thighs where I desired heat instead. I kicked back, an angry arc, dust rising around the soles of my shoes. I braked with my heels and got off the swing, then stalked to the edge of the meadow. I reached out and parted the grass, walked to the place where they had lain. I bent and pressed the palm of my hand to the ground, where she had been, the centre, where I had watched the unbearable beauty of it consummate.

A crow shot overhead, black crashing bomber, the sound of its engine: *raaaaaak.*

I stood and lifted my face towards it, and screamed.

There was silence in the shocked aftermath of my explosion, my detonation of... what? Rage? Frustration? Despair? The echo of it slapped around the dead walls of the town. I didn't care who heard it. It was gone now, discharged. I felt empty. I looked at the palm of my hand. I put it to my lips, stroked it with the tip of my tongue.

And then I went home.

I HEARD FROM my mother the next day that Geoffrey Dodd had been found beaten, was in a coma in a hospital in Canterbury, and Ann Bennett was missing, having not returned home that night. Shaun Bennett had been arrested and taken to a jail in Herne Bay protesting his innocence, reeking of drink, his knuckles scraped and bloody.

My mother was agitated. "I knew that man was going to end up like this," she said. I assumed she was talking about Shaun. I sat at the table in the parlour, its oilcloth speckled with breadcrumbs from my breakfast. I said nothing. The news had shocked me deeply. My mother spoke again, about Ann, and I was seized from my introspection. "What do you mean, Mum?" I asked.

My mother paused. She was preparing to bake. A little sugar, a little powdered egg. Nothing much, but a distraction. Her mind was not focused on it.

"In her condition," she repeated.

My face must have appeared blank, although comprehension was slowly dawning in my mind. My mother clarified it for me.

"Missing like that, just a girl, carrying Geoffrey's child. Poor mite."

I did not want to believe her; but I had seen Shaun's reaction, his rage, and the loveless abuse he had hurled after his terrified daughter. I had no choice but to accept what she had told me. I stood, feeling unsteady. I could not bear to be in that tiny parlour any longer. I left my mother to her listless baking and went out of the house into the street. It hurt, knowing Ann was pregnant. It was a hard, adult lump in my throat. It made what I had witnessed more than a moment, something permanent growing within her, a part of the man inside her forever. It was jealousy I felt, at this appropriation of her, and for a moment my fists clenched, and I was *glad* Geoffrey had been hurt.

Shocked by my own venom and sick with this new feeling, I stalked through the streets of Herne Bay and headed out of town.

*　*　*

RECULVER WAS MY sanctuary, my Kingdom. My leg hurt. Pushing off the swing, kneeling in long grass, treading the uneven dirt of the meadow ground, all brought my disability to the fore, made it a fulminous ache. I swore, kicked out at stones with my good leg, but the pivot on my bad hip made me wince and I stood in the empty street and tried not to cry. I could not differentiate between the levels of pain; somehow the heavy stone of jealousy around my heart hurt more. I could live with the pain in my leg, but this new torment seemed far worse. For a moment I did not know what to do with myself; I felt unmanned, helpless.

That was when I heard the plane.

Startled, the instinct to take cover ingrained, I ducked, looking for a place to hide, but I was on the seafront and there was nowhere to go except to drop to the side of the road and try to conceal myself against the low wall.

I could see it coming from the east: a bomber, heavy, roaring, coming in low. It ground through the air, solemn and smooth, less than a hundred feet above the water. I watched it pass, its noise fantastic, and saw the bomb doors fall open. It was such an arresting sight I could not start to make sense of it, I could only watch in fascination. Had it been shot down? Was it about to crash magnificently against the glass of the sea, its heroes battling to keep the nose up, to brace its convex chest in opposition to the forces of the water? There was no smoke, no sign of damage to the fuselage or the mighty, cruciform wings. The engines thundered, heaving it airborne, optimal, perfect.

Something dropped from the bomb bay. A barrel, spinning backwards as though the plane had shed a vital moving part. It followed the trajectory of the plane, dropping towards the sea.

And then it hit, gouging out a trench of white spray, the plane rose, turned, and I watched with wonder as the barrel skimmed from the surface, still revolving, and flew in a low arc across the water to come down again, tilted on its edge, breaking apart in a silent discharge of jagged fragments.

I had no idea what I had just witnessed. The bomber was now a distant thing, marooned in the blue sky, its eccentric, broken payload delivered. The sea was calm, emotionless. I looked across the beach and saw a solitary man standing at the shore, the cold shallow water washing around his boots. He held a clipboard.

I RETURNED THE next day, and the day after.

Ann was still missing. Geoffrey had not recovered from his injuries, and people were saying he might never wake up. My jealousy had not abated, but I could not remain hostile towards an injured man, not one so gentle, and that alone was some kind of relief for me. Shaun Bennett was in jail and there were rumours of murder and hanging darkening the talk of Herne Bay. My mother had been to visit with Mrs. Bennett but she would not speak of it to me. Instead we sat and read my father's most recent letters, and listened to the wireless, and found in his correspondence and Churchill's speeches an almost Biblical harmony, a revelation of something akin to prophecy. Churchill's iron words rolled out like tanks: we could win. We could destroy the evil that had threatened to darken the world forever. Once this great struggle was over and the world had returned to normal, we could go about our business again, our small murders, our parochial discord, within the newly ordered peace. I was less aware of my anger. I watched the planes. I dreamed my dreams of the monster in the meadow, the cup of pestilential iron, and imagined it a type of both conflicts: that without, raging across the world, and that within, no less savage and bloody.

AND I MET Barnes Wallis, that morning on the beach.

I had not been to school. I was sick of the taunts. The loss of Ann, the grief of her mother, had caused a sharpening of malice amongst the bullies and tyrants, and I was again the focus of their spite. As though kindness, however small, however fragile, remained as a bulwark against fear and derision; and its removal, or the threat of its removal, provided a gap of opportunity, like an infected gash, through which the ubiquitous germs of hatred could initiate a front.

I sensed in Wallis a determination mathematically inherent. The man was calm, good, *godly,* and yet uncomplicated in his awareness of what needed to be done. His accomplishments meant death, but there was no conflict in him as we stood together on that beach. I know this now. At the time all I can recall is a sense of my own smallness, my lack of impact on the world, against the vast screen of the sky, the drone of the bombers, the drone of *history* unfolding, for better or worse, and of minds imbued by a God who gave us the opportunities to use them and blessed their machinations, for His own, unfathomable sake.

I ONLY MET Wallis that once, and I am careful in telling this now not to superimpose too much of what I—what we all—learnt of him in the years following the War, to make him a fiction to myself, a false memory. Then he was just a man, a calm, gentle man, frankly unremarkable, mostly lost in tremendous thought. He did not spend much time with me and we parted with a firm shake of the hand as the second plane disappeared into the distance. I did not see him again, and that was the last of the planes to bomb the shallows of Reculver. The crews of 617 Squadron were on their way to immortality, and in completing their missions would inflate Wallis and his genius to the status of legend.

So it is practical to me to remember him as he was, without embellishment, because it composes my mind to recall the events that followed—and, I hope, reduces the astonishment of the facts.

THE COUNTRY WAS War-torn, tired, on the edge of defeat; so close, so close at times that it was as though Europe was one great black hand poised to claw us from the face of history. Our men, our small battalions, our blistered Navy and daring, hasty Air Force were sent crawling across the satanic flesh of it in attempts to weaken it, sever nerves, arteries, anything that might cause it to clench in upon itself and allow us more time. Britain was a factory, closed, smoking, pumping, harvesting, sparking along its edges with shipyards, its heart sooted with coal and iron. The big cities gouged from their sockets by German ordnance, the towns and villages producing the men to fight.

Mrs. Bennett had been to visit her husband in jail. He was ranting, self-absorbed, almost incoherent with wild stories according to my mother, who spoke often with Mrs. Bennett and supported her as best she could. Shaun had protested that he had had nothing to do with Geoffrey's beating or Ann's disappearance, that he had been drinking all afternoon and had got into a fight with a soldier on leave in the pub, who had accused him of abandoning his post and betraying his country. He had been thrown out, and on his way home had seen Ann and Geoffrey heading out of town.

Still enraged and smarting from the soldier's effrontery, he had gone after them but lost them, becoming disorientated amongst the alleyways and back streets of Herne Bay. He had stumbled through the increasing dark, falling in the dirt and rubble behind a row of small terraced houses, trying to find the main street for what seemed an age. Shaun admitted he'd fallen asleep propped against a back gate before coming awake with a start, vomit rising in his parched throat. He had pushed himself to his feet, swallowing bile, and seen something. Something that had filled him with such immediate, gripping dread that he had experienced a sublime sobriety there amongst the bins and muck in the guts of the town. Shaun Bennett said that he had felt more fear at that moment than he had ever felt amongst the dead and dying on the front. The ancient hostility radiating from the huge thing that rose hulking from the shadows had been directed solely at him: a personal, monstrous judgement come to fall upon him for all his sins, an embodiment of a scorched, demon-infested Europe sent to snatch him away.

He had found the strength in his legs to run. He was certain that if he'd looked into the creature's eyes he would not be here today, so savage was its presence, so morbid its bearing. He had glimpsed a long, domed head turning above great shoulders, its black face mercifully concealed in the gloom, hands raised and closed in heavy fists.

Shaun had fled, eventually escaping onto the street, and had run home to the tender arms of his family only to find out the next day that Geoffrey—'that fine young man'—had been found beaten half to death, and his daughter—'my beautiful little girl'—was missing.

"What wretched nonsense," my mother said and shook her head in disapproval at the utmost desperation of the man. "He swears he'll never touch a drink again. He'll only be good for that promise when they hang him."

MY MOTHER DISMISSED Shaun's testimony as the lies of a culpable man, but I was deeply affected by it. I could not shake the image of that creature rising from the filth and darkness in the throat of that alley, its black face tumorous with shadows, turning towards the sound of that stuporous drunk.

It was the creature of my dreams, I had no doubt. It was Guilt incarnate, something formed of matter from the shame of my preoccupations, and it had revealed itself to Shaun Bennett to get a message to me.

And my thoughts wandered further: perhaps Shaun *was* innocent of the attack on Geoffrey, perhaps Ann's disappearance was not connected to her father's rage.

I left my mother sitting by the fire, distracted by her sewing, let myself out of the cottage and walked out into the dark.

I went to Reculver.

I HAD NOT been to Reculver in darkness.

It felt even smaller, a locked trunk at the edge of the sea.

The moon was high, diffuse, through a fine layer of cloud. It silvered the wet pebbles of the beach, gave each stone a gleaming value. The sea crunched like something made of tin, hauling itself landward.

I walked along the front, past the road that led up to the meadow. I was not going there. Nothing could entice me to get lost amongst that high, cold grass tonight. I did not want to find the earth scored with decaying trenches of hoary moonlit iron.

The towers of St. Mary's were ahead. They were black stanchions against the wide strips of cloud. The body of the church crouched between them, derelict, broken-backed.

I headed along the coast road leading up to the monument. It is difficult now to recall how I felt, what I was expecting to encounter. Something about the church called to me. I was an iniquitous pilgrim slouching towards a bombsite Bethlehem to see what might have been born in the ruins. I brought no gift but guilt. Precious enough, I supposed, to what might feed on it.

My fantasies had placed Ann there in the past. Pale and beautiful, an icon bared against the rubble. I had met with her on the beach, upon the cold stones. My imaginings had yet again slipped into a dream and as she had dissolved, I had looked up to witness the creature standing colossal on the edge of the sea, the broad lintel of its shoulders tense with awful strength; and the dark waters of the shallows were washing against a thousand unearthed bombs, exposed like the shoreline's blunt, encrusted teeth. And I had wandered in shafts of dust through the rooms of the boarded homes and encountered her waiting there, gray-eyed, stocking-legged, and had heard the lumbering, heavy tread of the creature behind me, stalking me through the rooms I had just vacated. Reculver, my locked trunk, had consumed her, and now I limped towards the church: perhaps I had hoped to find her there.

*   *   *

BARNES WALLIS ONLY returned to Reculver once after the War. There is a single photograph of him, standing dressed in a white sports coat, in 1973, his head turned towards the turquoise horizon. You cannot see his face but one can imagine its expression, perhaps. I think of the frowning, serious aspect of the much younger man I had met. There were prototype bombs in museums by then, salvaged following storms that had lifted them from the seabed and thrown them to the beach. Concrete end caps hurled like discuses to be retrieved and venerated.

I would like to have met him again, there on the beach. I like to think he would have remembered me. Would I have told him about Ann? Would I have told him that Geoffrey had not succumbed to his injuries but had recovered in hospital with no memory of the events that had put him there, to remain no less a shell than if he had been carted back broken from a distant battlefield? That Shaun Bennett did not therefore hang, but had died from drink three years after the War had ended, mourning more for himself than for the loss of his daughter?

Would I have told him about the events of that night as I stood in the ruins of St. Mary's, my bad leg on fire from hip to ankle, and watched in sick apprehension as the creature came up from the bowels of the church to engage me?

No, not then. It is only now that I make Wallis a confidante, now that he is gone and I can use his memory as a lever. His impact on me was immeasurable, however brief. As I reflect, I think again of that verse from Jeremiah, and see a man fearfully and wonderfully made, born of a mother's womb with a great destiny knotted in every cell, and I compare him to the thing that heralded from the darkness, driven here like something pared from beneath the nails of that blighted European claw, into the empty sink of Reculver, drawn perhaps by the forces on display there, or by the power of that direct opposite of mind who stood deeply thinking. A filthy creation unborn, naive of any devout gestation, a vile antithesis but no less single-minded.

I think now of something Wallis once said: *There is such a very thin dividing line between inspiration and obsession that sometimes it's very hard to decide which side we're really on.*

It ROSE TO meet me, the rival from my dreams, and it was a terrible thing to behold. Its speed across the rubble was unearthly. It bounded like an ape across the space where long pews had once sat in rows but which was now a twisted deck of rubble. I stumbled, fell backwards and cried out as the rocks jarred my body. I remained supine, twisted, my leg a useless stick.

The creature stood over me, all shadows unravelled by moonlight, and I saw it revealed, naked, pallid, ancient and scarred. I saw the stitched wounds at its throat, beneath its mighty arms, its long, tensile thighs, the meat black and bloodless, congealed.

And its face—if it could be called a face at all, because faces are things of intricate muscular movement and interplay, and this visage had none—hung against old, dry bone, the circumference of stitches more like hooks in a swatch of skin to keep it there, to hold it against the skull. Only the eyes held expression, and that was fury. They looked the only thing alive about the brute, yet surely they were no more alive than the rest of it, because they bulged from their sockets, blown with putrid fluids. Their silver cataracts were a trick of the moonlight, not evidence of a soul, but they communicated its sentience nonetheless, and I fell back against the rocks, and moaned in fear.

The creature did not strike or attempt to molest me in any way. I cowered, expecting a blow from a massive black fist, or for it to fall upon me and use those yellow pegs of teeth to chew out my throat, but it did nothing more than stand balanced on the rocky floor of the church and watch me with those congested eyes.

And it spoke. The whimpers rising in my throat were silenced by the shock of it. It was a fine voice, strong, low-pitched, almost mild, the tone questioning. I did not understand the words but the accent was Germanic, of that I was sure. Was this the Enemy? Had Shaun Bennett perceived something of the truth when he had told his wife he had been sure this creature had come to drag him back to the battlefields of Europe? Was it some form of soldier, blown to pieces and remade, sent to sabotage the work Wallis was undertaking here, perhaps to murder him on Reculver beach? Had my presence here over the preceding weeks denied it its stealthy purpose? No, I did not think so. The creature spoke too softly, stood back from me and turned away when it could have savaged me. I am certain now that it had been driven here by War, forced across a ravaged Europe when all it wished was to hide, to exist, to evade the devastation that had uprooted it. It had found refuge for a brief while in a deserted town, but even that peace had been broken by the inescapable attendance of War.

It turned away and trod towards the darkness at the back of the church. It stopped once, turned its head. It spoke: "*Komme.*"

I STOOD, A gradual and agonising process. My knee felt like a cup of broken glass. My back was bruised from my fall to the rocks and my palms were deeply grazed. I breathed deeply, my eyes closed for a moment. I could hear the gritting sound of the creature's footsteps as it moved to what remained of the back wall of St. Mary's, a trapezium of stone between the fragments of two arched windows that gazed out across the town. I opened my eyes and started forward, following the path the creature had taken. I was cold, my muscles trembled, my abdomen rolled with a gaseous aftershock of fear, but I went forward, a grimace on my face, until I came alongside it and looked down at what it had to show me.

IN MY LAST dream of the creature, thoughts of Ann had moved to Reculver again, with me at the town's edge watching the creature on the beach. It was wading in the shallows, the water up to its waist. It went out further and slid beneath the surface. High overhead, against the night sky, a formation of bombers flew unlit, silent, just black scratches between the stars.

The creature's head broke above the water and it emerged, moving slowly, its broad, scarred back to me as it laboured to pull something from the seabed. Its strength was incredible. It gained the beach and ground its feet into the pebbles, dragging with it the cylindrical casing of a derelict bomb. I could hear it scraping against the stones, a sealed barrel weighing hundreds of pounds, as the creature heaved it to dry land.

The creature knelt beside the bomb and leant against it. It seized the end cap in its hands and I saw its muscles writhe with the effort of their work as the creature unscrewed the cap from its socket. The cap toppled to the stones, revealing the hollow interior of the bomb to me, a mouth round with astonishment draining black water, and that was when the creature noticed me standing on the dune. I could not see its face. It had no face, just a length of shadow from its hairline to its jaw.

Its arm came up, a slow movement, its fist clenched, a long necrotic finger extended. I thought it meant to point me out, but it did not, although the sweep of its arm encompassed me.

Instead, it pointed to the opening of the bomb, and beckoned.

I SANK TO the ground now. My leg sent bolts of agony through my body but I did not care. My grazed palms scraped against the rocks, but again I did not care. How could I care for physical pain? It did not even register.

Ann was here.

How many times had I imagined finding her here? Warm and sweet and alive, waiting for me. Innocent obsessions had become something more wildly carnal once I had witnessed her becoming a woman that day in the meadow, something I could never change however much I began each thought of her with naïvety of intention.

I reached out to touch her, and she was as cold as the ground.

IT IS A cold day in Reculver and there is still rain in the air, a leftover squall from the storm that passed over us last night.

I can see the towers of St. Mary's from where I sit in the day room. The church stands in grainy resolution against the gray sky, coming in and out of focus as the rain sheets across the town.

One of the home's carers, a young girl no more than eighteen, brings me another cup of tea. She is a sweet girl, but no beauty. She smiles and pats my arm. "Are you okay?" she asks. I nod and return the smile, hoping there is enough life in it not to disappoint her. She seems reassured enough, and goes off to see to someone else. She is not surprised to see—if she notices at all—that I have my coat on, and she does not remark on it. It's not the strangest thing to see in a place like this. I ignore my tea and push myself to my feet using the high arms of my chair. I take my stick and head towards the foyer.

I have to find someone to key in the number on the electronic pad on the outer door, because I do not know it and it changes all the time. Deprivation of liberties. I had to sign a consent form when I came here. It's all in my care plan. I'm not one of the ones who need locking in, but I understand the protocol. I'm allowed out on my own.

I think about taking an umbrella from the stand in the porch, but when I look out it has nearly stopped raining, so I don't bother.

I walk slowly down the drive towards the road that will take me to the front. My old legs ache—one much more than the other, of course—and the cold does not help at all. I continue at my own pace until I get to the road that runs alongside the beach.

The air is crisp, damp, with a fine, barely felt drizzle. It is like a ghost of rain, a whispering echo of the storm.

I walk towards St. Mary's, knowing what I will find up there on the beach.

I HAVE LIVED here all my life. I could not bring myself to leave and so gave myself a small and limiting existence, because it was all I felt I deserved. I could not countenance leaving what I knew was still here, or what I knew might one day come back.

The storm last night, and the dream I had in the midst of it, waking in terror to a room bright blue with electricity and throbbing from thunder, were enough to confirm I had been right to stay, even though I am very old now, and my confession almost done.

My room is at the end of a corridor on the second floor of the home. It has a window that looks out over the back garden. In my dream the garden was gone. In its place was a body of water, long and wide and black, stretching into the distance. The height to the water was immense, my window now hundreds of feet above it. I heard the bombers coming, and gunfire, and saw tracers streaking towards the planes.

I watched the bomb doors open, and watched the bomb roll out.

I AWOKE TO lightning and thunder. I sat up in bed, my breathing fast and shallow. As the sound of thunder died away I could hear voices raised in the corridor outside. I got out of bed and put on my slippers. I took my dressing gown from the hook on the back of my door and went out into the corridor. There were people in the hallway, night staff gathered at the open door to the room across and to the right of mine. The light was on in the room and I could hear more voices coming from inside.

A paramedic appeared in the doorway and spoke to the staff. He noticed me and nodded. One of the girls turned and, seeing me, came over. She did not need to tell me what had happened, it was common enough here, especially in the small hours.

I returned to my room and sat on the edge of the bed. I put my head in my hands and wept.

I wept for the man in that room. Because he was one of the

reasons I had not left. He was older than me, but not really by much. What's a few years between people in their nineties? Unlike me, he had been nursed for most of his life, and we had sat together, downstairs, and I had helped him eat, and read to him. And he had never smiled, or spoken. He was the reason I had chosen this home.

There was a knock on my door, and the girl came in with a cup of hot chocolate.

"Here," she said. "It's very sad. You two were friends for a long time."

One gets used to death here, her tone implied. I took the hot chocolate and said thank you. As she turned to leave, I reached out and took her arm. She looked concerned but I only wanted her to help me to my feet. I followed her to the door and watched her retreat along the corridor. I stood for a moment, looking across the hall at the door to the dead man's room, at the little metal nameplate screwed into the wood: *Geoffrey*.

I HAD SCREAMED in the ruins of the church. I had touched Ann's cold flesh, crawled across the dirt on my knees to reach her. I had seen the deep, dark bruises in the white flesh of her elegant throat, looked upon her pale, parted lips, the still lids of her eyes, her clear, unlined brow. I reached trembling fingers to her throat but could not bring myself to touch her there, instead I took one of her hands in mine and kissed her chill fingers. She smelled of the earth she had reclined against for days. Between her breasts, on a fine silver chain around her neck, her locket still lay. I did not touch it.

The creature had moved and now stood across from me on the other side of Ann's body. It stooped and put its arms beneath her and lifted her. I cried out as her hand slipped from mine, and I struggled to my feet. Fury was fuelling me now, entwined with the grief and horror, and I snatched up a rock, intending to smash the creature with it, but I did not get a chance. In one movement, the creature bounded away, Ann's body in its great arms, and cleared the rubble at the side of the building facing the sea, and was gone.

I stumbled after it, but I had no hope of catching it. I was able to follow its progress as it crossed the ground leading down to the beach. I stood helplessly as it jumped to the beach and carried Ann's body to the water's edge. The sea was churning, hissing, lashing against the creature's body as if in revulsion, as it plunged into the water. I took a few steps but could go no further, and collapsed in grief and exhaustion, onto the grass by the side of the church.

The creature carried Ann into the water, and as I fell to the grass in a faint, they both disappeared beneath the foaming waves.

I HAD COME to, freezing and distraught, in the shadow of St. Mary's, as day was breaking. Of the creature there was no sign. I was unsteady and miserable, but I managed to regain my feet and trudge down the path that led to the road next to the beach. There was a stillness to everything. My palms stung and my back hurt, evidence of my fall in the church the night before, but of the events of that evening nothing remained. I knew now that Shaun Bennett *had* killed his daughter, enraged with shame and jealousy, brutal with drink, but who would believe me? The creature had not come to kill, despite its wretched appearance. It had found an affinity with me, perhaps sensed a kindred spirit, another outsider. Reculver was silent, a repository of energies, of imaginings, and whatever I had brought here, enshrined in silent spaces, watched me from between the gaps and slots in the wood that boarded the windows along the front, and, I tried to believe, remained alive.

I REACH THE path that leads up to St. Mary's. Instead of taking the path, I cut across a verge and go down to the beach. It's not easy going, but it is a shallow slope and I manage, with a lot of help from my stick, to get down onto the pebbles.

I stop for a moment, and look at what is there.

It is not far from where I stand and so a few careful steps over the tightly packed stones gets me alongside it. I let out a breath I was unaware I was holding. With great care I lean forward and look inside, resting the hand not holding my stick against the barnacled rim. It smells of minerals, sluiced out by the sea, and a faint, distant suggestion of rot.

The bomb is empty, its cap smashed or thrown off in the storm that had washed it ashore. It sits on the beach, tilted a few degrees from vertical, and I peer inside. There is something in the bottom, beneath an inch of seawater, and I use my stick to hook it and lift it out. I hold it in my palm and smile.

Now old feelings of excitement are rising, a delicious and delicate fluttering I have not felt since I was a boy. I look up, and in the flat post-storm light, I could swear the windows along the front had been boarded up again. I am no longer sure which Reculver this is. I can hear a bomber coming in low. My heart is pounding.

I glance down, and see a trail of regular depressions in the pebbles, made by the remains of small feet as they walked away from the bomb casing.

Still smiling, I examine the locket and fine silver chain I hold in my hand. They are corroded, green as seaweed, the tiny links packed with dirt. I put them in my coat pocket.

As I walk up the beach towards St. Mary's, I let my fingertips linger against the other thing I have in my pocket, relishing the softness of the silk stockings.

I wanted to get a traditional gift for Ann. For my lady.

MADE MONSTROUS

MADE MONSTROUS
EMMA NEWMAN

Bury, Lancashire
December 1980

St Matthew's Church had always been a place of shame for McGregor. Over the past thirty years he'd done everything he could to avoid it. Walking up the path to the church's large oak doors, he reminded himself that he was a grown man now, that Sidwell was probably dead.

That it could never happen again.

A bubble of gas rose from his guts as he placed his foot on the stone step of the church porch. When Father Sidwell opened the door and intercepted him at the threshold, McGregor found himself snatching the flat cap from his head before he'd even realised what he was doing. He was ten again, late for choir and other abuses, palms sweaty.

Father Sidwell was hunched now, his neck practically parallel to the ground, his head tilted up to scowl at McGregor with milky eyes. Their dark blue had been leeched away by age, but they still had the power to root McGregor's feet to the spot.

"Been a long time," the priest rumbled. "Go elsewhere for confession now, do you?"

"No, Father," McGregor replied. "I haven't been to confession for a long time."

He was surprised to hear the truth emerge, having armed himself with a battery of lies on the way to the church. Perhaps it was the fact that he now towered over the priest, instead of the other way around. Now he was the one with some power, and the priest was nowhere near as terrifying as he once had been.

"I would be happy to hear your confession now," Father Sidwell said.

McGregor couldn't help but notice the spittle collecting at the corners of the priest's mouth. "Not when I'm on duty, Father. I came because you called the police."

The priest's thin lips pursed, reminding McGregor of his old cat's backside. It did nothing to help settle his stomach. "Mmm. I'd heard you work for them now."

"Catching the Devil's own, Father, that's right."

"Where's your uniform?"

"I'm a detective, Father. We get to wear our own clothes."

"Still as scruffy as you ever were, but then you could make Sunday best look sloppy." The priest's mouth puckered with disapproval again. "It would be easier to do God's work without the burdens on your soul, McGregor."

McGregor's patience, never strongly woven, was starting to fray. "It would be easier to do my police work without your... concern."

The priest's surprise managed to only fractionally raise the folds of skin over his eyes. McGregor suspected his parishioners were still too afraid to stand up to him. "You may as well go round the outside," Father Sidwell said, closing the church door fully behind him, "seeing as entering the house of God is too much of an inconvenience for you."

McGregor stepped aside, allowing the bent old man to shuffle past, tugging his flat cap back into place on his head. He belched, alleviating the pain in his chest, and checked his watch. Almost lunchtime. "There's been a few reports of churchyard vandalism over in Rochdale," he said as he followed the priest.

"This wasn't vandalism," Father Sidwell replied without turning his head. "I didn't want to tell the girl on the phone."

McGregor reached into his pocket for his notebook and pencil. "Control told me it was a disturbance. The vandals could have—"

"I told her the churchyard had been disturbed," the priest said. "But it was a grave. They dug up a coffin."

In his twenty years on the force, McGregor had never heard of grave robbing. For the first time that morning, he was glad the flu had stretched their manpower so much, sending him to follow up on a call that would normally have been handled by uniform.

"Whose coffin?"

"Mr Hebblethwaite's. He was buried yesterday. I haven't told his family. I..." He cleared his throat. "I don't quite know how to tell them."

"Was he buried with any valuables?"

"Not many."

"What did they steal?"

The priest stopped, making McGregor come to a halt so abruptly he almost pitched over. "His arm."

The priest had shuffled a few feet on before McGregor moved again. "What... they literally removed his arm from his body and—?"

"Come and see for yourself," the priest said, adding with a mutter, "See if you're really cut out for policing the Devil's work."

McGregor regretted the bacon butty he'd grabbed from Rhonda's Roadside Grub. He'd seen lots of dead bodies before, even some with severed limbs, but never *after* burial. He was so busy mentally preparing himself that he forgot to ask any questions before the disturbed grave came into sight. There was a tell-tale pile of dirt next to it, dumped on top of the grass instead of the usual tarpaulin.

McGregor pulled his scarf tighter round his throat, shivering involuntarily. How anyone could bear to be buried was beyond him. Obviously Mr Hebblethwaite didn't care now, but he must have *chosen* this. He must have known what they'd do with him... afterwards. Cremation was the far better option; all over and done with in a flash of fire, leaving nothing but ash to be scattered somewhere. He had no idea who'd scatter him, mind, but it was still preferable to rotting in the ground.

Father Sidwell shuffled round to the other side of the dirt pile, pointing down into the hole. "Didn't bring the coffin up. Did it all down there."

"He may well have been doing it alone, then," McGregor said, knowing how much of a palaver it was when an investigation needed to disinter a body. Back in his uniform days, he'd had to guard the perimeter of one of those operations. Thankfully he hadn't seen anything more than the equipment being moved to the site and the small tent erected around it. He couldn't for the life of him remember what the case had been about, and he usually had an excellent memory for these things.

Telling himself that it was all important information, he made notes about the hole and the dirt, observing that there was no spade left behind, but that there were clear marks in the sides of the hole that could be measured to determine the size of the tool. He quickly ran out of things to write. "Buried yesterday, you say, Father?"

"At noon. Well, the service was. But he was covered by... about 4pm, I think."

"I'll need to speak to the gravedigger."

"It wasn't him. He's worked here for nigh on ten years."

"I need to work out the timings, Father, and to ask him if he saw anyone hanging around as he worked."

"Oh. Right you are. He's over there."

McGregor's eyes followed the priest's crooked finger to a figure leaning against a shovel on the other side of the graveyard, watching both of them. He was wearing a black woolly hat pulled down so low it covered his eyebrows, along with a shabby overcoat that had seen better days in the 'seventies. The little of his skin that could be seen was pale: McGregor wondered if he was nervous, scared of being blamed. Not even his lips held any colour.

"Does he work here every day?"

"All days except Sundays, of course. He keeps the grounds tidy and looks out for vandals. St Mark's had its candlesticks taken, did you hear about that?"

"Can't say I did, Father."

"Some detective you are," the priest snorted.

"I investigate murders, Father, not petty theft."

Father Sidwell scowled at him. "This poor man was long dead, and yet you're here now."

"Half the station has the flu."

"Stretched, are they?" Father Sidwell nodded to himself. "It was the flu that took Mr Hebblethwaite. He didn't have a chance, with lungs like his. Will you be wanting a ladder?"

It took McGregor a moment to follow the non sequitur. He meant for the hole, the one he still hadn't looked down into.

"I'll..." McGregor coughed as he tried to think of a way to get out of it. Nothing came to mind. "I'd appreciate that."

Much to his relief, the priest moved off towards the groundsman. He took a deep breath and looked down.

There wasn't much to be seen, strangely enough. Only the top half of the coffin had been fully exposed; half of the lid was still open, resting against the dirt. The corpse inside was covered with soil, thankfully, and not the horror-movie monster his mind had fabricated.

Only two months before he'd watched a teenaged boy being dragged out of a river, his body bloated and face mottled, but it hadn't even stirred his stomach. It was something about this body being closed up in a coffin, laid to rest and left to rot that was disturbing him so much.

The late Mr Hebblethwaite had been buried in a tweed suit, one sleeve of which was now reduced to a sad pile of dirty fabric.

He needed to find out how the limb was removed, but it didn't feel right to get the whole team mobilised. The victim was already dead when it happened, of natural causes. Radioing into the station to ask for the photographer to come down—who was also ill, now he thought of it—seemed like overkill.

"Here you are, then," Father Sidwell called as he came back with the groundsman in tow. "A ladder for you. Frank will set it up for you, won't you, Frank?"

The grounds man nodded, not meeting McGregor's eyes. Up close, the man's skin looked almost chalky, it was so white. As he lowered the ladder into the hole, McGregor noticed a fearsome scar protruding from beneath the hat. The marks from the stitches could still be seen. *One hell of a head injury,* McGregor thought. *No wonder the poor bugger doesn't say much.*

The man stepped back and was about to leave when McGregor stopped him. "If I could just ask you a couple of questions?" The man nodded once, eyes focused on the hole in the ground. "I understand you work here, and that you dug this grave?"

He received a curt nod in reply.

"What time did you fill it in?"

"Four," the man replied. His voice was incredibly deep, with a slight slur.

"And what time did you go home?"

"Five."

"And he was back here again at nine, weren't you, Frank?" Father Sidwell said.

"Yes," Frank replied.

"Did you see anyone hanging around during the funeral, or afterwards?"

"No."

"Thank you, Frank," the priest said, patting his shoulder. "Why don't you get those leaves swept up from the porch steps and I'll bring a cup of tea out to you when we're done here?"

McGregor was about to intervene, angered at how the priest had shut him down, but Father Sidwell held up a hand as Frank walked off. When he was out of earshot, he turned and fixed those faded eyes on his former choirboy. "Frank didn't do it, and doesn't like being asked questions. And before you apply police thinking to that comment, you should know it's because he's a bit simple and he gets agitated easily."

"What happened to him? That scar..."

"I've never asked and he's never said. There's room for

everyone in my church, and just because he's not like everyone else, doesn't mean he shouldn't be here too."

Even room for monsters like you, McGregor thought, but he kept those words out of his mouth. Instead, he approached the top of the ladder, taking a couple of deep breaths as he tucked his notebook and pencil back into his pocket. After testing its stability, he climbed down and looked more closely at the dirt resting on the lower half of the coffin. There were no footprints and the earth was in loose clumps, still covered in frost. It looked like the thief was clever enough to break up the soil after they were done, before climbing back out of the hole. He gingerly stepped off the bottom rung of the ladder onto the dirt still piled on the lower half of the coffin. It creaked a little under his weight, but held firm.

Why steal a man's arm? Was it to steal a watch that couldn't be removed? A wedding ring? Why take the trouble to dig up a corpse when old watches and wedding rings could be found at the local pawnbrokers? Taking the whole forearm and hand just for the jewellery seemed unlikely, but *none* of this seemed sensible. Surely this couldn't have been done by someone in their right mind?

Or was it something to do with the victim himself? Some bizarre revenge?

"How well did you know him, Father?"

"He was a good man. Devoted husband and father. Came to confession"—Father Sidwell paused to glare at McGregor— "every week, without fail. They were standing at the back and on the church steps for his funeral, there were so many here to pay their respects. I dread to think what this news will do to the parish."

"I don't suppose you know if his watch was very—"

McGregor's question was abandoned as he saw the watch strap beneath the edge of the empty sleeve. "His watch is still here," he called up. "Was he buried with his wedding ring?"

"No," Father Sidwell said. "I talked to his wife about it. She couldn't bear the thought of not having it with her. She said she's going to wear it on a chain about her neck. He was buried with his war medals, though. Are they still there?"

McGregor pulled his pencil back out and with gritted teeth, began to prod the dirt around the top pocket of the dead man's jacket. The pencil point found something hard and McGregor brushed aside the damp soil to reveal a George Cross. "Did he ask to be buried with them?"

"He did. They meant a great deal to him. And Nora—his wife—she made sure it was all as he wanted."

McGregor fished out his handkerchief and picked up the watch with his pencil. It was good and solid, gold plated by the look of it, the sort companies gave to men who'd worked for them all their life. Worth a few bob, too. He wrapped it up and dropped it into his pocket in the hope there would be fingerprints.

"Aren't you going to look at his arm?"

McGregor directed a scowl up at the priest but bit back the words that came to mind. "Could you put the kettle on, Father?" he asked instead.

For a long moment there was nothing, save their pluming breaths in the cold morning air. Then, finally, the old priest shuffled off.

"At bloody last," McGregor muttered, and then lifted the sleeve of the jacket.

The arm had been severed just below the elbow, and judging by the precision of the cut, some sort of surgical instrumentation had been used. That, or a newly sharpened meat cleaver. There were no other wounds or any evidence of aborted attempts; whoever had cut the arm off had been confident and skilled.

The earlier queasiness had passed, now he was focused on the puzzle, and this was just another dead body. He checked for any other missing parts in the top half of the coffin and found none. It was clear from the compacted soil around the edge of the hole that the thief hadn't even attempted to access the rest of the coffin. Not all caskets had a divided lid, but the thief had known this one did, by the look of it, so he may well have been at the funeral. Or at the wake.

He measured the marks left by the spade and then climbed back out. The groundsman was leaning against a nearby tree, staring at him again. When McGregor stared back, the man pointed at the hole. "Done?"

"For now," McGregor replied.

The groundsman came over and pulled the ladder out, giving McGregor one last look before he moved off with it balanced on his shoulder.

McGregor looked down into the hole, at the waxy face of Mr Hebblethwaite and then up into the clear blue December sky.

"There's a cup of tea for you here," Father Sidwell called from the church porch.

"Sorry, Father," McGregor called back. "Got to get back to the station. Thanks anyway!" He marched out of the graveyard, smiling at the thought of the priest's irritation with the glee of a ten-year-old boy.

McGregor's HEAD WAS pounding by the time he got back to the station. Nobody liked breaking bad news to grieving families, but having to tell a grieving widow that the man she'd laid to rest the day before had been defiled in such a grotesque way was so much worse. He was glad the granddaughter was there to look after her.

There had been a picture of Mr Hebblethwaite on the mantelpiece, a portrait of him as a soldier looking far too young to have been given a gun to kill people, sporting the George Cross on his chest.

McGregor wondered if his own father had ever looked so fresh-faced and noble. No matter how hard he tried, he could only summon a memory of the man in a string vest and dirty trousers, standing in the council house yard, shouting over the fence at the bloke next door. If he wasn't shouting, he was hacking up his lungs between drags on the Woodbine always clamped between his fingers.

He stamped up the steps of Bury police station, shaking off that useless thinking and went up to the desk. "Anything come in while I was out?"

Jenkins rubbed his bulbous nose and shook his head. "No, sir. Everyone's too ill to go about murderin' each other, I reckon. Was it them vandals again at the church? I heard that St Mark's—"

"Wasn't vandals," McGregor said, grabbing the door handle to signal to Jenkins that he wanted to be buzzed through. "It was... something else."

He ignored the quizzical look and walked in. He didn't want to talk about it. It would only invite conversation and speculation and he wasn't in the mood for either of them.

The air in the main office on the third floor was cold and strangely fresh. Only one desk was occupied in the far corner of the room, by WPC Hannerty, who was wearing a scarf over her uniform. The window next to his desk was wide open. When he closed it, she yelped with surprise and whipped the scarf off hurriedly as she stood.

"I wasn't expecting you back until after lunch, sir," she said, cheeks reddening.

"If you're cold, closing the window usually helps."

"Just thought that some fresh air might be good, seeing as everyone was out."

He fished out his cigarettes and offered one to her. She declined and then he remembered she was into some fitness thing or another. Aerobicals, was it? Some silly fad or other. Just as he pulled one out for himself, he made the connection to the open window.

"I s'pose you'd rather I didn't?" he said, but she smiled and waved a hand and he lit up. "Quiet day," he added. "Catching up on paperwork?"

She nodded, sitting down again. She was a pretty little thing, even when she wore no make-up and had her dark brown hair pulled back into a tight bun. Petite. Too young for him, but it didn't stop him looking. Bright, too; he'd heard she had ambitions to be a DCI one day. *Good luck to you, love*, he thought, and went over to his desk.

He took a long drag on the cigarette as he took in the pile of paperwork waiting for him. Days like this were rare and he should be glad of a chance to do some of it here instead of at home, but he found it hard to get started. He couldn't stop thinking about Hebblethwaite's missing arm.

"You very busy, Hannerty?"

She looked up. "Need something, sir?"

"Fancy having a dig about in the files for me?"

"Has a case come in, sir?" she asked, grabbing her notebook and hurrying over. Eager. He liked that. Not enough people eager to work in the ranks, as far as he was concerned.

"I have a feeling I might have stumbled across one. Help me with this, and I'll see that you're in on it, if it turns into anything."

Her bright brown eyes sparkled with anticipation, pen poised. "What do you want me to look for?"

"Any reports of body parts going missing."

He was expecting some sort of disgust, or at least a pause as she took that in, but she just wrote it down and asked, "As part of a murder or after natural causes?"

"Doesn't matter. Both."

"Even accidents?"

"Yup, that's fine. The most important thing is that the limb has been removed from the scene."

She nodded as her pen flew across the page. "How far back do you want me to go?"

"Start with six months."

"I'll get onto it right away, sir."

She marched off towards the archive with a purposeful stride. She was smarter than the others gave her credit for, he was sure of it. Maybe he'd underestimated her too. He waited until she was gone and switched the radio on. Blondie's new song was playing, something about a high tide and holding on. He looked at the in-tray pile as he stubbed out his cigarette. It seemed fitting.

THE PILE IN the tray was half gone and the ashtray was half full, by the time Hannerty returned.

"Anything turn up?"

"Yes, sir," Hannerty said, dragging over one of the empty

chairs. "I looked in current cases, the archive and I made a few phone calls."

She placed a piece of paper in front of him with a look of pride. There was an itemised list in her neat handwriting.

> *Royal Liverpool Hospital: Torso disappeared from*
> *morgue*
> *Manchester Royal Infirmary: Left leg disappeared from*
> *pathology after post-mortem exam*
> *West Cheshire Hospital: Right arm stolen from body in*
> *morgue*

His head snapped up. "All in the last six months?"

"The last three, in fact, sir. All of the bodies were of people who'd died from natural causes. At least, that's what was concluded. The Chester case was from last month. All the thefts were reported to the local police forces and all are still considered open."

"I'm impressed, Hannerty. Nothing more local?"

"No, sir. I made a few phone calls to the hospitals in a hundred mile radius and dug those up. Has there been another theft, then?"

"There has, but from a graveyard rather than a morgue."

"That's interesting," Hannerty said, tapping her pen against her lips. "I hope you don't mind, but I took down some details about each of the, er, victims. Seems strange calling them that when they were already dead."

McGregor nodded. "It does. And I don't mind at all." Indeed, he'd found a gem in Hannerty. "What did you find out?"

"All were men in their late fifties. All seemingly fit and healthy when they were alive, and all put forward for post-mortems due to unexpected death. All were declared to have died from natural causes, though. The Liverpool man had a massive stroke. The Manchester man had a blood clot that had moved to his lung and the Chester man had a fall and died from internal injuries."

"This morning's case was an older man. He died from the flu, apparently."

"Not sure we have enough to be able to identify a pattern, sir," Hannerty said, staring at her own list. "But…"

She flipped to a new page of her notebook and drew a rough outline of a body, then lines defining the different pieces she'd listed. "Which limb was stolen from the one this morning?"

"The left arm."

He watched her add a line to indicate that one. She ripped the page free and placed it on the desk in front of him. "There are no duplicates," she said, leaning back in her chair. "That's interesting."

"That we know of," McGregor said. "Widen your search. And get hold of the pathologist reports for each of those ones on your list. Bring them to me as soon as they come in."

"It might take a few days, sir."

"That's fine. Doesn't look like the thief is murdering anyone to get what they want. But prioritise it, okay? I've got a feeling about this one."

She nodded and stood up. "Oh, sir, I had another thought," she said tentatively. At his nod, she took a deep breath. "It seems to me that if the thief is targeting men of a certain age, he may well be monitoring the intakes at the various morgues. There can't be many people with easy access to that sort of information. Even doctors and nurses at those hospitals would have to go out of their way to find out about new intakes. I…" She hesitated. "If it was okay with you, I could look into that."

She was pushing, desperate for a chance to take a bite at something more interesting than the crap the rest of the team usually gave her. He'd never really thought about it before, but perhaps having the rest of the men in the office out sick or filling in for others was a relief for her. Even an opportunity.

"Good idea," he said. "Tell Jenkins to give you one of the pool cars. And if he gives you any shit, tell me."

Hannerty beamed. "Right, sir!"

After she left, he looked down at the picture she'd drawn. No head. No right leg. Assuming the thief was collecting all the pieces of—

Collecting?

He shuddered. Something about this was bothering him on a deep level. Not the morbidity of digging up dead bodies, not the tastelessness of hacking a limb off a corpse, something else…

It finally coalesced in his mind: what was this *for?* What could someone possibly plan to do with limbs stolen from different dead bodies?

He rummaged in his desk drawer until he found the small address book from his old life. He flipped through pages of people he hadn't spoken to for over five years, until he found the one he was looking for. Would she still be there?

He pulled the phone towards him, picked up the receiver and started dialling the number before he could change his mind.

"Dr. Spencer, please," he said to the receptionist.

"One moment."

It was a terrible idea. He reached across to press down the cradle arms on the phone when he heard her voice. "Dr. Spencer. How can I help you?"

There was a physical pain in his chest. Images of her hair on her pillow, her face tilted back in the shadowy bedroom as she screamed with passion, her scowl as they descended into yet another argument. He could still remember what the skin on the back of her neck felt like, the sound of her laugh. The sight of her slamming the door in his face.

"It's me," he managed to croak.

The awful pause ended with her clearing her throat. "It's been a long time. How are you?"

At least she didn't ask who it was. "Oh, you know."

"That bad, eh?"

He clenched his teeth, torn between slamming the phone down and pouring it all out to her. "Listen, could I ask you about trophies? As in things that killers take as a memento?"

"God forbid you'd actually ask me how I am."

He sagged in the chair. Truth be told, he didn't want to know. He wanted to extract the information he needed as quickly and painlessly as possible. It felt like reaching into a box of primed mousetraps to look for a piece of cheese. He didn't want to spend any longer in this dangerous place than he needed to. "Clare..."

"What do you want to know?"

McGregor wished he had some water. He settled for a cigarette instead. "Ever come across limbs being taken as trophies?"

"Entire limbs are less common, but not unheard of. Feet, breasts, heads... all sorts of body parts have been documented. Have you found limbs in a suspect's property?"

"No. I've uncovered thefts of body parts. But the bodies are of people who died of natural causes."

"Hmmm..." She was clearly intrigued. She'd be slipping her shoes off now, he imagined, wriggling her toes in that way she did whenever something had caught her keen mind. "I can't recall any cases where souvenirs have been collected from non-violent deaths. The ones I'm familiar with are related to murders; and the trophies are collected by the one who committed the crime, like a souvenir. They use them to relive what they did, to fuel fantasies of the next crime. Where are the limbs being stolen from?"

Anyone else, and he'd have told them it was privileged information, but this was Clare. He knew this wouldn't go any further than this phone call. "Morgues. And one from a fresh grave."

"Fascinating," she murmured. "All the same limb?"

"No, different one every time."

"Does he have a whole body yet?"

"He's missing a head and a right leg. Or we just haven't found out about those thefts yet. It's like he's collecting all he needs to make a body. But... but why the fuck would anyone want to do that?"

"Disturbed individuals do disturbing things. Sounds like this one is getting to you. Where was the grave he dug up?"

"St. Matthews."

"Oh. Well, that explains it."

He regretted telling her. He'd handed the mousetrap his whole bloody hand!

"Do you want to talk about why this is upsetting you so much?"

"No. Thanks for the input, Clare."

He dropped the handset back into the cradle with a satisfying *thunk*, hating the way he'd just treated her. She did this to him; she made him into an arsehole. She always had to try and worm her way into his head, always had to try and winkle out his feelings like they were juicy meat to feast upon.

McGregor lit the cigarette and went to the window. Hannerty

was climbing into one of the new Cortinas, a big grin on her face. *You go for it, love,* he thought. *You get stuck in while you're still young and you don't realise how fucking hopeless all of this is.*

The phone rang. He almost didn't answer it, but when it persisted, he knew it wasn't Clare. "McGregor."

"Just had a call from Bury General Hospital," Jenkins said. "There's been a break in at the morgue and they want someone down there. All the PCs are out on call and—"

"I'll go," McGregor said, abandoning the cigarette. "Did they say if anything had been stolen?"

"That's the thing, sir... I must have heard wrong, but she said it was a leg."

"I THINK I'VE got something, sir!" Hannerty blurted out as McGregor walked back into the office.

"Bloody hell, let me at least get my coat off," he said.

Jackson, one of the other uniforms that shared the office, sniggered. "She's been here for an hour already, looking up every time that door's opened like a puppy waiting for its owner to come home," he whispered as McGregor shrugged off his wet coat.

"Maybe she's been doing some actual work and is keen to share the results," McGregor snapped. "How come you've got so much time on your hands?"

Jackson blinked, taking a moment to process McGregor's reaction. "I... I was just getting some paperwork finished before my patrol starts."

McGregor glanced at the clock. It was almost ten. "You'd better get gone. Don't want to be late now, do you?"

Jackson looked out at the rain lashing the windows. "Yes, sir." He had time to throw a scowl in Hannerty's direction before he left, but she was too busy gathering up a sheaf of papers to notice.

"Well, what is it then?" McGregor asked, dropping into his chair. His neck ached and his skull pounded. Probably just the poor night's sleep he'd had, rather than the flu. At least it was only the two of them in the office again. He couldn't cope with a full house today.

Hannerty came over with a bounce to her step that McGregor could only dimly remember ever having himself. "I went to the three hospitals on the list yesterday and interviewed the people who work at the morgues."

"All three? What time did you get home?"

She shrugged. "Some time after nine. They're open late, so it wasn't a problem."

She laid out several sheets of paper. Photocopies, by the look of them. He grinned at the large circles drawn on them. "Go on."

"I took photocopies of the sign-in books from each morgue. Anyone who goes in other than the morgue attendants has to sign in at the desk, you see. Well, sir, there's a pattern! At each hospital, a Professor Wilson visited the morgue in the week before the theft. That's the only name that appears in every one. I didn't see it until I got home and compared them, but as the attendants are there twenty-four hours, I phoned them and asked them to check further back in the records. Professor Wilson didn't sign in at any other times."

McGregor scratched the stubble on his chin. He hadn't got round to shaving that morning. "The week before each theft?"

She nodded.

"You don't think it's a bit strange for a thief to sign their name in a book just before they nick something?"

Her eager smile flickered for a moment, but she said, "Well, the visits were a couple of days beforehand, so I thought it might be that he was casing the place each time."

"But, even so—"

"Sir, that's not all. I phoned a friend at Liverpool Uni. He's studying medicine, and he told me there's a Professor Wilson who's one of the most famous surgeons in his particular field. Guess what that field is?"

McGregor shrugged. He needed to get some paracetamol down his neck, and some coffee too.

"Reattaching severed limbs."

She beamed at him and he forgot the headache.

"You're bloody joking."

"I'm not, sir. I phoned Manchester University bang on nine o'clock this morning and confirmed it with the medical school. They told me that he's a pioneer of a new technique that's brought millions of pounds of funding into his department. He's managed to reattach a finger on a man's hand that was cut off completely, with full movement and sensation after healing. The bloke on the phone was dead excited about it. They're right proud of him."

McGregor pulled out the photocopy he'd made from the sign-in book at Bury Hospital's morgue the day before. None of the staff had been any use, none of them having seen anything unusual. He spread the pages on his desk and Professor Wilson's name leapt out.

"There he is!" Hannerty cried, stabbing the name with a finger.

He nodded. "Let's go pay the good professor a visit, shall we?"

Hannerty's jaw dropped. "What... both of us?"

"Got something better to do, have you?"

"No, sir! I'll get me coat!"

McGregor had only ever visited Manchester University on the job, and most of those occasions as a PC called in to sort out some incident involving too much drink. He struggled to manage his loathing as he and Hannerty passed the clumps of students. All that loud chatter and misplaced confidence set his teeth on edge. He couldn't admit how much he envied them. He'd risen through the ranks, taking pride in the fact that he had a degree in common sense that his super, an Oxbridge man, seemed to lack.

"You never been tempted to do a degree, Hannerty?"

"I was, sir," she said, after smiling at a young man who held the door to the School of Medical Sciences for them. "But then Mum got ill and I had to stay at home. It was easier to fit police training in around her care."

"Oh, right. How is she now?"

"She… she died, sir."

Shit. This was why he didn't do small talk.

"It was a couple of years ago now, sir. It's fine. Just me and Dad now."

"Right. Good." *'Good'? You stupid bastard, keep your trap shut.*

"Professor Wilson's office is on the second floor. He isn't lecturing today, so he should be there."

Staff and students alike parted ahead of them, the sight of Hannerty's uniform leaving whispers in their wake. He took in notices, signs, posters, all giving glimpses into another world. A small crowd was heading through double doors at the end of the corridor, past which he caught sight of a lecture theatre. Hannerty steered him towards the stairs and they climbed them together, his breathing more laboured than hers by the time they reached the second floor. She gave him a concerned look but didn't say anything.

A young woman in a white lab coat saw them knocking on the professor's office door and directed them to a lab on the third floor. With a heavy heart, McGregor slogged up another flight of stairs with Hannerty pulling away from him. He didn't like the way she had to stop and wait for him, and would have said as much, if he could just catch his breath.

By the time they reached the lab, he could speak again. "Let me lead this, Hannerty."

"Of course, sir."

He pushed open the door and glanced around the alien environment. All the furniture was white, with microscopes and all sorts of equipment he couldn't fathom the use of—arranged upon two rows of tables. Six people were in the room, five of them hunched over their work, all wearing white coats.

One man was standing, watching one of the people working, a young woman with shapely legs with a pipette in her hand, dropping some liquid into a tray with lots of tiny compartments. The man had his hand on her shoulder as he peered down at her work. "Yes, that's it, good."

He was in his late fifties, by the look of it, with a neatly clipped white beard and wavy grey hair that was thicker than McGregor's had been in his thirties. He glanced over at the door, eyebrows rising at the sight of Hannerty in her uniform, and then said something quietly to the student he was helping. She glanced over too and then all work ceased.

"Can I help you?"

"Professor Wilson?"

"Yes. What can I do for you?"

"I'm DI McGregor and this is WPC Hannerty. I'd like to ask you some questions."

"I'm just in the middle of helping my student with a delicate experiment. Can it wait a few minutes? Laura, show them to my office, will you?"

While he didn't like being delayed, McGregor could see some value in talking to one of the man's colleagues. When he saw the young woman cross from the other side of the room, he mentally corrected himself. She was obviously another student, a petite blonde with big eyes.

"If you'd like to follow me?"

Once they were out in the corridor, Hannerty fell into step alongside her. "Are you one of Professor Wilson's students?"

"Assistant," she replied. "I was a student, but I've finished my surgical training and he asked if I could stay to work for him before my placement starts next month."

Following behind them, McGregor took in the curves that the lab coat failed to hide and suspected it wasn't just her mind the professor wanted to keep around.

"What is he like to work for?"

"Oh, inspirational!" The assistant flicked a smile back at McGregor, trying to involve him in the conversation. "He's taught me so much. His work is simply incredible."

"Something to do with reattaching severed limbs?"

"That makes it sound far simpler than it actually is," Laura replied with a laugh. She proceeded to gabble about nerves and tissue and bones and McGregor's stomach turned. He distracted himself by thinking about how effortlessly Hannerty was interviewing the woman, gently probing for information without seeming invasive. He recalled Jackson's behaviour back at the office, how he'd taken the piss out of her enthusiasm. He couldn't remember Jackson ever impressing him this way, yet he was up for promotion. He made a mental note to speak to the super and ask why.

"It's a privilege to work for him, really," Laura said, bringing him back to the conversation as they went down the stairs.

"How long have you been his student?"

"Well, he was one of my lecturers for the last 2 years of my degree, and then he was one of my tutors in my surgical units over the past two years. So... on and off for the past six years or so."

"And now you're off to be a surgeon too?"

Laura laughed. "Oh, wow, no! My placement is for another six years of training."

They reached the office and she showed them in. "Is there anything else you need? Coffee? Tea?"

He wanted a coffee, but didn't want her to leave yet. "No, thanks. So... how did he perfect this reattachment technique? I mean... there must be a need to practise, but how do you practise something like that?"

Laura frowned briefly and then went over to the radiator and kicked it. "Bloody thing isn't working again," she muttered. She smiled at McGregor. "Sorry. You asked about practising? Well, people leave their bodies for medical research after death. I'm sure the professor will be very happy to explain the process, if you're interested. He doesn't have to go and murder people or be a body snatcher!" She laughed, awkwardly, and Hannerty joined in to put her at ease. "Is that what you're here to find out? Only, I'm not sure he has any time to be an expert witness these days."

"Have you assisted on any of those procedures?" Hannerty asked. At Laura's frown, she added, "I'm just curious about what they involve."

"Oh, I see! No, I haven't, though I have attended his lectures on the subject. I'm not at the level where I can assist in surgery yet. That's many years off."

"Something to look forward to," McGregor said, failing to keep all of the sarcasm out of his voice.

"It really is," she replied brightly.

The door opened and Professor Wilson entered. "Thank you, Laura," he said, holding the door open for her. Once she'd left, he closed it and smiled at them both. "How can I help you?"

"We'd like to ask where you were between 6pm Monday evening and 9am the following day," McGregor asked.

The professor's eyes widened. "Good grief," he said, unbuttoning his lab coat. "That sounds like something from *The Sweeney*!"

"Could you answer the question please?"

Seeing the lack of joviality on McGregor's face, Wilson dropped into his high-backed leather chair and gestured for them to take seats opposite him. "I was in Paris on Monday," he said, leaning back, relaxed. "I was giving the keynote address at a very high-profile conference. At 6pm I think I was probably at a lovely little restaurant just off the Champs-Elysées. I was staying at the Hôtel Du Louvre and flew back late on Tuesday evening. I probably have my ticket stubs somewhere if you need them. I definitely have the hotel receipt. Why do you ask?"

McGregor ignored the question. "And what about yesterday evening, between 9pm and 1am?"

The professor frowned and scratched the bridge of his nose. "I was here, going through some data with Laura."

"Until one in the morning?"

"I'm at a critical point in my latest study. I needed to be certain of the data before proceeding with the next stage." His eyes flicked to Hannerty, standing in full uniform with her hat in her hands. "Am I in some sort of trouble?"

"I don't think so," McGregor said. He leaned across to Hannerty and whispered, "Check the alibi for last night with Laura, get her details too, and meet me by the car."

She gave a nod and left. Wilson stood and moved round the desk. "Is there something going on that I should know about? Is it one of my students?"

"Am I right in thinking that you specialise in reattaching severed limbs?"

Wilson leaned against his desk, folding his arms, relaxed. "I've only been fully successful with digits so far. I'm hoping to have the chance to use my technique on a whole hand soon."

McGregor schooled his face to hide his disgust. "But... isn't it... the finger or whatever... isn't it dead, once it's cut off?"

"Well, it depends on how one defines 'dead.' The window for reattachment is really quite narrow, and the cut has to be very clean to have a good chance of success."

"Could you... theoretically... attach one person's hand to another person's arm?"

"I had an interesting debate with a colleague about that in France, strangely enough," the professor said in a matter-of-fact tone. "If you could find a hand, say, from a person of similar size, the mechanical aspects of reattaching another person's hand to an arm would not be very different to reattaching the same person's hand. I'd speculate that there could be issues with some form of rejection, just as there is in organ transplants. Now, we're finding better drugs to manage immuno-suppression, and it could just be a matter of managing it the same way. But there is an argument for—" He paused, frowning again. "Perhaps I should stop there, eh? Looks like you don't have the stomach for this sort of thing."

McGregor's lips were tingling in quite a distressing manner. He coughed and moved towards the door. "Thanks for your time, Professor Wilson."

"If there's anything else I can do for you, just let me know."

"Oh," McGregor said, hand on the door knob, a question coming to mind as the ringing in his ears stopped. "You practised attaching digits on... on corpses before doing it on a living person, right?"

The professor chuckled. "Yes, of course. It's not the sort of procedure where one learns the basics on an actual patient."

"Where do you practise that sort of thing? In the morgue at one of the hospitals?" He doubted that was the case, but wanted to be certain.

"Heavens, no," the professor replied. "Here at the medical school."

"So the morgues ship the bodies to you here?"

"Perhaps if you explained where your curiosity is coming from, I could better satisfy it."

"I'd rather not, at this stage."

"All right then. No, the bodies are not moved from hospital morgues. We train students and practise new techniques using cadavers that have been left to us in someone's will. Some people leave their bodies to medical science. There's a robust system in place that means they are referred to the local facility—this being the one for Manchester and surrounds, for example—once they are approved."

"Approved?"

"The manner of their death may preclude them from being accepted. I have some literature somewhere on it, if you're interested."

"Do you go to the morgues to decide if those criteria are met?"

The professor's smile was a perfect blend of smug and condescending. "My dear man, there are others who do such work. Those who have not reached my level of specialisation."

"Right. Of course. When you're not practising though, when it's for a living patient, I assume there's a narrow window of time for the procedure?"

The professor nodded. "Indeed. Of course, it depends on what is being reattached. Digits can last longer when severed from the body than an arm, for example. That's where I've been specialising. Even if the finger was cut off seven hours before, the surgery can be successful."

"And for an arm or a leg, how long can they last?"

"Oh, three or four hours at best, and the temperature makes a big difference too. I'm talking about maximising the chance of a full recovery, you understand."

"So if the limb had been... detached for longer, it might still work?"

"The odds decrease as each hour passes. One finger I reattached had been cut off two days before, but was iced pretty much immediately."

"What if..." McGregor paused, wondering if he should ask the question. But he needed to know. "What if someone attached a limb that had been dead for a while?"

The professor's mouth turned down in disgust. "No one worthy of a medical licence would even consider such a thing."

"So stitching a dead limb to a living person would be pointless?"

There was a flash of alarm in the professor's eyes. "Why on Earth would you ask such a question, inspector?"

"Would it be, though?"

"It would be pointless," the professor said. "And more than that, utterly tasteless. If there is any possibility that someone in my medical school is experimenting in such a manner, I'd want to know about it immediately and have them expelled. Do you understand? That sort of thing is simply disgusting!"

A red flush covered the man's neck; he seemed quite appalled.

But McGregor couldn't help but think there was something else beneath the man's protestations. "I will take that literature about donating a body to science, if you don't mind," McGregor said. Not just to fill the gaps in his knowledge, but also because he wanted to inconvenience the self-satisfied git for just a few minutes longer.

"WILSON'S HAVING AN affair with Laura," Hannerty declared as they drove out of the main gates. "She confirmed they were together that night. At the lab, so she says."

"What makes you think it wasn't what he said it was?"

"Oh, come on, sir. You saw the way she talked about him. She was so full on. And keeping her on as an assistant before her placement? That rang alarm bells. Anyway, he's such a creepy guy, I'm not the least surprised he's cheating on his wife."

McGregor raised an eyebrow at her as they waited at traffic lights. "You really didn't like him, did you?"

"No," she said, folding her arms. "I didn't like the way he put his hand on that student's shoulder in the lab, either."

"He was helping her."

"Does his hand help her use that dropper thing better?"

"Oh, give over," McGregor laughed. "He was just being friendly."

"That's what they all say," Hannerty muttered.

An ambulance raced passed with blues and twos, distracting McGregor. When the traffic was moving again, he mulled over the conversation with the professor. "He's got alibis for when the grave and Bury morgue were robbed, and no reason to go to the morgue anyway. The bodies he uses for his work are donated to the university, would you believe?"

"Fancy leaving your body to be chopped up by medical students! Who'd want to do that?" Hannerty said. "Oh, and I asked the front desk about the conference and it checks out. The woman at the desk gave me this." She waved a newspaper. "There's an article about Wilson in it. They're very proud of him there. I had the feeling he's a bit of a celebrity in those circles."

"If he didn't go to those morgues, why did the person who did sign his name in the visitor's book?" McGregor mused aloud.

"Maybe he thought that if someone looked back through the records for some reason, it would make sense for Wilson's name to be there, given the field he's in."

"Yeah, but that should raise an alarm bell for anyone in the know," McGregor replied. "That professor has no reason at all to visit any morgues. He can get access to as many dead bodies as he likes without having to leave his place of work."

"Something else that bothers me, sir, is that one limb was stolen from a grave and all the others were from morgues. It breaks the pattern; it must be significant."

McGregor nodded. "I'm going to drop you off at Bury morgue. Find out who was on duty the night the leg was taken and get a description of the person they thought was the professor."

"Yes, sir. I was also thinking that it might be useful to look at the victims more closely. Perhaps they're linked in some way. If they are, that could lead us to the thief."

McGregor smirked. "Who's in charge of this investigation?"

"Sorry, sir! I didn't want to overstep the mark!"

He laughed. "I'm only pulling your leg, Hannerty. That's exactly what I'm planning to do. Tell you what. I'll take you to the station so you can pick up that Cortina again, then after you've been to the morgue, go and speak to Mrs. Hebblethwaite and find out more about her husband."

"I thought you've already spoken to her, sir."

"I did. But maybe she'll open up to you some more. We need to make some progress on this, and soon. That bugger has got the whole of a body now, except a head. I'd like to catch him before I have to tell another grieving family that their loved one's corpse has been decapitated."

McGREGOR SPENT THE rest of the day looking into the other victims, plagued by a headache that simply wouldn't shift. It seemed that the only thing they had in common was their gender and age range. From what he could tell over the phone, none of the local constabularies had done more than a cursory investigation. It wasn't murder, so wasn't flagged up as that urgent; but it wasn't a straight-forward kind of theft either. He had the feeling that the crimes had fallen between two stools.

He spoke to the officers who'd written up the paperwork for each theft. All they could tell him was that none of the victims had criminal records, and all were employed, but in different industries. He ended up requesting the full files, determined to trawl through them to find something that connected them.

By the time Hannerty returned to the office, McGregor was

ready to call it a day, but the young officer looked pale cheeked and nervous. "Out with it then, Hannerty," he said. "What have you found?"

"Sir," she said, a tremble in her voice. "Oh, sir, I think I've made a terrible mistake."

"Sit down, love. Start at the beginning."

She sat, after hanging her coat and hat on the stand in the corner. She was shaking. He readied himself, getting his temper in check nice and early, not wanting to put off a promising officer after she'd got stuck in to the case with such enthusiasm.

"I spoke to one of the administrators at Bury Hospital, and he told me they sacked the morgue attendant who was on duty at the time of the theft. I got the man's details and went to see him."

"You should've checked in with me, Hannerty."

"I hadn't spoken to anyone in connection with the case yet, sir, so I didn't think I should bother you. I radioed into Control, they knew where I was the whole time, sir. That's not where I made the mistake."

"Go on, then," McGregor said, seeing she was building herself up to something.

"I went to this bloke's house and spoke to him about what happened that night. He was hard work at first—"

"You shouldn't have gone inside alone, Hannerty!"

"I can take care of myself, sir! That wasn't the problem. He didn't want to talk about it at first, but I laid it on thick with him. I said that if he didn't come clean with me now, he could end up in court as an accessory. I pointed out that he'd already lost his job, so he didn't have to hide anything from me, as I was helping him avoid getting into more trouble."

McGregor nodded. She'd played it well, by the sound of it. "I've not heard anything worth this drama yet. What happened?"

She looked down at the desk, her eyelashes longer than he'd appreciated before, now they were cast against her pale cheeks. "He told me a woman phoned him. Said she would give him two hundred quid to take his tea break at midnight and leave the door unlocked. He thought it was like a student prank or something. Apparently the junior doctors play tricks on a consultant pathologist there, and she said something that made him think it was that. She said it would be a laugh and that no one would find out anything had happened on his shift. He agreed—didn't seem that bright, sir. She left the cash in an envelope under one of the bins in the alleyway outside. He'd already spent it by the time I got to him."

"So it was a woman who arranged it?"

"Yes, sir, and…" She sighed. "And that's the mistake I made. When I heard him say that, I went and double-checked who is on the staff at Bury General and… and we've been talking to the wrong Professor Wilson, sir. The professor we spoke to has a wife, and she's a professor too!"

"Bloody hell," McGregor sighed. Hannerty bit her lip, looking like she could burst into tears. "Oh, give over, Hannerty, I thought it'd be much worse than that. I should have checked your work better. It's not just your mistake."

She nodded, still crestfallen. She'd been so desperate to impress him, she was being too hard on herself. He wasn't himself either. Since that bloody grave robbery, he'd barely slept. And he couldn't shake the hammer in his skull. He was being sloppy, and expecting a green officer to do the hard work for him.

"So, what have you done to make up for it, then?" he asked, as cheerily as he could muster.

"I've got her CV here, and her home address, sir. She's been married to the professor for thirty years. She was the first female pathologist to qualify in her university, and she's well respected. She's a professor of Pathology at Leeds University, but also a consultant pathologist at Bury General a few days a month."

"Pathologist, eh? That's why no-one batted an eyelid at her signing the book?"

"Well, it's still a bit odd, sir. She's staff at Bury, and should never have to sign in there. And she's never had a professional reason to sign in to any of the other places either."

"You've been busy, haven't you?"

"As soon as I realised what I'd done, I went straight back to Bury General and found out as much as I could. I'm so sorry, sir. No wonder the professor had alibis; we were talking to the wrong one."

"Let's go and see his wife," McGregor said, standing up. "She home by now?"

"Yes, sir."

"And put this behind you, all right? It's a good learning experience, for one thing; and for another, you realised early on, did the legwork when you did, and came and told me right away. We've only lost a few hours and it's not like it's a murder case now, is it?"

She brightened. "Thank you, sir. It means such a lot to me that you're letting me work this case with you. I've wanted to get stuck in on something interesting for ages, but Jackson always weasels his way in somehow."

"Funny that," McGregor muttered as they both put their coats on. "I wonder how he manages that."

*   *   *

McGREGOR PULLED UP in the wide, leafy street and they both stared at the huge house. "Bloody hell," he said as he turned off the car's lights. "Seems that chopping up dead people and stitching bits back onto people for a living pay well."

The Victorian red-brick house was a far cry from the terrace he lived in. It was detached, with a sweeping driveway. He didn't want to park on it, though; better that she didn't hear a car pull up.

There was a BMW on the drive.

"That's her car," Hannerty said.

"His might be in the garage," McGregor said, looking at the double garage to the side of the building.

"Or he might be staying late at the lab," Hannerty said. "You know, going over that very important data with Laura."

McGregor smirked at her tone. "C'mon. Let's go and disturb the other Professor Wilson."

Even the doorbell sounded posh. The woman who opened the door looked tired and a little red around the eyes. She was in her early fifties, but hadn't let herself go completely, wearing a jumper and long woollen skirt with a tartan design woven into it. She frowned at McGregor and then noticed Hannerty; the scowl was rapidly replaced by concern.

"Has something happened to Paul?"

"No, Professor Wilson. I'm Inspector McGregor and this is WPC Hannerty. May we come in, please?"

She stepped back and he was glad to enter the warm hallway, with its original Victorian floor tiles and wide staircase. It was grand but still homely, a vase of fresh flowers on the console table and the smell of baking bread making it feel welcoming. He'd like to come home to this at the end of the day.

"Has something happened? Is Paul all right?"

"This has nothing to do with your husband," he said, wiping his feet thoroughly on the mat and stepping in so Hannerty could do the same. "We'd just like to ask you a few questions, to assist us in an investigation."

"Oh! Is this about the theft from the morgue? Come through to the living room. Would you like a drink?"

"No, thank you."

"That bloody theft has thrown my whole schedule off this week," she said, leading them through into a beautiful living room with an original fireplace boasting a roaring fire. "Those junior doctors are really going too far. It's bordering on harassment and I'm not going to stand for it much longer. It's unprofessional on their part and distressing for me. I have been thinking about getting the police involved, but if there's one thing I've learned, it's that the more fuss you make about something, the more they gun for pushing you out." She glanced at Hannerty then, before retrieving a glass of red wine from the coffee table.

"I need to ask where you were on Monday evening between 6pm and 9am the following day."

She frowned at him. "I beg your pardon?"

"Please answer the question."

"Am I under suspicion for something?"

"Please, Professor Wilson. Answer the question."

"I was here, at home. Why?"

"Alone?"

"Yes. Paul was in Paris." There was venom in the words.

"He didn't take you with him?"

"Oh, no, he doesn't bother taking me anymore!" She glanced at the newspaper resting on the table next to the coaster, her scowl deepening.

"And what about yesterday evening, between 9pm and 1am?"

"Wasn't that when the leg was stolen from the morgue? Bloody hell! You don't think I did that, do you? I don't bloody believe this!"

"Please answer the question."

"I was home, alone. Again. I didn't take that leg and I resent the implication. This is a campaign to discredit me, and I can give you the names of the junior doctors behind it! They can't stand the fact that I'm a woman. They want to—"

"Professor Wilson," McGregor cut in. "WPC Hannerty will take those names in a moment if you want to take this further. Is there anyone who can verify you were at home on those evenings?"

She blinked at him. "I spoke to my sister at about ten, actually. She phoned up in a bit of state. My nephew is ill and she thinks I'm her on-call doctor. I spoke to her for at least an hour. Other than that, no."

"Did you speak to the morgue attendant about a payment of two hundred pounds yesterday?"

"Two hundred pounds? I have no idea what you're talking about. I resent being asked these questions without any context whatsoever, and the implication that I'm under suspicion. Ask Tom about what else they've done in the morgue. He knows how long this has been going on. I refuse to be accused of something that's clearly intended to make me resign. It was just bullying before. This... this is..."

Tom was the administrator that Hannerty had spoken to. "Your husband wasn't at home last night either?" McGregor asked. He wanted to understand where that anger was coming from.

"No, he wasn't!" she said, slamming the glass back down. "He was 'at the lab.' That bastard!"

She closed her eyes, visibly shaking with rage. "In all honesty, Inspector, this isn't the best time. I've had a total shit of a day and I don't want to talk about it."

She was staring at the newspaper again.

"I heard there was an article about your husband in that paper," Hannerty said. "It must be dead exciting being married to such an accomplished man!" *Smart girl.*

"Oh, you silly, bloody..." Wilson snapped, and then looked appalled. "Good lord, I am so sorry. I'm... I'm just not myself."

"Is your husband at the lab now, Professor Wilson?" McGregor asked, prodding that raw nerve once more.

"I doubt it very much. In fact, perhaps you have the wrong Professor Wilson. It's usually the other way round with us." She snatched up the paper and unfolded it. "If you want to speak to the other Professor Wilson, I suggest you find *that bitch* and ask her where he is!"

She stabbed one of the three pictures of her husband. It had been taken at some sort of gala event, by the look of it, and Wilson was there in black tie and a big smile. The smile was very much focused on the young woman in a stunning gown right next to him, one hand on his arm, laughing. McGregor recognised the student he'd had his hand on at the lab.

"She's called Chloe," Professor Wilson said through gritted teeth. "The journalist calls her his 'glamorous assistant,' but, funnily enough, he's never mentioned her. I bet she's one of his simpering students. You may as well go and find him with her, Inspector, and when you do, tell him not to bother coming home tonight. Now, if you'll excuse me, I'm going to go and knead some more bread and get pissed. It's better than hunting him down and punching his lights out, as I'm sure you'll agree."

She showed them the way out and slammed the door behind them.

"How many glamorous assistants does one surgeon need?" Hannerty asked with an arched eyebrow.

"Get on the pipes to Control and get them to patch you through to Jackson. He'll be getting back to the office about now. Get him to phone Manchester University for us and get this 'Chloe's' surname and address. We'll pop in to see her on the way home."

"But, sir, we know he was in Paris with Chloe. Neither of them can be involved."

"We know he was in Paris when the grave was robbed. But where was Chloe when Bury morgue was robbed? He could have got her to pay off the desk clerk."

Hannerty nodded, went off to the car and radioed in as McGregor took a short stroll down the road and lit up. By the time he'd smoked down to the filter and got back to the car, head clearer, Hannerty had what they needed.

Chloe Atkinson shared student digs with another young woman a couple of miles away in the sort of red brick terraced house that was more in keeping with what McGregor knew. She was just returning home as they arrived, keys still in the lock.

"Do you remember us from earlier today, Miss Atkinson?"

"Yeah," she said quietly. "You'd better come in."

They followed her inside, the dingy hallway with a pile of junk mail crushed behind the door a stark contrast to the house they'd just visited. Chloe mumbled an apology for the mess and led them through to the kitchen where a plump young woman was stirring a pan of baked beans.

"Hey, Chloe! I hear you're in the paper with—" she caught sight of Hannerty's uniform. "Oh. Hiya. I'm Peggy."

"Can you give us a few minutes, Peggy?" Hannerty asked and the girl nodded, turned off the hob and squeezed past them all to dash upstairs.

Chloe moved past McGregor to shut the kitchen door. "Is this something to do with Professor Wilson?"

"We saw the picture in the paper," McGregor said. "We thought Laura was his assistant."

Chloe's cheeks turned a remarkable shade of puce. "That was just something the stupid journalist wrote. Laura really is his assistant."

"So why did *you* go with him to Paris, and not her?"

Her cheeks darkened further. "She wasn't free," Chloe croaked. "And..." Her eyes filled with tears. "Am I in trouble? I've already had crap at uni today over that bloody photo, but the police? What's going on? It was a conference in Paris! I went to help him! It's not a crime, is it?"

She'd pulled the sleeves of her coat down, hiding her hands, and backed herself against the sink.

"I need to ask you a question and it's very important that you tell us the truth," McGregor said, taking care to sound as serious as he could. "Where were you yesterday evening, between 9pm and 1am?"

She wrapped her arms about herself. "I... I was... I was at the lab. Working."

"That's very late. Were you alone?"

"No, Professor Wilson was there. We were checking data. For an experiment."

She was a terrible liar. "Was anyone else in the lab with you?"

Chloe shook her head.

"Are you absolutely sure about that?"

"It was just the two of us, I'm positive."

"And were you there the entire time, with the Professor?"

She nodded, eyes glistening.

The door swung open, almost hitting Hannerty. "Chloe! Tell them the truth!"

"Piss off, Peggy!" Chloe yelled.

"She wasn't at the lab, but she was with the Professor. They go to this swanky hotel in Chester and he gets his assistant to cover for him."

"Peggy!" Chloe started to cry.

"Look, I know you think you love him, but he's not worth getting into trouble with the police for, is he?" Peggy's hands were on her hips. "My granddad was in t'police, and he told me that the ones who don't have to wear a uniform are the ones to pay attention to." She jabbed a finger at McGregor. "Look at 'im! This is serious, Chloe, and I'm not going to stand 'ere and listen to you get into proper trouble just because of that cheatin' bugger. He'll never leave his wife. He's just not worth it!" She looked at McGregor. "Sorry I listened in, but I'm her best mate and someone has to look out for her!"

McGregor smiled at her, and then Chloe. "That's all we need to know, Miss Atkinson. Don't you worry about a thing."

"You've got a good friend there, Chloe," Hannerty said to her as McGregor left the kitchen. "Don't be angry with her."

Peggy showed them out and they went back to the car.

"You know, the more we find out about the professor, the more I dislike him," Hannerty said once they were inside and pulling away. "And as much as I want him to be behind all this, it's looking like we're barking up the wrong tree."

"Mmm," McGregor grunted. "I'll drop you home, if you

like? Then first thing in the morning, we'll pop round to Mrs Hebblethwaite. I take it you didn't get a chance to see her today?"

"No, sir, sorry. Once I found out about the other Professor Wilson I came straight back to the station."

"Not to worry. If Wilson is involved, he may not be stealing the limbs himself. Whether or not the thief is working for him, someone wants us to put him or his wife in the frame. And his wife doesn't have an alibi, for either of the two most recent thefts. Neither does Laura, for that matter."

"Yes, but she lied to cover for Wilson," Hannerty said. "There's dedication for you: telling a bare-faced lie to the police to cover up for the randy bugger."

"Mmm. If we could work out how the thief is choosing which bodies to steal from, it might throw some light onto all this."

"Maybe it's someone with a grudge against the Wilsons, and he's writing their name in the book to make us look into them."

"Maybe," McGregor said, tapping his finger against the steering wheel as he waited for the traffic lights to turn green. "But it seems like a bloody strange way to go about it. And I keep coming back to the same question: someone's going to a lot of trouble to steal those body parts. What the hell are they planning to do with them?"

THE NEXT MORNING McGregor arrived at the office early. Not because he'd made a special effort to offset his lateness the day before, but because he'd been up since five in the morning.

He'd woken with a jolt, certain he'd heard someone coming into his bedroom. He'd even switched on the lights and checked the whole house for an intruder, like all the silly sods did in the horror movies. He'd concluded it was a bad dream, even though he couldn't remember it, but by then he was awake for the day.

The internal post arrived not long after he'd got to the office, delivering the files held on the other thefts. He'd only had time to skim the first summary sheet when Hannerty arrived, carrying a large paper bag.

"Oh! Morning, sir," she said, far too fresh-faced for his liking. "Are you all right, sir? You're not coming down with that flu, are you?"

"I'm fine," he said, ignoring the headache that still hadn't left. "Just woke up too early, that's all. And Hannerty, love, call me 'guv,' will you? 'Sir' is for supers, and people you're pissed off with, okay?"

She reddened slightly. "Right you are, guv. Are those the files on the other thefts?"

"Yup. Let's both review these; by the time we're done, it'll be a sociable enough hour to go and see Mrs Hebblethwaite. I want you to lead that one, Hannerty. Like I said, I think she might open up to another woman better. I'll hang back and see if I spot anything interesting in the house. Okay?"

"Yes, guv!"

An hour and two cups of coffee later, neither of them could find any connection between the victims. "I'm not getting anywhere with this," Hannerty said. "They all lived in different cities, none of them went to the same school and none of them went to college or university, so they couldn't have met the thief there either. The only thing these blokes had in common, other than their gender, was that they were all horrible." Hannerty pulled out the piece of paper with the divided body sketched onto it. "Mr Left Leg had been reported to the council for animal cruelty, but never prosecuted. Mr Torso was sacked from his last job after accusations of embezzlement but the case was never brought to court for lack of evidence. Mr Right Arm was charged for assault ten years before he died, after a punch-up in a pub. Mr Right Leg was involved in some far-right groups and was arrested for disturbing the peace at some weird rally a few years ago. What was Mr Hebblethwaite like?"

"A pillar of the community, by all accounts," McGregor replied. "He used to go to the same church as me when I was a boy."

"Do you still go to church, guv?"

"That's a very private question."

"Sorry, guv. Only... I thought maybe we could talk to the vicar if—"

"No need, I've spoken to him already." There was no way he was going back to St Matthew's again. "C'mon, let's go see the Mrs, and see if she has anything useful to say about her husband."

Mrs Hebblethwaite's cramped post-war bungalow was only fifteen minutes away. Her granddaughter's blue mini was parked on the drive. McGregor parked up on the road outside and looked at Hannerty. "Gently does it with her, Hannerty? She was a mess when I last saw her."

Hannerty nodded earnestly, taking a moment to check her notebook one last time before they left the car. "And the granddaughter is called Mrs Miller, right?"

"That's right. She was nice enough. Young, not far off your age."

They walked up the garden path together, McGregor knocked on the door and stood back. Mrs Miller answered the door, looking better than she had the last time he'd visited. Her blonde hair was tied back and she wore jeans with a fluffy powder blue jumper that brought out her eyes. "Oh, Inspector McGregor! Come in."

"This is WPC Hannerty," McGregor said. "Mrs Miller, is your grandmother up to speaking to us?"

"She's much better. And call me Karen. She was in shock before, but she's much more herself now. Come through. I'll put the kettle on."

The bungalow smelt of the same lavender water that McGregor's mother used to wear, sending his thoughts tumbling backwards. He pushed aside memories of laundry day, when he and his brothers used to play hide and seek amongst the huge sheets hung up in the communal yard behind the house he grew up in. It had been torn down after being declared a slum and he'd not thought about it for years.

In the living room Mrs Hebblethwaite looked like a different woman. Her hair had been curled and set and she sat in the armchair by the window wearing a pink twin set and pearls. She smiled at him, then at Hannerty when she was introduced, and waved at the sofa for them to sit down.

"WPC Hannerty is going to ask you a few questions, if that's okay?" he said.

"You can call me Nora too, love," she said to Hannerty. "Have you found out who did it?"

"Not yet, Mrs Hebblethwaite—sorry, Nora—but we do have several lines of enquiry, and we're doing all we can to find the person responsible."

"Disgusting business, digging up graves," the old woman muttered. "It really knocked me for six, it did. But I've rallied now, and I'm angry. It's not just a crime against my Donald, it's against God. That was holy ground he disturbed."

Hannerty pointed to the photo on the mantelpiece. "Your husband was very handsome," she said.

"Oh, aye, too handsome," Nora said, pursing her lips.

"And a war hero, I understand?"

"Aye, he were that too. I think he would have been happy if the war had gone on longer, truth be told. He never seemed to settle after it were all done and they came back home. We got engaged the day his draft came in; to be honest, I think he was shocked he'd survived and that he had to go through with it once he came back."

"Go through with it?"

"Marrying Nana," Karen said, coming in with a tea tray. "Tell them about Great-Granddad, Nana."

Nora laughed. "Dad thought he were going to do a runner. He asked him to play a game of billiards with him, and by the end of it, Don had settled the date with my dad, which church it was going to be in and that the party afterwards would be at the club. We were married a month later."

"Great-Granddad was a bit scary," Karen added.

"Did Donald have any feuds with anyone, or fall out with anyone badly?"

"No. Everyone loved Don," Nora sighed.

"Not everyone, Nana," Karen said. "There were a few husbands who took a dislike to him."

"That was nothing, love," Nora said, shuffling in her chair a little.

McGregor stood, knowing Hannerty would handle the rest. "Can I use your loo, please?"

"It's just down the hallway and on the right," Karen said. "Would you like some biscuits too, Nana?"

"Yes, love. This lovely police lady needs a biscuit or two, don't you, pet?"

Karen followed him out, closing the living room door behind her. "Inspector?" she whispered. "You should know that Granddad wasn't as popular as Nana says he was."

He stopped to face her. "Go on."

"I know he cheated on her. Lots of times. I overheard my mum and dad arguing about it when we came down for the funeral. There was a woman who came to the house with flowers the night before, and Nana wouldn't accept them. It all came out then. She was one of his... bits on the side. What a cheek, coming to his widow's house with flowers! And she wasn't the only one. There were at least four wreaths at the church from his 'floozies,' as Mum calls them. No-one wants to say anything bad about the dead, do they? But this is different. What if one of their husbands wanted to get their own back?"

"Thanks for letting me know," McGregor said. "I'll just..." He gestured to the bathroom, and Karen gave an embarrassed nod before hurrying to the kitchen.

His plan was to wait until she went back into the living room and have a quick nose about the rest of the bungalow, but a picture on the wall stopped him before he'd even reached the bathroom.

It was a photo of Karen on her graduation day, beaming at the camera in her gown, arm in arm with a woman he recognised immediately: Professor Wilson's assistant, Laura.

"Err, Karen," he called. "This is you, isn't it?"

She came back out of the kitchen. "Oh, yeah, back when I was a brunette. I look quite different now, don't I?"

"Who's that?" he pointed at Laura.

"Laura Cartwright. My best mate."

"Met at university, did you?"

"No, way before then! My nana was friends with her

grandmother, they used to go to school together. Laura was brought over for the day with her grandmother, when my nana was babysitting me, so we first met when we were like six months old or something. Funny that, in't it? Ended up going to the same university and we were thick as thieves."

"And you decided not to stay on with postgraduate studies? Like Laura did?"

"I... I was going to, but... it wasn't right for me."

There was a whole story behind those words, but not the one he was interested in. "Did Laura come to your grandfather's funeral?"

"She did. There were so many people there. I hadn't seen her for years and I was so chuffed she'd come. It was really kind of her."

"But if you were best friends, why hadn't you seen her for so long?"

She frowned slightly. "Why are you so interested?"

He tried on his best smile. "Occupational hazard. I'm curious about everything."

"We had a bit of a falling out a few months after graduation. She... she was upset I wasn't carrying on with my medical studies. She didn't understand. We made up at the funeral."

"And how did she seem that day?"

Karen leaned against the wall, hands in pockets. "In some ways she was exactly the same, but... I don't know. She seemed... harder. But she's had to be, I suppose. I mean, what she's been through." She saw his face and grimaced. "Her parents died while we were at university. She's had to take care of herself and handle lots of difficult stuff. No wonder she threw herself into her work. There isn't much else in her life. She's an only child and so were her parents. But I am worried about her.

She's working too hard, I could see it, just talking to her." She shrugged. "I don't know how she does it, meself. That wasn't the life for me."

He nodded, gave a brief smile, and went back to the living room. Hannerty was scribbling something in her notebook as Nora sipped her tea. "I understand you know the Cartwright family, Nora," he said.

"Oh, yes. Sad story that. Only little Laura left now."

"How did her parents die?"

"Car crash. Both at the same time. It were terrible, weren't it, love?" she said to Karen.

Hannerty twisted round to look at McGregor, and he gave her an urgent look.

"Well, that's been very helpful, thank you, Nora," she said. "We'll leave you in peace now."

Once they were in the car, Hannerty said, "The 'little Laura' she mentioned isn't the same Laura who works for Wilson, is she?"

"One and the same. I saw her picture in the hall. She was best friends with Karen at university. They studied medicine together."

"Bloody hell! That's the first link between one of the victims and Wilson!"

"When we get back to the station, I want you to dig up everything you can on Laura and her parents. They died in a car crash, apparently. I'm going to phone the university and have a poke about in Karen's student records. She hinted that something happened that put her off medicine. It made her and Laura fall out; they didn't talk to each other for a couple of years."

"If she was on the same course as Laura, maybe it was the lecherous professor?"

"My thoughts exactly. I don't know how this connects to stealing dead limbs, but I've got the feeling we're on to something here."

McGREGOR DIDN'T GET much from the university on why Karen abandoned her course. No official complaints were made and all the administrator could say from looking at the file was that it seemed rather sudden. There hadn't been a decline in grades or attendance problems, as is often the case before dropping out. The record cited 'personal reasons' with no further explanation. "Lots of students can't take the pressure of postgrad studies," the man said down the phone. "It's not like being an undergraduate, but lots of them think it will be."

Hannerty's call ended soon after his and she dashed over from her desk. "Right, guv," she said, sitting down. "I've got something! Laura's parents were killed in a car crash that Laura survived. They were just outside of Geneva, on holiday, apparently. Her father was driving and both parents were killed instantaneously. She had some broken bones but made a full recovery. Her parents were the owners of the Northline Haulage Company. It was a very successful business and made her parents millionaires."

"Northline..." McGregor muttered, looking at the files scattered on his desk.

"It's familiar, right? That's because Mr Torso worked for Northline and was sacked. Laura's father accused him of embezzlement, but the charge didn't stick. And look!"

She flashed a page of her notebook at him. "This was where the company was registered when it first opened. It was just a tiny business to start with, and their home address was the official company address too. Look at where it is! It's next door to Mr Left Leg!"

"Blood and sand," McGregor muttered.

"And Mr Right Leg worked for a company that serviced Northline's fleet of delivery trucks!"

"What about Mr Right Arm?" McGregor said, grabbing the relevant file. He flicked through the notes about the assault case as Hannerty flicked through her notebook.

"Where did that assault happen?" Hannerty asked.

"The Ship Inn, in Chester."

Hannerty grabbed the relevant road map from the shelf at the other side of the room and flipped through to find Chester. "There you go, guv! It was only down the road from where Laura grew up! What if she was in the pub when it happened?"

"She's not listed as a witness, I would have noticed her name."

"Her parents were already wealthy by then, maybe she was kept out of it."

"Not as strong a link as the others, but it's enough for me," McGregor said. "We need to go and have a serious conversation with Laura."

The phone rang and he answered it. "Got a Professor Wilson on the phone for you, sir," said Jenkins. "She said you spoke to her last night and you'll know who she is. She asked for you by name."

"Put her through." There was a click. "Hello? DI McGregor speaking."

He recognised Professor Wilson's voice, but not the tremulous uncertainty. "Inspector… I don't want to be a bother, but I've just had a call from the university and it seems that my husband didn't arrive for work this morning. He's already missed a lecture and is now late for an important meeting with the trustees. I… I hate to ask this, but did you find him at that Chloe's house last night? It's just that I don't know where else he could be and… oh, this is so embarrassing."

"He wasn't with her, Dr Wilson. When did you last see your husband?"

"Yesterday morning. His car isn't here. I assumed he'd spoken to you and that's why I hadn't heard from him. Oh, God, do you think he could have had an accident? It isn't at all like him to miss work. He hasn't missed a lecture in over ten years."

"I'll look into it, Professor Wilson. Are you at home all day?"

"Yes, I am. I'll stay near the phone and call you if he turns up."

McGregor put the phone down and looked at Hannerty. "Mr. Wilson has gone missing."

She stood up. "Oh, shit. What if he's involved in this thing with Laura?"

McGregor rubbed the stubble on his chin as he looked down at Hannerty's sketch of the body's parts. "The body doesn't have a head yet," he said. "What if they were looking for one, and something went wrong? Phone up the Medical Schools and find out if Laura has been in today. And get me her home address. I'm going to put out a call to look for his car."

HANNERTY CONFIRMED THAT Laura hadn't been in the Medical School that morning either. A patrol car was only five minutes from Laura's house; the officers confirmed that neither her Ford Capri nor Wilson's Audi were parked on her drive or in the nearby streets.

They tracked down the details of the hotel he liked to take Chloe to, but Wilson hadn't been seen there since his last visit with Chloe, and the staff confirmed his car wasn't in the small car park outside the hotel. As Hannerty called his wife back and asked her for more places he could be, McGregor reviewed the notes Hannerty had made about Laura.

"I've got a couple of suggestions from her, but flimsy at best," Hannerty said. "They have friends in Wales, and—"

"Wait. What happened to the haulage business when Laura's parents died?"

"It was left to her. She sold it for a few million quid."

"So there are no warehouses or distribution centres or anything that she still owns?"

"No," Hannerty said. "But she didn't sell her parent's house; it's out in Altrincham. I've got the address somewhere. Should we send a squad car over there to check it out?"

"Sod it, let's go ourselves," he said. "Patrol cars are thin on the ground and I'll feel like a right chump if there's no-one there."

"Do we need to run it by the super, guv?"

"He's still off with the flu." McGregor grinned. "C'mon."

IT WAS ALREADY getting dark by the time they reached the address, the thick clouds bringing the night early. They'd left the busy main road and were now in a tree-lined avenue with wide pavements and detached houses, all huge, each one a different design to its neighbours. There were Bentleys and Jaguars parked outside double garages, along with an assortment of brand new small cars, probably bought for wives and kids to go and do things without the old man.

"That's Wilson's car!" Hannerty said as they passed a huge house with an art deco design, set back off the road with its own drive. "There are no lights on in the house, though."

"Call it in to Control and let them know we're going to the property," McGregor replied. He kept driving to the end of the street, to park without being seen from Laura's house.

"You sure she doesn't live here anymore?" he asked Hannerty after she'd called in.

"Positive, guv. She lives near the Medical School."

"But she kept this place?"

"Last connection to her parents, I suppose."

"Mmm."

They got out of the car and headed back towards the house. The headache was reasserting itself, like a drill through the back of his head. McGregor rolled his shoulders a couple of times, to try and ease the tension. His body was gearing up for a confrontation before his mind was certain of what they'd find there.

"I've got the feeling Wilson isn't playing away here," he said to Hannerty. "He never misses work, for one thing, and he knows we're sniffing about his business. I want you to be ready for trouble, okay?"

"I'm ready, guv," Hannerty said, checking her radio was set to silent before tapping the truncheon hanging from her belt.

They went up the drive and were soon out of sight of the road, thanks to the overgrown hedges on the boundary of the property. There was a pair of eight-foot-tall wrought iron gates, but they seemed to be rusted open. He paused to rest his hand on the bonnet of Wilson's car. It was icy cold to the touch.

The house was in darkness and looked unkempt and unloved. The windows were dirty and leaves had been left to mulch down in uncleared drifts around the front steps. Paint was peeling on a couple of the window frames and weeds were growing through cracks in the footpath up to the house.

"We'll check around the property first," he whispered to Hannerty. He couldn't see anyone watching from the windows, but still steered her to the wall of the house, just in case.

She unclipped her truncheon, her breath pluming in the cold air. It was hard to see her face properly now, away from the streetlights, but he could still see the thumbs-up she gave him.

Quietly, carefully, they went round the side of the house. It was surrounded by lawn on three sides, the grass so long at the sides that it came up to his knees, making his trousers wet. The building went back further than he'd appreciated from the front, and he wondered whether he should call for a squad car at least.

Hannerty stopped and tapped his shoulder, making him twist round to face her. "Can you hear that, guv?"

He shook his head. "What?"

"Music… I think it's coming from the back of the house. It's muffled, though. I think it's Blondie."

He pressed on, and as he reached the edge of the house, finally able to see into the jungle-like back garden, he could hear something like music. Trumpets, maybe. Then it clicked; it was the song he'd heard on the radio the other day.

He peeped round the corner, seeing a small rectangle of light spilling across the path that ran down the back of the house. It came from a very small window set at ground level.

"I think they're in the cellar," he whispered to Hannerty.

She peered round the corner too. "There are steps going down at the far end of the house, by the look of it. Might be an old servant's entrance or something."

Her eyesight was clearly better than his.

The professor had been missing less than twenty-four hours and he still wasn't sure if it was Laura or Wilson behind the thefts. Either way, it wasn't strong grounds for entering the property without creating a tonne of paperwork and having to justify himself to his superiors. "I have reason to believe someone may be in danger, Hannerty, do you agree?"

She knew what he was doing, thankfully. "I do, guv," she said, tapping the truncheon against her palm. "I say we get in there and sort it out."

He could just about see her grin in the deepening gloom; her enthusiasm surprised him. "I'm going to have a look through that window first, hang back until I say go, okay?"

"Yes, guv. You might want to get behind me if things kick off in there," she added. "I move quick and I'm armed. You're not."

"You're bloody joking, aren't you?"

"My black belt in Wing Chun says I'm not."

There wasn't time to ask if girls did martial arts or if she was pulling his leg, so he just nodded and tiptoed to the window to crouch down and look through the filthy glass. All he could see was a dingy corridor running parallel to the rear wall of the house.

"Come on," he whispered to Hannerty and she was off, whipping through the long grass to the back door before he'd even had a chance to ready himself. As he hurried after her he thought he heard something move in the garden and snapped his head round, only to see a fox slink past and race for the driveway.

By the time he looked back at the steps down to the old servant's entrance, Hannerty was already down them, standing ready at the back door. As he reached the top of the steps she tried the handle. Locked. He was about to ask her to move aside when she crouched down, lifted an old coir mat and revealed a spare key.

"Didn't think that happened in real life!" she whispered as she unlocked the door.

Before he could pull her back, she'd opened the door and gone inside. The last time he'd entered a building on suspicion of someone being in danger was when he was a newly minted PC and someone had asked the duty officer to check on his elderly mother who wasn't answering the telephone. He'd broken in and found her dead in her bed, looking like she was sleeping peacefully.

Even then, when he was just as youthful as Hannerty, he hadn't gone in with the same enthusiasm as her. She moved silently though, even in her regulation flat shoes that made most PCs sound like elephants. She was holding her truncheon differently to the way he'd been taught in basic training, reminding him of Bruce Lee in a movie he'd seen back when he was PC. He didn't like the way she was taking the lead, but not nearly as much as the way he was letting her do it.

He felt a drop of sweat run down the side of his head and his heart hammered so hard it was painful. With every step along the cellar corridor, the walls blooming with mould and an awful smell of damp filling his nostrils, a sense of terrible dread gripped him tighter.

They passed an open door on the right which led to a hallway into the house with a flight of internal stairs running up at the far end. There was a door halfway along, ajar, revealing what looked like an old pantry, complete with dusty jars and rusting tins of food. He pushed it open with his fingertip as he went past, seeing two huge chest freezers plugged into the far wall, rumbling away.

There was only one other door, closed, and it sounded like the music was coming from the other side of it. McGregor's mouth was dry, his tongue felt like a slab of salted beef and the pain in his chest was worsening.

Then he was ten again, in the corridor at the back of St Matthew's Church, the one leading to the room where Father Sidwell disrobed after his fiery sermons. It was the smell of the damp and dust, the quality of the light, the way the single bulb filled the corridor with shadows. It sent his mind back to that place, made his legs shake again as he walked towards something awful, something he did not want to see and did not want to do.

"Guv?" Hannerty's sharp whisper snapped him back. She jerked her head at the door she was now standing next to, the music blaring on the other side.

All he could do was nod, stripped as he was of his strength and confidence. She took a couple of steps back, drew in a deep breath and then kicked the door open.

"Police!" she yelled as her own momentum took her through the doorway and out of his sight.

He picked up the pace, panicked by how far the situation was from his control, and burst through the doorway behind her.

The room was so much colder than the corridor, and darker too, save for the pool of light where a huge lamp hung over an operating table.

He saw the leg first, waxy white, the foot flopped to the side. Then he saw the stitches running around the top of the thigh.

More stitches around an arm, around the other leg, joining it to the torso. It was as if he could only see in images, in frames, as if that was the only way his mind could handle what it was seeing.

There was no active violence taking place, but his body reacted as if there was; he felt his muscles tense, his limbs go rigid with shock as he saw the second table in the shadows. A body was lying on it, wearing a brown suit. The collar of the shirt was stained a deep, dark red around an awful stump of a neck.

A woman wearing a white lab coat was standing next to the stitched corpse, head and shoulders bent over it with her back to them. She was doing something with her hands that he couldn't see. Hannerty had stopped, thrown by what she'd found, by the lack of reaction from the other woman.

The song came to an end and the tape player clicked off.

"Just a minute," the woman said, and he knew it was Laura.

"Step away from the table!" Hannerty said, but Laura ignored her, carrying on as if nothing had happened.

The dread that had clogged his mind cleared, and McGregor grabbed Laura's shoulder and pulled her away.

"No!" she yelled. The thread running from the needle she was holding pulled taut against the last stitch in the corpse on the table. It snapped as McGregor wrestled Laura's hands behind her back for Hannerty to cuff them. "Just let me tie it off!" she whined as he pulled the needle from her fingers. The cuffs were on, and as Hannerty wrestled her away from the table, he saw the front of her coat was drenched in blood.

"Jesus Christ," he gasped as he saw the whole body for the first time, with Professor Wilson's grey face staring up at him, his head mostly sewn on to the stolen torso.

"You can see him now!" Laura said ecstatically, even as she strained against the firm hold Hannerty had on her. "Yes! Yes, you see him for what he really is! A monster! Now he has the body he should have!"

His gaze fell upon the stolen right leg and a Nazi swastika tattooed over the upper thigh. It felt into place in his mind then, pieces of monstrous men, stolen and remade into a new monster, one befitting a man she'd hated to the point of madness.

He shook his head, aghast, and then helped Hannerty manhandle her out of the room. "Call it in, Hannerty, I've got her," he said and then, as Laura begged him to let her go back and finish the stitches, he recited her rights. He spoke them loud and slow, using them as bricks in the wall between his mind and her view of justice, something behind which he could hide until his colleagues arrived.

When the street outside was awash with blue lights, and a gathering crowd watched Laura be put into the back of a squad car, McGregor went and stood next to Hannerty. "Good work, Hannerty."

"But we didn't get there in time, Guv," she said, her voice cracking. "If I hadn't made that bloody mistake—"

"That's enough of that," McGregor said, pulling out his cigarettes and lighting up. "That's not going to do anything except drive you mad. It was your first case and you stepped up like a good 'un. And when my next one comes up, you're my first choice to assist."

"Thanks, guv. I'm going to go with her to the station, get her booked in and then get started on the paperwork."

He turned and looked back down the side of the house, into the dark garden. It felt like they were being watched. "See you there," he said, shrugging off the paranoia. The lads were checking it all now. No one was there. "I'm going to see his wife and then I'll be with you."

His HOUSE WAS dark, empty and cold when he finally got back to it. He switched on the light, put the fire on in the front room and made himself a cup of tea with his coat still on. Ten minutes later, when the fire had taken the chill off the room, he took it off.

For a while he just sat there on his sofa, hands wrapped around the mug, letting snippets from the day pass through his mind. He'd tried shutting them out in the past, with booze or TV, only to find them come out in his dreams. Now he knew better. He let the cellar room, the stitches, the headless corpse and the newly assembled one, pass through his mind until they lost their power.

Snatches of the interview came to mind too, of Laura's pale face in the bleak interview room at the station. How calm she was. His wife would have said something about dissociation, probably. They'd talked about it before, he was certain.

He grabbed the phone and dialled her number without thinking. Just as he was about to hang up she answered. "Hello?"

"It's me."

"It's late."

"Sorry."

Her voice softened. "What is it? Tough case?"

"Yeah."

"The one stealing the body parts?"

"Yeah. Caught her. She murdered for the last part. The head. She was making a body to stitch it to."

"That's… really interesting."

He couldn't help but smirk to himself. She never stopped working.

"So was there a pattern to the thefts?"

"Yeah. All the men she took limbs from were nasty pieces of work. Each of them represented a thing the last victim did, but covered up. She said she was making sure the world could see how monstrous he was."

"By stitching them together? I'd really like to interview her."

"I know. Listen, she mentioned a scientist, someone who inspired her. Frankenstein was his name, apparently. Her parents came across some notes of his when they were on holiday in Geneva. They were inside an antique box they bought. You heard of him?"

"No, never. Not my field though, is it, chopping people up?"

"He brought dead people to life or something. I don't know, she wasn't making much sense at that point."

"Was she planning to bring her creation to life?"

"I don't think she'd thought that far ahead. She was... pretty far gone, you know. She said that her knowledge of Frankenstein's work gave Wilson the breakthrough he'd needed. He never credited her in his work, though. Then he raped her best friend. It tipped her over the edge, I reckon."

"It wasn't only that. If women chopped up men when they found out what they'd done to their friends, there would be a lot more women in prison and far fewer men on the streets."

"Yeah. Listen..." Somehow the words fizzled out in his head. She coughed. "I'm listening."

"Listen, there was a moment... tonight... when I had to..."

"Do you need me to come over?"

He was shaking. She must have heard it in his voice. "No, don't be daft. I'm fine. I'm just tired."

"Jack. Tell me. You want to. Otherwise you wouldn't have phoned. What happened tonight?"

And he told her. The words came in a trickle first, then a torrent. The corridor, the lightbulb, the way it had felt like he was walking through thick mud the closer he got to the door.

"It felt like I was just a kid again," he whispered. "And it got in the way, Clare. I let a green WPC go in ahead of me. What if it had been a bloke with a knife inside that room? What if she'd been hurt because I was having a funny turn?"

She was silent for an age. Then he heard her sigh. "Okay. You need to listen to me. You know why that happened tonight, don't you?"

"No! That's the point, I don't. What if it happens again?"

"Jack, there will always be some part of you being that kid in that corridor and being that kid in that room you were scared to go into. And until you meet that part of you and face this, you'll never get over it."

"Over what?"

"Over what happened to you at St Matthews. I have a suspicion about what that was, but this is the most you've ever said to me about the way you feel since we were engaged."

"Oh, this is bloody psychobabble claptrap! It isn't—"

"Oh, for God's sake, Jack! There was a monster in the room at the end of the corridor tonight and there was a monster in the room at the end of the corridor in the church, wasn't there? When you were a boy. Wasn't there?"

And then he was crying. He let the handset fall from his grasp and surrendered to the rasping sobs that took his body. He didn't hear her car pull up outside, nor her old key in the lock, not even when she opened the front room door. All he felt was her arms about him and the shame, the shame that had been there for as long as could remember.

At some point, tea appeared and he drank it. A blanket was wrapped around his shoulders and Clare put a piece of paper on the sofa cushion next to him.

"Phone that number tomorrow morning, first thing, and ask to speak to Nathaniel. He's a good friend and an even better therapist. Get some help, okay?"

"You could help me," he said, looking up at her.

"I tried, Jack. I'm not the right person to do that now. Call that number, okay? I'll speak to you tomorrow."

He listened to the door shut and the quiet roar of the gas burners. He thought about Laura, in the cell at the station, about how the monster in her life had made her monstrous. How she'd tried to make the man hiding in plain sight look as disgusting as he really was.

In some twisted way, he knew how that desire felt.

McGregor picked up the number and tucked it into his notebook. He would get help. He would find his courage. One day, he would face his own monster.

LOVE THEE BETTER

LOVE THEE BETTER
KAARON WARREN

WE WERE IN the heady days of love, Declan and I, when the accident happened. Fortunately we had already spoken our vows, albeit in an office rather than a church, or I believe he would have insisted I leave him, find an able-bodied man.

His was the fifth accident on the worksite, enough to have it close down for inspection, leaving Declan out of work in two ways, and with a 'sick worksite' on his resume to boot.

Most of the men, and the office staff, believed the building site at best haunted, at worst cursed.

They're a superstitious lot, in the building industry. They don't like it when you point out that accidents happen when standards slip; they'd rather believe in ghosts, or burial ground curses.

Declan's was the worst of the accidents, his arm caught in the lift mechanism and literally ripped off; I can't even think about it without feeling queasy. Luckily he was only on the first floor scaffolding, so when he collapsed he didn't have far to fall. When I glance at his face I sometimes catch him looking down as if at what's missing.

He's still the same Declan, though, with a sense of humour and a gentle nature, like the shy kid at school with the beautiful eyes you could get lost in.

And he is still my amorous sweetheart; no easing off in that department, although his balance is somewhat askew.

They never did retrieve his arm. Some pieces of bone, which we have in a jar and which he wants to display, though I prefer to hide it in the cupboard. That's all that's left of his strong, smooth arm.

One man lost three toes when a concrete block dropped on them. Another lost his left thumb when a huge pane of glass shattered. The others were minor incidents: torn muscles, concussions, that sort of thing. And many, many cuts, blood spillages, enough for the men to start calling the site the Suez Canal, which really was quite a clever nickname.

We got stuck, though, with him sitting on the couch surrounded by an ever-growing pile of empty painkiller packets. He swore his missing arm hurt and nothing would persuade him otherwise. He didn't like the light, he didn't like my voice and I was at the end of my tether when my parents called with an amazing offer.

To be honest I'd been avoiding them. They were so filled with pity (always had been, but it had eased off with my marriage) and I couldn't bear it. I was trying to be strong, to carry on, and they weren't helping.

My father said, "Do you remember my old school friend Firth Franklin? You used to love him! Don't you remember? He always brought the most gruesome things for you to look at."

I did remember him. An apple-cheeked man who looked much younger than my father.

"I spotted him in the paper last week. Would you believe it? He's chief medical officer on a cruise ship these days. What a life, eh? It's the sort of thing you and Declan might like. Especially Declan. They do a lot of…" Here he paused, as he always did when he was going to say something he worried would hurt me. "A lot of corrective work. For people like Declan, who've been damaged in one way or another. Your mother and I thought you'd like to go. Our shout. What do you think?"

I looked at Declan, slumped in the dark lounge room, and said, "You bet."

DECLAN TOOK A while to convince. He hated to be seen by anybody, even though no one really noticed his missing arm. He hadn't been out on his own since the accident, relying on me to drive and hand over money or cards when shopping, all of it. I didn't mind looking after him; that's what love did. But I hated the way he'd lost his spirit, his confidence to be amongst people.

In the end it was my parents, coming around to have stern words with him, convincing him that this was best for both of us. It would scoot us out of the doldrums and back into the real world, in the luxury environment of a cruise ship.

My daddy got angry. He was livid with Declan for the injury, thinking it a terrible burden on me. I told him I didn't mind, and he called me his stoic warrior, which I guess I am.

It was a week or two after Daddy lost his temper that Mummy called with the exciting news that they'd booked us on that cruise—"to get you out of the house," she said. It was fully medically supported and all expenses paid, and Declan and I couldn't believe our luck. Our honeymoon had been rushed because I couldn't get enough time off work, so this was very welcome.

*   *   *

A MONTH LATER, we walked down an old cement path leading into the pier where a small transport boat waited. The edges of the path were covered with shells and moss and the concrete was cracked. Once upon a time it was smooth, I suppose. I couldn't understand why we were boarding here rather than in Sydney or Melbourne, where the cruise ship could have pulled into a massive harbour. Avoiding fees, perhaps. "Avoiding police, I reckon," Declan said. Already he looked brighter, and I loved that he could throw a conspiracy theory into the mix.

I stumbled and Declan reached to grab me with an arm no longer there, but I caught myself by clutching his coat.

We were the only ones to board this small transport boat, and we sat in silence, smiling every time we caught each other's eye, as the boatman took us through the water to the large ship waiting at sea.

"Quite a distance!" I said.

The boatman nodded. "Speed this baby reaches, we'll be there in half an hour. Hold on," he said, and we took off. I was pretty soaked by the time we got there ("Oh, sorry, forgot to tell you to put the raincoats on," the boatman said), but exhilarated at the same time.

We watched the ship grow closer. It seemed monstrous in the distance, far too big to stay afloat, and momentarily I worried how Declan would cope with all the people, with the space. He'd turn inward if he hated it, and he was hard to dig out when that happened.

The boatman came to a halt where a sturdy ladder waited for us, and helped us both to climb up. Declan struggled manfully, pressing his face into the rungs for further purchase and climbing over the top as if without a care. "Enjoy yourselves," the boatman said. "Make the most of it, eh? Lucky for some." I shook his hand and felt deep ridges at the base of each finger. "Yeah, I had a turn on this ship," he said, as I looked down and frowned. "Changed my life."

I didn't ask him for clarification. I barely realised it was needed.

WE WERE SHOWN to a tiny cabin with two small beds and little else. I looked through the porthole, though, and saw a great expanse of sea and thought, *at least I'm not paying for this*, and I knew I wouldn't complain.

Declan was tired from the trip (this from a man who used to pull all nighters if the job required it, and all nighters if the party was a good one) so he flopped on the bed. "Sleep with me," he said, half-sexy, half *I wish*.

WE WERE WOKEN up in the dark by a knock at the door. It was a purser (I think they're called pursers) letting me know the captain wanted to welcome us, and that we could join his table for dinner. "He always invites the new passengers to sit with him for the first night. After that, you join the lottery!"

We dressed quickly, and I tied my hair back to keep it off my face. I should have had a shower and washed the salt water out, but there was no time. I caught sight of myself in the dulled mirror and wished I hadn't; I'd felt okay about myself until then.

"You look great," Declan said. "Healthy country girl," and he kissed me hard on the mouth.

*　*　*

THE CAPTAIN, AS it turned out, *was* my father's old school friend Firth Franklin. Doctor, captain, collector. He was a smooth, baby-faced man, still looking far younger than my father. "Nina!" he said. "Oh, this is marvellous. Isn't it? I'm so glad your father tracked me down the way he did. And look at you. Declan, isn't it?"

We had a delicious meal. So much wine! And Japanese food was the theme that night, so lots of sushi and flavourful rice and raw fish and veggies and just delicious.

ALL OF OUR meals were taken at tables of four. The captain had a system whereby you took a number at the doorway at breakfast and that was your table for the day. He told us that one meal with new people was an introduction, two was getting to know you, three was old friends.

"There is nothing sadder than loneliness, and I will have none of that on this ship," he told us. "Even the worst of us deserves companionship. Even one considered a monster, a creature so unusual none are like him. We are all Aliquot parts here, making a greater whole of friendship and community."

I wondered who the captain was talking about. Did he have someone particularly monstrous in mind? Did that person sit amongst us; was the game to identify him or her?

At breakfast on the first day, I was seated with three men. On my left was a dapper old fella wearing a purple La Coste shirt tucked into neat, ironed pants. His eyes were the brightest blue, sparkling, but his mouth drooped as if he was always unhappy. On my right was a young guy—thin, black t shirt, black woollen beanie—slumped forward in his chair. Opposite me was a man with a very bad wig who seemed to have suffered some kind of brain trauma. He didn't have a helper and managed to feed himself but little more. He flashed his genitals at us whenever he got the chance; hung like a horse was the consensus. He made us all laugh with odd sayings. "I'm as full as donkey on the rocks," he'd say, or "If the horse runs, make it trot," or "What's for snacks?"

The old man dominated the conversation, telling us all sorts of things about Doctor Firth. "Obviously he's a good man, none of us would be here if he weren't. He means well. But you need to keep your wits about you, don't you? Keep your centre." Here he tapped himself on the chest. "He's one of those characters who'll take you over if you let them. Powerful, if you know what I mean. He's the guru type, isn't it? Ran a sweat lodge once. Three people died, far as I know. He got twelve years' jail for that, set up a self-help circle inside, got out early on good behaviour. He likes to think he reformed them in there. He's reforming us day by day, isn't he?"

"Not me," the young man said. And I said, "I've only been here a day!" and they all kindly laughed, even the poor man with brain damage ("I've been here since Monkey was made of brass," he said), although I think he just went along with the others.

"What is it you do?" the old man said, and that was a tricky question. What I did mostly, these days, was keep an eye on Declan. I'd nearly lost him and I didn't want that to happen again. I hadn't told anyone, I barely admitted it to myself, but he'd left me for a bit. He wanted to live in filth, was the thing, and I'm no neat freak but I do want the rubbish put out and would prefer not to have maggots and ants running the house. That's just me.

I had to find him and drag him home when I got the call about the cruise, so at least he was there when my parents came to talk us into it this chance to start over.

When I think of the state of him…an old mattress on the floor. No bed base. Mouldy underneath, spreading to the carpet. Pile of old newspapers, probably unread, in the corner. Floor covered with old takeaway boxes, empty wine casks, torn. Empty wine bladders, twisted into silver men to wring out the last drops of warm alcohol. All of his clothes dirty, in piles on the floor. Full ash trays. It smelled like a skip behind a pub the day before rubbish collection.

He never went back there and neither did I. There was nothing of value there.

DECLAN AND I didn't get to sit with each other at all, but met up at the bar after dinner. The drinks were free and we made fine use, Declan more than me. He was unused to spirits, usually choosing beer, but here he thought (as many did) that you'd get your money's worth better with expensive alcohol.

Not that we'd paid: thank my parents for that.

ON MY SECOND day, I shared meals with a heavily-pierced postal worker. He was the kindest man! Very focussed on the rest of us. One ear had a dozen or so piercings, the other was the most utterly perfect ear I think I've ever seen. If I was a poet I'd write about that beautiful ear and how well he listened. Next to him was a very short, old, thin woman. Her clothing looked like blankets draped over her. She was the whitest woman I'd ever seen except, for a large red nose. She wore a colourful hat worn low and was hilarious, full of jokes and quips. She told us a long involved story about the size of her feet and how hard it was to find shoes, but somehow it was not boring at all. She ate with her mouth full, constantly, lettuce and asparagus vying for greenness in there, and lean steak on her fork ready to go in, and the other hand ready with a piece of orange.

On the other side of me was a very large woman, maybe three times the size of my other companions. She told us she'd been an Olympic runner and later on she showed us, dashing around the ship in record time. I'm sure she didn't cheat. And she was barely puffed when she returned. Sea gulls and pelicans scattered as she neared them and someone said, "Look at that. Birds of a feather flock together, don't they? Lovely with lovely, ugly with ugly."

At dinner, the Olympic runner said, "Now, have you been warned? That there are ghosts that walk at night? If you see one of them, you'll drown within a year."

"Or a loved one will. Which is worse, isn't it?" the postal worker said.

We all pondered if this was true.

DECLAN WAS SO paralytic the next night one of the crew rolled around a wheelchair for him. Then everybody wanted one, and we had races up and down the deck until someone went flying off their chair and bashed their skull against the railing. Blood everywhere! It was only an eyebrow, everyone said, and the passenger (a man of about 50) got wheeled off to the infirmary. They called it "Hospital without Borders."

"I've heard of them," I said.

"That's Doctors Without Borders. This is *like* that, but not it. Mind you, we get donations all the time from people who think we are." I liked this nurse. She was tiny, reaching up to my waist and so vibrant I felt as if touching her would recharge tired batteries. Doctor Firth called her 'his next wife' and she told him to stop it every time, but clearly she liked it.

He paid very well, she told me.

You'd think Declan would have sobered up by then, but someone had brought out a bottle of champagne and we'd been guzzling that while racing up and down. One of the lovely pursers helped me get him to our room.

"How'd he lose the arm?" the purser said. His name tag read *Benjamin, at your service*. I told him.

"So not disease? A clean wound?" he asked. "He looks very fit, otherwise."

"Oh, he is, believe me," I said. We laid Declan on the bed and I scrabbled for my purse.

"No need to tip, Ma'am. We get paid very well." He reached into his jacket pocket. "Aspirin for the morning if he needs it. And for you, too. My tip is to take it the night before, just in case."

He smiled at me and I figured out what was not quite even about him; one of his hands was much larger than the other, with a scar around the wrist.

I wondered if he'd survived a suicide attempt and tried to remember to smile whenever I saw him.

DRUNK DECLAN SNORED fit to shake the porthole, so I took a blanket and went to sleep on the deck. I loved it out there. The air so fresh, the gentle whoosh of small waves against the walls of our ship and the creak of the deck were the only sounds.

I had just snuggled down and was gazing at the clear, bright stars when I heard a shuffling. A snuffling. I hunched into my deckchair, made myself invisible, not wanting to talk to anyone. Covered my head so I saw nothing but still heard the slow shuffle of heavy feet. Then I lowered the blanket to peek.

The next day I was sure I'd dreamt it. Dreams are so vivid out at sea. Because a huge man stumbled by me, not once but a dozen times, lapping the deck, like our ex-Olympian had done just hours earlier. In the darkness all I could see was his shape and his lurching walk. There was nothing ghostly about it, but still I felt certain I was better off staying hidden.

MY MEAL MATES the next day included Claudia, a woman who ran the canteen at a large primary school. We learned her life story over breakfast and then her current woes over lunch. Claudia hated her left leg with a passion I had never seen before. She said that all of her suffering (and there was plenty: she lived in a world of sleazy brothers-in-law, debt, drinking, family members who killed each other and themselves, sisters who died in drink driving accidents) meant she hated her body parts; and at the moment it was the left leg she wished someone would cut off. "I just hope he does," she said.

We had a middle aged man who looked like he thought he was in an ashram. He smelled of incense and he had that blissed-out sense to him of a person who thought they'd sorted out the afterlife. He'd made his money selling organic grains, apparently (a major supplier of this cruise line, he told us) and was now enjoying a philanthropic retirement. I was envious of that, a life handing out money—and more—to people. He said, "I've got two kidneys, don't need 'em both. Same with most of the rest of me. I see how people manage and how they become stronger with adversity. Don't you? I mean men like your husband. Isn't it?" I'd noticed how many passengers parroted that *isn't it?*, which Doctor Firth said often.

He drank only green tea, only raw food. Even healthier than the rest of us.

And a terribly smelly old man I'd seen on the deck, smoking a stubby cigarette, holding it with nicotine-stained fingers, hiding around the corner from his half-blind wife. I couldn't see which table his wife was on. He told us he didn't smoke, that he only smelled that way because a young woman with big breasts blew smoke in his face and then rubbed her smoky, stinky breasts against his back. He wasn't joking, he said. His white hair looked clean and it was neatly brushed. Shirt ironed, pants pressed, tidy shoes. He looked like he should smell fresh, but I could smell his odour across the table. He wore the same shirt I'd seen him in every day, a grey-striped nylon thing that hung on him like loose flesh.

The rot of old age. The terrible cruelty of a withered body. Surely we should be able to avoid that.

DOCTOR FIRTH CAME to our table. "Ah, what a marvellous group you have here!" he said. He smiled at me and started to speak, but the canteen lady stood up and was in his face. "It's my leg," she said. "If only it was gone I'd be a new woman," and he led her to the bar where they sat in close conversation. I felt a slight envy of this, and perhaps all of us did; certainly our conversation stalled as we all watched them together.

THE PROGRAM KEPT us very busy. Lots of marvellous rehabilitation for Declan and others like him, many of whom had also come from construction sites. It worked wonders, and it didn't hurt me at all to join in. The only annoying thing was how happy it made my mother; my whole life she'd been on at me to be more active. We exercised at the front of the ship, which was shaded by a carefully-contrived sail that blocked the sun but let through the breeze.

After a particularly good session, Declan and I took a quick dip, then found deckchairs in the sun. Pursers brought us drinks and I lay there in a form of bliss. From there we could see the bridge, and I got the feeling then, as I did often on the cruise, that someone was watching us. That couldn't be right, though, because the shadowy figure I thought I saw was enormous, almost filling the window up there. I could relate to that, the being too big. My father used to call me Fairy Princess until that became ridiculous, and now it was Amazon Warrior.

I thought it must be a flaw in the glass, a dark shadow somehow etched into the pane. Declan had teamed up with Jacko, a glazier whose right leg had been sheared to the bone in an accident. I mentioned it to him and he said, "There are some cowboys around, that's for sure. My team wouldna left it like that. We'd've replaced it, free of charge." But he winked and I wasn't sure where the humour was directed. A couple of days earlier he'd hooked up with Claudia, the canteen lady. Jacko had never married—never seen the need, he said—but he fell like a tonne of bricks. From my perspective, she seemed to be having fun, but I wasn't sure if it would last beyond the cruise.

But then again, I wasn't sure how long the cruise would last. It wasn't specified, which was part of the attraction for a lot of us. We should have been given an end time, a day where reality returned, but I didn't speak to anybody who wanted such a thing.

I sat quite happily between Declan and Jacko. They spoke to each other over me and I felt lulled by their voices as they chatted, talking about things I didn't understand. Every now and then Declan would lay a hand on me so I would know he knew I was there, and Jacko did the same, both of them with their rough hands resting on me.

I loved it.

By the pool the men were bare chested, strong arms tanned, shiny from the water, quite beautiful.

"Any you like in particular?" Doctor Firth asked us. He'd joined us, making me sit and talk.

I laughed.

"What an odd question," I said. I hoped they couldn't tell I was blushing out here in the sun, because I had been looking at their arms wishing just for a moment that Declan was like them.

"Declan?" Doctor Firth said.

Declan answered. "The one with the purple shorts. He's the only one without tattoos. If I have a tattoo I'd like to choose my own."

"I think he does have an old burn scar across the forearm."

"That's okay."

It was such an odd conversation, one I felt left out of. I asked Declan about it later and he said it was a surprise, and he kissed me, but little else happened.

TIME PASSES SO strangely on board the ship.

MY HUSBAND TOOK a shower in the tiny cubicle. "Wash my back, will you, love?" he called out. He still liked me to help him, although he is more than capable of managing things himself. Both of us enjoy the intimacy. I love his smooth skin, he loves the touch of my soapy hands.

I was curled up in my bunk, reading to take my mind off my queasy stomach (my turn to be wheeled home in the wheelchair last night, as far as I can remember), so I was slow in responding. He poked his head around the door. "Come on, love," he said softly. Such a beautiful voice.

I was a bit wobbly on my feet and he stepped out, naked and wet to steady me as I stumbled. "You settle back," he said, kissing me as he tucked me into bed. I felt those physical stirrings but seriously was too ill to act on them. He kissed me again as he headed out, telling me he would hunt down some biscuits for me, dry ones I might be able to keep down. I made him let me pin his shirt sleeve over properly, then was asleep almost as the door snicked shut.

SOMETIMES IN THE cabin I got the sensation of being watched and wondered if some of the pursers had drilled peep holes to spy on the travellers. I strip-teased every time I got undressed, enjoying the fantasy.

DECLAN WAS NOT back in our cabin when I awoke close to dawn. I lay in my narrow bed feeling more desperately lonely than I ever had been when I'd had no husband and few friends, when my sister disowned me and my parents were physically ashamed of me, their every action an avoidance, a pulling away from me.

Even this cruise I thought was part of that. The chance not to have to look at me for a while.

Declan says I'm beautiful and he means it. He looks at me in the way other men look at beautiful women. I don't doubt his adoration for a minute. There are women galore aboard this ship and many opportunities for him to dally, but he seems not to be interested in them. He is interested in dancing, singing at the top of his voice and sliding on his arse on the shiny dance floor, though, as are we all.

I know I've led a particularly quiet life, and while I regret none of that, it's so much fun to cut loose for a while.

Now Declan left me alone to be with his new friends. He said he needed air, but what he meant was, "I need to get away from you," because he found my scent nauseating, I was sure of it.

I was not sure of it. These thoughts are pointless and damaging. Declan does love me, and when he returns I won't demand to know where he's been. Instead, I'll laugh as he tells me masculine secrets, things done behind doors.

And time passes strangely onboard and he has still not returned.

Declan has not returned and a terrible small part of me made me think he was with another woman, all flesh and skin and legs wide open, but I needed to stop that. I was feeling physically much improved and, with the sun peeking over that wide, wide horizon, I thought I'd explore the ship on my own. There were always people around. So much noise. The partying continued day and night; Even now there were people slumped in doorways, bottles everywhere, piles of vomit and other spillages. You see what happens here? People become other than themselves. They are all strangers, there is nothing of their old selves, their past, their real selves, nothing of that here. All of it is the now, the who we are at this moment.

I was hungry, I realised, so I made my way to the dining hall, thinking to eat at the first breakfast session. This was the quietest meal of the day; often you could eat alone, if you got there early enough, as I did today. I ordered a huge breakfast. I felt ill, but the kind of ill that food could cure. So I had eggs Benedict, cereal, French pastries, coffee and another French pastry. I liked that they had this kind of breakfast available, even while all around me ate fruit and dry wholemeal toast.

I sat with one of the injured building workers. He looked very depressed, barely managing to raise a smile at me. They get very little support on the mainland, especially at an emotional level. They're supposed to just put up with it. Be a man. It's really hard for the ones without good friends or lovers to talk to. This guy was just an apprentice. Lost his foot below the ankle. He reckons he could have been a footballer if it hadn't happened.

Our other companion was a middle-aged man, so white if he lay his head on the tablecloth he'd disappear. Fat, too, in a slobby way. He said to the apprentice, "Look at the size of you. You'd be no good on the field. In the old days, skinny little shit like you'd be fine on the AFL field. These days we're a lot bigger, aren't we?"

The young man deflated even further, as if this horrible fat man was right. "Don't listen to him," I said, and I called over Darren, an actual grade-level footballer. He was so badly injured in a car accident he'd never play again. Painkillers helped him carry on and let loose a part of his personality we all found delightful. Desirable. He was very popular onboard, but I had no interest in him beyond watching him and Declan enjoy a game or two together.

The apprentice had bitten the tip of his tongue off in the accident, so he didn't bother with sweet food and hated talking. He sounded okay, but a bit like kids do when they're pretending to be brain damaged. His body was lean and he spent a lot of time in the sun so he wasn't unattractive.

He and Darren had a great old chat. We all ignored the fat white man, which was made easier when Doctor Firth came to join us. He liked to eat early so he could get on with his day.

"How are your parents?" he asked me. I hadn't spoken to them in days (I'd lost track of how many).

"They never change!" I said. "Nothing bothers them."

"Ah, but that isn't true, exactly. You haven't seen it. I did see how they changed, after your house fire. After you survived death."

This floored me. No one knew about that; not even Declan. I didn't want to be one of those people, the special ones. I told the captain that.

He said, "But you *are* special. There are very, very few of us who know that there is nothing on the other side, who understand the importance of staying here for as long as possible. I'm working towards that and you are all helping me."

"You survived death too?"

"I was electrocuted 20 years ago. They say I died for seven minutes; it felt like I lived a lifetime in those moments. But there was nothing, nothing but my memories and what I had hoped for. It's about fear of death and what comes next."

Six or seven other passengers had clustered around to hear him. It was always like that. He told us about the cruise line, which I hadn't known was called The Forever Company, a nebulous group of loosely affiliated parties. 'Regeneration Cruises,' they called themselves. At the centre of it all was my father's old school mate, Doctor Firth Franklin, a campaigner for the acceptance of body transformations. "I like to call myself a mathematician. I am discovering the aliquot parts that make a perfect whole. Whole selves are different. Shared selves, a body made of many different people, become something new. A re-invention of the self or the brain, with new memory and signals. And this is why, while you are all precious, some of you are more precious than others."

He put his arm around Claudia, the canteen lady, Jacko's true love. Jacko was nowhere in sight and I wondered if he and Declan were partying together somewhere. "We have that special walk we've planned, don't we?" the doctor said to Claudia. She limped off, which irritated me no end. It looked fake to me.

The rest of us were a little jealous of the attention the passengers like her the ones who hated their body parts—received from the captain. He squired them about the place, ordering drinks on his own tab, making sure they ate well. "Need to be healthy," he said to them. "Nothing more vital than your health. Isn't it? Ask any chronically ill person."

We had those, too, the quieter ones who seemed grateful just to be here. One told me she'd come for the painkillers, another for the medical marijuana.

As Doctor Firth and Claudia left, he said to me, "Don't you worry about Declan. He's in sick bay, but he'll be fine. Totally fine."

He left me there alone, surprised and unsure what to do.

"Call your father," the doctor said.

THAT NIGHT AT dinner I sat with Jacko and a woman with the most beautiful long fingers; I felt very embarrassed by my short stumpy ones. I tried to keep up a happy face, but I was terribly worried. The conversation with my father had frightened me and angered me at the same time. Firth had told me to call him, but my father was not forthcoming about why.

"Don't you worry," he said, dismissing me as he always did. "Everything will be fine. Things are under control."

"What things?"

As dessert was being served, the purser Benjamin whispered in my ear, "If you'd like to come with me, your husband is ready for visitors." Doctor Firth called Benjamin 'my right hand man,' and anywhere else you wouldn't think about that; but here, I looked at the doctor's right hand, and at Benjamin's, and wondered if they'd done a swap.

THE FIRST THING I noticed was Declan's smile, pure radiating happiness. He hadn't smiled like that since the accident, no matter how hard I tried.

"Nina!" he said. He kissed me, properly, and I felt the most wonderful stirrings.

I also felt two arms around me.

I COULDN'T SLEEP that night. Declan's new arm rested heavily on my waist, elbow bent, fingers cupping my breast. It felt quite cold, a dead-weight, and I wasn't sure I liked it. His vigour I enjoyed, although he still couldn't put weight on his new arm.

I slid out of his grasp, pulled on some clothes and went out onto the deck. I do adore that about being on a ship; instant access to sea air. Marvellous.

It was very chilly and fresh out there, with the wind quite high and whipping my hair about my face. The brain-damaged guy swept the deck with his left hand, using his right to hold his wig on. There really wasn't much left of him, but he looked happy enough, sweeping away and not seeming to care that he didn't get anywhere.

A light glowed in the bridge and I saw the dark shadow up there. Instinctively I raised my arm in greeting.

The shadow waved back.

Feeling adventurous I walked through the corridors towards the bridge. There was much evidence of frivolity; many empty bottles outside doors and signs saying *do not disturb* or *enter if your naked* or *party in progress*. I could hear laughter from one room and was tempted to knock, looking for ordinary companionship.

But I continued towards the bridge.

On approach I saw the door was ajar, so I could peek through without being seen.

He was huge. It was no illusion; this man stood close to the ceiling, seven foot or nearabouts. He was broad across the shoulder and his arms so long his fingers dangled near his kneecaps. The room smelt like pure alcohol, like a bottle of metho. He turned toward me. His hair was sparse and clumpish, steel gray in the low light. His neck was squat, tucked into his collar.

His face. I have looked at many things in my life, from a miscarried calf to a three-armed man, but nothing as odd as this creature's face. Eyes set well back in the skull, bushy eyebrows casting a shadow, flat and broad and apparently sewn on, chin bulbous and spongy-looking. He smiled slowly when he saw me and held his arms wide as if asking for a hug. He'd crush me. Look at the size of him. He made a noise at me, like a bird burping, I thought.

"Sorry to bother you... I was looking for the captain." A

ridiculous thing to say, but I had nothing else.

"And you've found me," I heard. "He doesn't talk." The captain sat on a stool in the corner, as if he was sitting observing a creature in the zoo. He bade me enter, had me sit. Closer up and with the light now shining on the enormous man, I saw there were surgery scars on his face and fingers, around his neck. He stood comfortably, though, as if used to his disparate parts.

"I've learned by hard experience never to make his face perfect. People are frightened by perfection, in awe of it. We are made in the image of God, but who is to say how God looks? All we can do is control how we look."

The creature moved his head around as if showing it off. So he could hear all right.

"We've learnt that people neither trust terrible beauty nor terrible ugliness," Firth said. "I try to find a happy medium that barely causes a reaction."

I wasn't buying that he'd got the face right. You take this guy out onto the street, you'd get a reaction. Look at him, towering over me. His shoulders twice the width of mine, but he was hunched over, as if in pain.

"I call him Adam. He seems to respond to it."

"Handsome devil," I said, meaning it.

He lurched towards me.

"It's okay," Doctor Firth said. "He's gentle as a lamb. I took out the bit that causes anger last time I replaced the brain. Shake hands, Adam," he said. The creature lifted his arm. I reached for it impulsively, but stopped, the horror of what I saw freezing my actions.

The creature grabbed my arm, his fingers so strong I could almost feel my bones crack.

I tried to pull away, but it only made him tug me closer.

"Go limp," Doctor Firth said. "Pretend to be dead. He doesn't like dead things."

So I did that, collapsed in a heap, and he let me go.

"Let me show you something. I've been experimenting with this stuff for years; you probably remember! You seemed fascinated as a child."

The tall man's shoulders slumped, as if disappointed that we were leaving.

"He seems lonely," I said.

"He is. Who wouldn't be, in his place? We're doing what we can. I let him out to walk each morning between three and five. And I keep him company when I can."

Firth led me to a room beside the bridge, well lit and sparsely decorated. There were jars in the room, filled with scales and noses and eyes. I thought he'd shoved animal skin in there and wondered at the point of it.

And then I saw movement.

"Lobard's chameleons. Grow to adulthood in sixty days, which is about as long as they can live in these circumstances. I put them in there as newborns and feed them until they've grown to fit the space. There is no reason why we can't change how we look. Really, it is quite a natural process."

The chameleons had no real space to move and I couldn't understand how they stayed alive. "It's mostly electrical impulses," Doctor Firth said. "Any body shape can be changed. I worked with rats for a while, but there is so much superstition about rats it wasn't worth the trouble. Isn't it?"

It was awful, these creatures in jars with nothing but suffering and death.

The worst thing, though? Was that my first thought was, *why didn't you help me? You've known me since childhood. Why didn't you make me into a more beautiful person?*

I FOUND DECLAN in the bar. His new arm was paining him, he said, and he needed whisky to dull it. "Whisky makes me frisky," he said, and he pulled me towards him so we tucked together like spoons. He ordered me a gin and tonic.

I told him about the huge man, and the chameleons, and I showed him the bruise on my arm. He kissed it gently and got me another gin and tonic; he didn't seem bothered by any of it.

WE HAD AN upset a couple of days later, when the man who'd given Declan his arm passed away. He was 'having a routine procedure,' is how it was described, but by then I'd realised that we were all here for transplants, to give or to receive. I guess this had become routine to all of us onboard. Was he getting a new arm? Rumour had it he still thought the old one was there and had stabbed into his armpit, wanting to cut it off.

It was terrible; so many of us witnessed it. He bled to death, and you could see it in the corridors near the hospital, because he'd run out (the nurses said they'd only turned their backs for a minute) as if he was trying to escape, and the blood could be seen from one end of the corridor to the next. He'd come short just as he reached the deck, collapsing for all to see.

This wasn't the first death on board, although it was the most public. There was also the woman in her forties, travelling with a group of women who met online seeking adventures. I'd never shared a meal with her. She was found naked and choked to death (rumours differed as to what on, but most believed it was a horse tranquilizer). We had an onboard security guard who seemed the man to go to for all these things; his report stated *To Be Determined*.

An old man had fallen asleep and not woken up on one of the deckchairs.

Four or five had gone missing or at least couldn't be accounted for, but this was absolutely standard, the staff said. People came on cruises in order to disappear; that was the plan. So if a relative kicked up a fuss, no one did anything apart from share details of the last port of call.

There were rumours that the hospital performed late term abortions and that one woman had died from it, but no one had any evidence of that.

Of course you had to feel sorry for all of them, each one missing a limb of one kind or another, some of them despising their own bodies to the point of physical illness. Those like Declan who'd been injured on the job seemed to stand above the others, as if they had more worth or something. I don't know. That's just how it seemed to me.

Every building site you see a death or two, pretty much. Accidents happen. People are lazy. Contractors cut corners, take the cheap way out. Some reckon you need these sacrifices for a building to stay up. You need the blood and if you don't get it when you're putting the thing up, you'll need it after. Suicides, domestic violence, miscarriages, overdoses; it'll keep happening until there's been enough, then it'll stop.

What we had on the cruise were a lot of people who'd sacrificed limbs; three or four arms, dozens of fingers, some feet, two legs, about 20 toes. An ear. Not all from the same building site, of course.

Declan was superstitious, as many building site workers were.

He was sure the accident was his fault, because he hadn't worn red socks, or touched his nose twice, or whatever it was that day he believed failed to keep him safe.

On board he was an encyclopedia of knowledge of ship-side superstition.

There were the unlucky words he had everyone avoid: knife, salmon, rabbit, egg, salt. They become a joke, but still the list was kept and added to.

Then all the things that were bad luck: Beginning your journey on a Friday. An overturned bowl. Losing a mop at sea. A dead body at sea is bad luck, so that's why they liked to bury at sea as quickly as possible. No one seemed bothered by it all; it seemed right, out there in the doldrums.

You had to stop a ringing glass or a sailor would drown.

And whistling brought winds. We'd all learned not to whistle.

AND I ONLY knew time had passed when I called my parents and they told me so. "It's been weeks!" my mother said. Had she worried, I asked her? Did she miss me?

"Of course we do. We miss you terribly. The cruise must be heading for home soon."

I didn't think so and I told her so. I said, "We're going to stay on the boat. We like it here. Declan is doing so well." He was helping with maintenance, getting stuck in with the plumbing and the electricals, fixing all the problems that presented themselves. "You could come to join us," I said, thinking of my mother's dicky knees and my father's poor hearing. The doctor could help them both.

"What a lovely idea," she said, and I thought perhaps she meant it.

*   *   *

I SPENT A lot of time on the deck. Declan sat with me, tanning his new arm. He looked far happier; he'd lost his moroseness and was the most helpful man on board, always bringing drinks and towels.

We didn't really talk about the operation. We just enjoyed the results. He was far less curious about the shadowy man in the bridge than I was. To me, up there was all philosophy, all reason and meaning. Down here we existed and enjoyed the warm sun. We ate and we drank and we made love, we laughed, we built friendships.

Only the captain seemed to share my fascination.

"He is astonishing, isn't he?" He'd caught me staring up, holding Declan's hand while he somehow managed to read a potboiler novel and drink a huge cocktail at the same time, me staring up at the window, wondering if that big man was looking down at me. He was like an elusive guru or a secretive god. Rarely seen, but with a powerful presence nonetheless.

DINNER TALK WAS interesting, to say the least. My companions today were a man called Graham, an ex-soldier and, we'd discovered, sex offender. He was on anti-libidinal medication which caused him medical problems he didn't mind telling us about. He wasn't supposed to drink, but he did, scoffing a bottle of wine at lunch and two at dinner. It made him sleepy and slurry rather than anything else, thank goodness. Nonetheless I kept an eye on him to make sure he didn't go near any of the children on board. I also had a self-described 'gamer geek,' who said dull things in precise tones and nodded at everything I said, and a couple ("we can't be apart"), a blind man and his wife, and she wiped food from his mouth after every bite as if he made a mess, which he didn't.

The gamer geek and I spent the meal laughing and talking. I really enjoyed his company and I think he enjoyed mine.

The ex-soldier said to me, "You needn't think you've got a chance with any of those young men once your husband runs off." He said it after I'd laughed out loud at something the clever gamer geek said.

And the ex-soldier said, "Birds of a feather stick together."

It was a saying I'd heard a lot onboard. They meant it literally, looking at all the birds that hitched rides; and metaphorically, meaning that we were all deformed in one way or another.

This old soldier seemed to think I was worse than the rest of them.

Then conversation turned to the latest death on board.

The blind man's wife said, "It's that monster up on the bridge. Tell me you've seen him. He's getting out in the middle of the night and murdering people. Why do you think there have been so many deaths?"

"All of those deaths are explained," Graham said. He sounded as if he was used to forming a defence. "He didn't murder that poor woman who lost a leg. And he didn't chuck anyone over board."

"So you say," she said, and her husband and the gamer geek murmured their agreement.

"I'm sure you'll be able to deboard at the next dock," I said. The woman annoyed me; had she even met the man up there? Had she been close, seen how astonishing the work was, how lively his eyes, how gentle his touch?

* * *

TIME PASSES SO very, very slowly and strangely.

DECLAN AND I booked in for a stay in the sensory deprivation tank, one of the many cleansing things on offer. I'd done plenty of them; I loved the sense of utter quiet in that coffin-like box. Declan always refused, but everything was free on board so he gave it a go.

I was in there for a long time. Hours, I think; certainly when they let me out, Declan was long gone, showered, fed and returned to wait for me.

I remember nothing of it but pure rest. Just an emptiness, a lack of thought. I was aware of every part of my body, from my toes to the top of my head, and all of it was beautiful. How did people despise their bodies?

When they opened the lid I felt reborn, as if all of my old self was gone and all that remained was the now. No past. No history.

"You look amazing," Declan said. He stood fresh and handsome himself, his fingers warm on my arm as he helped me out, his body hard as he helped to dry me.

"What did you see in there?" I asked.

"I saw you," he said.

DECLAN AND I went to look at the chameleons in the jars. I wanted to set them free, or kill them at least, because they were doing little for Doctor Firth's research. They were just there for his curiosity and that didn't seem to be a good enough reason for their suffering.

"You always were fascinated by such things," Doctor Firth said, joining us in the room. "How's the arm, Declan?"

Declan swung it around as if it was a baseball bat. "Bloody brilliant. Never would have imagined it could feel so good. The bloke really looked after it."

"All our donors do. Strange that so many of them despise their limbs, which are so beautiful to all of us."

"But they aren't all happy with the donation, are they?" I said. Declan nudged me; he wanted me to stop asking questions. But I'd seen a bitter fight between two women, one missing a left thumb, the other the woman who'd received it. They were at the stage of beating each other with champagne buckets (I'm not joking; this actually happened) before they were pulled apart. The donor wasn't happy with the way her thumb was being used; the new owner said it was none of her business.

Such are the dangers of a cruise. You're stuck for the duration.

"Most donors are happy. They get this cruise for free, including all transfers. And most are disgusted with the limb they donate, and would struggle elsewhere to find a doctor to remove it."

"Is that why we're in international waters?"

"That, and of course your new friend. My adopted son. Those who can afford it pay a lot, of course, and they think it is value for money. Your parents could afford the tariff. He's done very well for himself, your father! I'm proud to be a school mate of his."

I never liked to talk about what my father did, and Declan loved me enough not to mention it either. We'd decided we'd accept the spoils of it all, though. What good would it do to refuse?

"You say 'adopted' son? How old is he?"

"His mind is over two hundred years old. He's an observer of life rather than a participant. Like the great seers, he stands by and watches. He's old enough to be my great-great-great-grandfather. I would love to hear him speak about his good old days, wouldn't you?"

"But all he does is watch from up there," I said, waving my arm at where I thought the bridge might be. "Like a cat stuck inside, staring out at the birds."

And like these chameleons, I thought.

"He does get lonely. He is functionally immortal. He hasn't aged, but then of course I upgrade his bits every now and then. Modernise him, I guess you could say."

"Using bits from broken people."

"I don't break anybody; I pick up the pieces. You always want your children to have friends, don't you? All he wants are more like him."

I could relate to that. My mother used to invite children over, provide the best afternoon tea, but they would sit and scoff all the food, watching me or avoiding watching me, until they were collected again.

"Your child is over two hundred years old."

"He still can't make his own friends, though."

"Mate, I'll be his friend," Declan said.

"I like that," Doctor Firth said. "Let's drink to it."

I HADN'T SUFFERED a hangover like this before, and felt almost as if I had completed a rite of passage. At the same time I couldn't help but stand in judgment, just the smallest bit, of the women who were so drunk they danced on tables, no underwear. And the men who held their shoulders while others poured more alcohol into them and then, in groups of three or more, carried these women off. Not for their own safety; no doubt about that.

* * *

IT WAS GROWING close to dawn when I awoke. Declan was snoring, dead to the world. I wasn't sure which of us had been the drunkest last night, but I certainly felt bad enough.

There was a note under our door. *See you below*, it said, and I assumed it was from Doctor Firth, but I couldn't be sure. Declan wasn't rousable but I felt restless, ill, so I decided to go exploring on my own, throwing caution to the wind. We'd been warned about 'down below' by some of the other passengers. There were things happening below we didn't need to know about. Whole floors of debauchery too awful for a nice couple like us to contemplate.

The passageways below were narrower, and showed the same signs of partying. Booze bottles, food plates, other forms of rubbish I didn't look at too hard. I wanted to knock on one of the doors, see who was inside, but I wasn't that courageous. I'd heard so many ghost stories, at dinner and late at night. Many were about disembodied body parts, desperately seeking sanctuary. A hand that crawled like a spider. A screaming skull used as a drinking vessel. Others were about below deck, where it was dark and there were no portholes. Down there, there were no rules. I heard about babies born and reared down there without ever seeing the sun. And of people who died, even those drowned at sea, crawling along the deck in desperation, as if reaching for something that would give their life back.

I didn't see any ghosts, but I did accidentally see the Adamites.

I'd heard rumours about them as well. They believed all sins are absolved, that there was no original sin. So they lived naked, and had lots of sex. They asked all the big questions: *Why am I here? What is the point? What is next but the great nothingness?*

They had been contained on this floor to avoid bothering people with their philosophising, although they came upstairs to eat. I'd heard their theories and I couldn't say I was tempted. I could hear loud noises as the lift reached their floor. A high buzz of conversation, of champagne corks popping, women who were too pissed to play games upstairs. The corridor here was full. I was pushed out by the others, moved out of the way.

They were all naked. "Just like Adam and Eve. We don't even believe they wore fig leaves, you know."

I wasn't interested in taking part. To be honest, they looked a bit bored themselves, and I stepped back into the lift to escape before more of them spotted me and dragged me along to join in. "You remind me of my daughter," one said, over and again and again.

There were always people who wanted you to join in.

I FOLLOWED THE route down below. As I reached a lower floor, I saw a red glow. It was an unusual light, bright and yet diffuse, steady for the most part, a warmth that I followed along the narrowing passageway. Down here there were no human noises, just a rhythmic thrumming. The ground was rubberized, slightly bouncy. The wall lights were dim.

I think it was the bilge area? I don't know what it's called. But the glow came from there, and that sense of warmth, so I stepped through the oval door and inside.

The smell of singed hair, of… not formaldehyde, but something similar, and the floor grey with greasy smear.

The ceiling was covered with a bizarre artwork, criss-crossing lines of copper wire forming intricate patterns and lines. It was almost hypnotic, to stare up at it. I saw shapes and figures and patterns and wondered who had made such a laborious, painstaking, beautiful piece of art.

I heard a low moaning sound, as if someone was trying to talk through a mouthful of food, but no one was there. It sounded perhaps like the huge man, learning to speak at last. He used sign language or made noises, had learnt like cats do how to communicate. Chirrups, almost grunts, guttural noises.

It would have been the first time I had seen him away from the bridge, apart from those night time circumnavigations on the deck. Others had seen him, and we walked with him now, at a respectful distance. The longer we are on board, the more we move like him. Mimicking his slow walk, the way his toes drag slightly. We talk in chirrups and gasps. Dinner conversation is less than it was but then we all know each other now. We all know everything about each other.

I left that strange room and went back to my cabin, where Declan was stirring and we could talk about the night before as if we remembered it. I told him about the copper ceiling below, about the Adamites, but he laughed, thinking I was telling stories to amuse him.

MOSTLY AT MEALS we listen to Doctor Firth tell us stuff, about why he does what he does and why we are here. He makes us feel special, as if we are in a position the rest of the world envies, and it's hard to deny that as we sit here drinking champagne, eating this beautiful food, afloat at sea without the worry of law or country or anything else at all.

"There is code in movements, in the number of breaths and swallows. The number of times we chew," he told us. He made us all want to be cryptographers with stories and mysteries, of Gorgo, wife of Leonidas, who divined a message in a blank slate. She dreamt you needed to scrape off the wax to see it and she was right. Of the Rossignols (father and son), who created the Great Cipher but both died, and the cipher lay undeciphered for 200 years. We wanted to be the ones to decipher these things.

"You need a long life for genius. Imagine if those men, that father and son, hadn't died? What they would have discovered."

As time goes on we are more separated and yet more combined, as one takes the arm of another, one takes the leg of someone else. And time passes in strange ways and people swap rooms. There are so many rooms and beds. People are swapping here and there, but Declan and I are true to each other. The man whose arm he has watched me for some time, but that man is gone now.

Doctor Firth spends time alone with the body part donors once or twice. It rarely takes three visits and never takes four.

The young woman at first appeared to have only one arm, but the other was strapped tightly to her side. When Doctor Firth unbound it, he said that it would be of little use to him. She'd tried to cut it off herself, and the deep gouges and tight binding had turned the arm a green-grey.

"You'll need a strong course of antibiotics. The infection has barely set in," Doctor Firth said, but she wouldn't be here if she wanted that solution.

"The arm is more than infection," she said. I wondered if he'd remove it as a charity case, given the state of decay. Not quite charity; this kind of operation cost upwards of ten grand, not covered by any health insurance. She had paid the full amount; I knew because she had the necklace, a gift given to the highest-paying passengers.

* * *

SHE PROVED USEFUL otherwise, though.

She died on the table and was revived.

She said, "I dreamt I died. And there was a great black hole in front of me. I didn't want to go forward, but I had to. And my arms"—she started to cry— "my arms were still there." It was this more than anything else that frightened her: that she had been through all that and her despised arms were still attached.

"Your arms are gone," I told her. She was still sluggish, so I held up a mirror for her to see her bandaged armpits.

"Both of them?" she said. Her throat was croaky and dry so I gave her an ice cube. "I thought just below the elbow?"

"Always best to take the whole limb," I said, and she smiled. She would see her good arm daily, attached now to a woman in her eighties, insanely wealthy and quite wild. The arm was always dressed differently to the rest of her, naked most often. And the nails were beautifully looked after, painted, glorious.

THE DONOR'S OTHER arm was thrown overboard.

I WAS HELPING Doctor Firth in the clinic by now. He treated me especially well and I realised I was at the top of his heap: a survivor, someone who has seen the other side and returned. The woman, too, who had given us her arms. She was put to work in promotions, making all the announcements, and spent many nights in Doctor Firth's cabin. Declan too, acting as orderly, using his two strong arms to move people about, to carry anyone who needed carrying. I tried not to be jealous, but

I knew some of them did it on purpose, asked for his help just to be carried by him. I can't say I blame them, though. To be carried by Declan was to feel safe and secure and loved.

My father was very pleased with me. "You've found your feet there. At last," he said. The conversation almost made me cry, because it seemed to me that for the first time in my life he didn't pity me. He really felt happy for me, that I had found my place.

I was certain Doctor Firth didn't keep me here out of pity. I truly was good with people; I had an empathy born of a lifetime looking odd and out of place.

He could perhaps relate at that level as well. Because he was filling the shoes of a man long dead, following in the footsteps of others before him: surgeons, artists, scientists. The guardians of the creature.

How strange for a creature to outlive its creator by so long.

A RESTLESSNESS CAME over the ship. Were we perhaps drifting through the doldrums, physically and spiritually? There were words said during our meals, especially amongst the older passengers still with us. They wanted to see land again, some said, though others said, never again. One night as we sat on deck the electricity buzzed as it sometimes did, and we talked about that, about this idea that Doctor Firth was creating a family for his creature and we were all a part of it. Doctor Firth told us this buzz occurred, this physical response, when the matches were good.

ON THE TENTH night, or the twentieth, or the thirtieth, the lights flickered while we were in the bar drinking Negronis. I had intended to race down to the room I called Copper Ceiling, next time the electricity did this, but I was too settled. Declan was next to me, his arm on my thigh, his finger drawing figure eights, and the feeling of love was so intense I wouldn't leave it.

THEN I SWEAR that there were two shadows in the bridge, although I was not keen to visit them.

IT WAS THE tenth night at sea, or the thirtieth, or the fortieth, that the child went missing. That morning at breakfast, someone said, "I feel as if our numbers are thinning." I looked around the room and realised he was right. The brain damaged man who'd made us laugh so hard at his odd sayings was gone. The blind man was gone; I couldn't remember the last time I'd seen him. His wife was still there, wearing brighter colours than I'd seen her wear.

"How is he?" I asked her, and she stared blankly at me as if forgetting she'd ever been married. I thought he'd paid a fortune for a lung transplant; perhaps things went wrong. I felt sad for him, if that was the case. Of all of us, he was the one who'd sought immortality, who'd really believed he could live forever, given enough money.

WE SEEMED TO float in those doldrums for a long time. A child went missing and I feel as if his mother was too tired to care very much. She was one of our wheelchair passengers now, blissfully happy with it, I thought; although, too, I thought she had little connection with reality.

"What's good," Doctor Firth said, "is that the child now lives forever in her mind. There is no death, there is only uncertainty, and with that comes eternal life."

I imagined this would bring little comfort to the rest of the family.

WE CELEBRATED CHRISTMAS at sea, and Evensong, and Valentine's Day and Easter. He told us that those destined for greatness need long lives to achieve their destiny. We had great people on board, very great, the gifted and talented.

THERE ARE TWO shadows on the bridge. The second communicates even less than the first, using gestures he mimics from Adam. Adam, Doctor Firth calls him, even though I have told him this is both shallow and ridiculous. Adam is, strangely, the shyer of the two, like a young boy whose mother has invited a new friend over to play, one unknown and unmet. He liked me to sit with them, as if that would make the friendship stronger somehow. There was a level of that, I guess, but really Doctor Firth was not happy.

This new creature's face was smooth, pink, undamaged.

He had bits I recognised.

The old man's blue eye, the blind man's hands, the postal worker's perfect ear.

THEN HE BEGAN to fall apart. His fingers first, one by one dropping off as the stitches dissolved. The parts beginning to rot on him. Then the light in his eyes faded, his mouth slumped, and we needed to wheel him away before Adam witnessed the 'death.'

"He hates the loss even more than he hates the loneliness," Doctor Firth said. He asked me to sit with Adam, distract him. He said, "What did I do wrong? Did I make inadequate substitutes? We will have to try again. Gather our features, our Aliquot parts, and begin again."

We buried the failed creature at sea.

DOCTOR FIRTH TOLD us, "We should live forever. What sort of God builds a universe where we *expect* to die, leaving behind grief-stricken loved ones who are changed irrevocably by our departure?" He told us he had performed dissections from a young age, that he understood the sinews of the human body better than most. I remember his visits to our house when I was young, how much I enjoyed his admiration when I didn't faint away, as the others did, with his descriptions and his demonstrations. It's only natural, isn't it? What's inside us? The connections and what makes us tick. I think I remember him so well because he spent a fortnight with us when his fiancée died. It was the first glimpse of grief I'd had and as a child was fascinated. There was no music in the house and my parents lost their usual joie de vivre, which, to be honest, annoyed the hell out of me usually. It was my mother who tired of it, who wanted to open up the house and let the warm breeze in, so that Doctor Firth had to go.

I had forgotten most of this, to be honest. I told Declan about it, but he was tired of it now, and keen to get home, get back to work. His arm was functioning well and he felt adrift here, I think, and wasted.

*   *   *

I SAT WITH Doctor Firth to tell him perhaps Declan and I needed to leave the ship. Get back to our reality.

"I would hate that," he said. "I think that you are the ones who can help me bring some magic to the process. I really do. I've replicated precisely the original scientist's actions. I've had so many failures. So very, very many."

I said, "But what have you learned? What have you added? Surely the result will be the same."

"It's about the sonic vibrations. We need to understand the sympathetic nervous system before the implantation of electrodes. The physical horror of it is too much for most, but you were always hardy in that regard."

He drank his gin. He drank a lot of gin, claiming that it helped numb him to doubt. "It's about the blood flow," he said. He knew what it was about, but he wasn't sure how to bring long-term success.

"You need to stay," he said. He told me he had taken on this task in direct line from the original creator, and how he hoped I'd be next in line. "It's all circumstance," he told me. "There's a certain magic in it all."

"I have no scientific knowledge. No medical knowledge."

"Others will do that work. There are unlimited funds for that, thanks to early investments. But he must be kept safe, and out of the authorities' hands."

Speaking of hands, I looked at his; solid, dextrous, unscarred, if somewhat wrinkled.

THE NUMBERS THINNED.

The lights buzzed.

There were burials at sea.

All of us knew the risks. Even those so wealthy they wore $10,000 diamond necklaces to dinner knew the risks and took them.

ON THE FIRST or the hundredth or the fiftieth day, Jacko almost drowned at sea, but we saved him.

"That isn't a place you want to go, is it?"

Jacko was exhausted, his eyes almost black, his whole self shivering.

"No, sir," he said.

"You saw the afterlife. What's ahead. A great awareness and a great nothingness. You are there, but nothing will ever happen again, for all eternity. There is no real afterlife. This is it. These moments of death are precious. My son has many moments of death, each of his body parts carrying with it that moment, especially the brain."

I eyed off his new girlfriend's fingers as she stroked his brow. Jacko was so alive, I loved to be around him. But I was twice his size, and the woman he chose is a tiny thing, sweet like a butterfly. Fingers like tiny needles flying through the air.

MANY OF US walk before dawn with Adam now. He travels with a limp. One arm longer than the other, and hairy. Arms dangle. Fingertips on one hand blackened. He needs a new arm. I wondered whose arm it would be, and was glad that Declan got his.

I liked his arm.

He still didn't talk, though; he communicated (if indeed it was that) with his dear little noises. We tried to communicate back.

He always wanted to walk and walk and walk, and Doctor Firth did give him more time. But to me he felt trapped, always trapped.

At least when he was surrounded by large, odd people he could actually go out and about more. So I fit in well. The point of a long life is to enjoy it. And to learn, expand the mind. Otherwise, what's the point?

I wasn't sure if was poignant or tragic, to see Adam with a book he couldn't read.

WE DON'T LIKE dreamless sleep. Too much like the emptiness of death.

Breakfast conversation always started with: what I dreamt.

"I don't really dream," I said, because I hadn't remembered a dream for years. The last one I dreamt I was beautiful and it was so hard to wake up and find I wasn't. I'd trained myself not to remember. I think the others were relieved; more time to tell their dreams.

One woman said, "Dreamless sleep equals death." She had dreamt the night before that all of her teeth were tiny houses with tiny people inside them, and that anything hot made them sweat, anything cold made them shiver. "I want to walk around with my mouth open to stop them from suffocating," she said. "But I know that's nonsense." Still, she did sit there with her mouth open and I couldn't help peering in, just in case.

Doctor Firth wasn't present that morning, his place for breakfast still set. When the lights flickered, I wondered if he was down in the Copper Room. Declan said he wanted to swim some laps and I wasn't in the mood to watch him, so I went for a wander. I didn't trust the lifts when the lights flickered and I could almost hear the electricity buzzing, so I took the stairs.

"DOES THE SOUL rest in the heart or in the brain?" Doctor Firth asked me. He didn't seem surprised that I was there. He worked alone, behind a locked door he had allowed me access through.

On the table lay… what would be a man. I've been on this ship long enough to recognise some of the parts.

A young man's arm.

A short old lady's feet.

A fat lady's thighs.

And someone's left leg. I lost track of that one.

There was no head. Not yet.

"We can't be choosey about the heads. Limbs are lost, with no questions, but a person has to die to donate the head. Anyone worthwhile has somebody to miss them."

I thought that was a bit harsh. I was set up, but not everyone had family and friends. Didn't make them bad people.

Adam turned slowly to look at me. He was almost handsome. Almost not terrifying. He'd been watching the procedure, waiting for his new friend to wake up.

ON THE TENTH or the twentieth or the thirtieth night, they had a trivia quiz, with quite marvellous prizes, including a helicopter ride to a luxury island resort with a six-star chef ("Only one in the world!") and a diamond necklace with papers and 'an armed guard for life' and tickets to shows in New York. All sorts of things.

"Who's got a good head on their shoulders?" the MC asked. I nudged Declan; he was always so good at remembering details of things.

I wasn't keen to join in, but they needed teams of four, "No more! No less!" and my dinner table didn't want to miss out. I had the blind man's wife, Jacko and the football player.

Declan was on a table on the other side of the room and I could hear them easily. They had one of those women with a high-pitched squeal for a laugh.

First prize was a helicopter flight to an island resort 'for a meal not cooked by these miserable bastards,' and the kitchen staff came out and bowed while we all booed and cat-called. The food was excellent, really and that was part of the joke. "And," the captain said, "a free cabin upgrade on return."

That got everyone going. We competed properly then.

I had a couple of dummies on my table, so we didn't have a chance, but Declan has always been brilliant at this stuff, and he had a TV addict and a college professor at his table. Everyone was dressed up—the women with too much make up, the men with too much cologne—but that didn't stop them shouting and standing on tables and all the rest of it.

The table winners all got huge hampers of booze and bits of food, but only one would get the helicopter flight and cabin upgrade.

Doctor Firth sidled up to me. "How much do you love your husband?"

"Utterly," I said. I realised we were all under this man's spell, that all he had to do was lift his arm and we'd all be quiet. He'd brought peace to so many, with his words and the work he did, and just bringing us together, those of us who'd suffered.

I was so busy watching him I missed the fact that Declan was up on stage. He was joking around but intense, I could see that. One more question right and he'd win.

"So, Declan," the MC said. "How are you feeling?"

"Have you ever sat on your hand until it was numb before you masturbate? This is even better." He raised his new arm and everyone laughed hysterically.

He had the whole room in stitches with his jokes. His mates were always on at him to do stand up, but he didn't like the pressure. He liked being funny when no one expected him to be funny. I looked at him up there, with his skewiff nose from a long-ago cricket incident, his floppy hair, his huge smile, and thought *how do I deserve him?*

The last question was about the precise location we were at. I didn't think he'd know it, because he'd taken little interest once the boat stopped moving, but somehow he knew it. He winked at me and I wondered if he'd been given the answer, because Doctor Firth, up on stage also, barely looked surprised. I loved them both in that moment, because really Doctor Firth was giving me the room upgrade as well—if not the trip to a resort, because that was only for one.

Of course Declan offered the helicopter ride to me. "You should go," he said. "You're the one who loves adventure." But the captain said it wasn't transferrable. I helped Declan shower and dress, just for old time's sake; and we did that, too, even though we knew people were waiting for us. He wore a beige safari suit, thinking that would give everyone a laugh.

"You don't have to come and wave me off," he said, but as if I would miss the helicopter landing and all the rest of it.

Very little happened on the ship.

"You'll need to stand there," one of the pursers said, and Declan kissed me good bye and waved theatrically to everyone else, as if he was a grand dictator going off to subdue another country, and the cheering took all my attention. I heard a *thwock* like a hard tennis stroke and I turned around to see Declan standing red-suited, as a joke, swaying from side to side. I wanted to catch him before he fell. There was something so very odd, the light in my eyes and the glinting off the helicopter blades, because it seemed to me he had somehow tucked his head into his shoulders like a bird going to sleep.

And then he crumbled. Crumpled? Collapsed in a heap. Someone held me back, saying, "Wait until the blades have stopped."

WE WERE A long way from home, and short of flying out by helicopter—the very idea of which made me ill—I was there until we arrived at a port. We had been to ports before, and people disembarked, but mostly they didn't. They wanted to get their money's worth. So they ordered food they didn't eat. Drank too much. Non-drinkers ordering boozy drinks because otherwise it isn't fair.

Declan took me out of a sad and lonely life. I didn't think I'd ever have a husband, let alone one I so loved.

We'd had no time for children.

I dreamt (day-dreamed) of a baby growing inside me. A girl. She wouldn't know her father, but she would know he'd loved her, because I'd tell her, show her photos, play his songs for her.

I was so certain, so absolutely positive that this baby existed that I cried when my period came on time, cried as if I'd miscarried at six months.

There would be no child for me. The chances of finding another man like Declan were slim indeed. The funny thing was, I had not previously thought *any* of it possible. I'd been resigned to, if not happy about, the idea of a life alone. Declan had changed that, but now he was gone and I curled up in bed wishing I were... dead? Not quite. But wishing I could feel nothing.

We had met so serendipitously. Both of us reaching for the last issue of *Good Weekend Food* at the same time, and he allowing me to have it. I dropped my driving license (and you know what Freud would have to say about that) and he returned it to me, and he said, 'you look nothing like your photo' which was the nicest thing anyone ever said to me.

I never doubted him, not really.

And now?

I'm dreaming now. I dreamed about a helicopter and that I once had a husband called Declan who loved me.

They tell me he is enjoying the resort and will come back to me soon.

On the fifth night or the fiftieth, they told me Declan had returned. They took me to the copper room and I could smell him, I thought; but how could that be?

"The miracle of life," Doctor Firth said, but Declan's eyes stared blankly, lifelessly at me. There was no recognition. His skewiff nose, his floppy hair... it was my husband. It was him.

"Talk to him," Doctor Firth whispered. "No need to be quiet. Whish-whish-whish," he said. What he meant, I have no idea, but I did talk, about the world's biggest nonsense. Gossip about our fellow travellers, complaints about the weather. There was no response until I said, "Well now. I'm tired and I think you'll have to excuse me to go to bed."

Then Declan reached. His whole body (not *his* body) turned

toward me and he regarded me carefully, up and down, an inspection.

I wondered whose body he had. Whose chest, whose torso, whose penis, whose legs. He walked well; Doctor Firth hadn't let me see him until he was certain he was steady.

"It's a miracle," Doctor Firth said. "Your man did the trick. Your magic man."

I led him to the cabin. He reached for me before the door was shut but I managed to close it, thinking as I did, *Should I leave it open? Am I safe?*

He felt cold, hard, unyielding, like an iron bar, and his face displayed no emotion. Declan always gave a little coo, and his eyes crinkled at the edges, and he'd kiss my shoulder so gently.

This one thrust at me until I had to beg him to stop, then call, then scream for help and to accept the humiliation as three men pulled him off me.

STARING INTO THAT once-beautiful face, I wonder where we would have been, if not on this cruise.

But I had dragged him from the pits of self-despair. I had saved his life, bringing him here.

IT FEELS SOMETIMES as if we are in old castle, with floor upon floor of strange things, and the captain is the lord of it all. In every room, at every meal table, are new creatures waiting for creation. All these passengers waiting.

Not me, I don't think.

I'll stay me.

Doctor Firth's offered to keep me up to speed. Replace my bits as time goes on. I'm eyeing off the passengers (the new ones, that is; the old ones are too piecey). I'm looking at their hands and their feet.

"How much do you want from a person, to be a true companion?" I asked.

"I don't have a percentage," Doctor Firth said, "But I imagine you will need to replace at least half of your body to qualify. When your limbs are no longer your own, you will be a creature. A created."

I'm thinking I should think about a child before that happens, although I'm not sure about bringing a child into this company. There are hard choices we make every day, hard instructions to follow, and I don't know if a child should be exposed in this way.

Adam is beyond needing a bride. All of that is the last thing on my mind. And his, too.

Not on my mind.

I felt terrible, but there were men already catching my eye. I'm checking them out, choosing a leg here, an arm there. Wanting my man to be perfect.

I CALL MY parents once a week, so they don't worry. Oh, the relief each time, when they know I'm not going home.

You might say this is like a prison. But it's a happy one. I have my lovely husband and plenty of friends. Declan still is very good with details, with remembering things. Part of him still exists.

ELIZABETH BARRET BROWNING wrote the sonnet 'How Do I love Thee' which ends, *And if God choose, I shall but love thee better after death.* I didn't think I *could* love Declan any better, but I do.

I do love him.

So very much.

THE TWO CREATURES spent most of the time in the bridge. Doctor Firth let me take Declan-face to our cabin in the evenings. Each time I did so, Adam tried to follow, his shoulders twisting to get through the door frame. "You stay here," I said to him. He clutched at me, and I kissed my fingers at him. How strange, to have two men interested in me! Declan, while not so much Declan any more, still followed his instincts. He didn't talk and I miss his jokes greatly, but so good to have him near me in the bed.

ON THE TENTH or the ninetieth day at sea, I was delayed an hour or two in visiting my men. There was a disturbance on the Adamite floor; two men charged with rape, a charge they hadn't thought possible. If I were captain I'd have them sent off in a rowboat, sent away, but our captain didn't make that decision. Instead, he looked them over.

"Handsome feet," he said of one.

"Mediocre shoulders," I said of the other.

The men quivered and shook as we spoke, which made us laugh, and we let them go, assuring them they would be sent ashore at the earliest convenience.

By the time we reached the bridge, Declan and Adam were agitated.

"It's all right, boys, she's here now. She has lots of boys to visit, you know," the doctor said.

"Don't be ridiculous," I told him, hands on hips, cross that he would say such a thing about me.

Adam moved to the doorway, filling it completely.

"Let her out, Adam," the doctor said, his voice thin, nervous. He saw something that I had not; Declan reaching for me.

Oh, God.

Then Adam too and I'm sandwiched between them, breathless, feeling such pressure, such awful pressure.

"Doctor?" I said, but he shook his head helplessly. I went limp but that had the opposite effect; they simply held me tighter.

He stood there just as helplessly as Adam pressed his fingers to my throat.

"I'll bring you back," Doctor Firth said. "Small and beautiful and perfect."

I tried to shake my head no; I tried to beg him no.

"You won't know," he said, so quiet in my ear I thought I was dreaming. "At least that," and I hoped to God he was right.

ABOUT THE AUTHORS

Rose Biggin is a writer and theatre artist based in London. Her published fiction includes "A Game Proposition" in *Irregularity*, "The Modjeska Waltz" in *The Adventures of Moriarty* and "The Gunman Who Came In From The Door" in *Defenestration*.

Her writing for theatre includes genderqueer retelling *Victor Frankenstein, Plunge*—a play about coffee and culture that flows backwards in time—and Live Art performance *BADASS GRAMMAR: A Pole/Guitar Composition in Exploded View*. Her book *Immersive Theatre and Audience Experience* is published by Palgrave.

Paul Meloy was born in 1966 in South London. He is the author of *Islington Crocodiles* and *Dogs with Their Eyes Shut*, and the collection *Electric Breakfast*. His work has been published in *Black Static*, *Interzone* and a variety of award winning anthologies. He lives in Devon with his family.

Emma Newman writes short stories, novels and novella in multiple speculative fiction genres. She won the British Fantasy Society Best Short Story Award 2015 and *Between Two Thorns*, the first book in Emma's *Split Worlds* urban fantasy series, was shortlisted for the BFS Best Novel and Best Newcomer 2014 awards. Her science-fiction novels, *Planetfall* and *After Atlas*, are published by Roc.

Emma is an audiobook narrator and also co-writes and hosts the Hugo-nominated, Alfie Award winning podcast *Tea and Jeopardy* which involves tea, cake, mild peril and singing chickens. Her hobbies include dressmaking and playing RPGs.

She blogs at www.enewman.co.uk and can be found as @emapocalyptic on Twitter.

Tade Thompson lives and works in the south of England. He is the author of *Rosewater* (winner of the Nommo Award and John W. Campbell finalist), *The Murders of Molly Southbourne* (nominated for the Shirley Jackson Award and the British Science Fiction Award), and *Making Wolf* (winner of the Golden Tentacle Award). His interests include jazz, visual arts and MMA. He is addicted to reading.

Shirley Jackson Award Winner **Kaaron Warren** published her first short story in 1993 and has had stories in print every year since. She has lived in Melbourne, Sydney, Canberra and Fiji. She has published five novels (*Slights*, *Walking the Tree*, *Mistification*, *The Grief Hole*, which won all three Australian genre awards and her latest, *Tide of Stone*) and seven short story collections, including her latest, *A Primer to Kaaron Warren* from Dark Moon Books.

Kaaron was the Established Artist in Residence at Katharine

Susannah Prichard House in Western Australia and will be Guest of Honour at the World Fantasy Convention in 2018, New Zealand's Geysercon in 2019, and Stokercon 2019

You can find her at kaaronwarren.wordpress.com and she Tweets @KaaronWarren.

David Thomas Moore is the Fiction Commissioning Editor at Rebellion Publishing, and the editor of Holmesian alternate-universe anthology *Two Hundred and Twenty-One Baker Streets*, Shakespearean shared-world *Monstrous Little Voices*, Stokerian pseudohistory *Dracula: Rise of the Beast* and Kiplingesque anti-colonial anthology *Not So Stories*. Australian by birth, he lives in Reading, England with his wife and daughter.

FIND US ONLINE!

www.rebellionpublishing.com

/rebellionpub /rebellionpublishing /rebellionpub

SIGN UP TO OUR NEWSLETTER!

rebellionpublishing.com/sign-up

YOUR REVIEWS MATTER!

Enjoy this book? Got something to say?

Leave a review on Amazon, GoodReads or with your
favourite bookseller and let the world know!

MONSTROUS LITTLE VOICES

New Tales from
Shakespeare's
Fantasy World

Jonathan Barnes ~ Adrian Tchaikovsky ~ Emma Newman
Kate Heartfield ~ Foz Meadows

Monstrous Little Voices

Mischief, Magic, Love and War.

It is the Year of Our Lord 1601. The Tuscan War rages across the world, and every lord from Navarre to Illyria is embroiled in the fray. Cannon roar, pikemen clash, and witches stalk the night; even the fairy courts stand on the verge of chaos.

Five stories come together at the end of the war: that of bold Miranda and sly Puck; of wise Pomona and her prisoner Vertumnus; of gentle Lucia and the shade of Prospero; of noble Don Pedro and powerful Helena; and of Anne, a glovemaker's wife. On these lovers and heroes the world itself may depend.

These are the stories Shakespeare never told. Five of the most exciting names in genre fiction today – Jonathan Barnes, Adrian Tchaikovsky, Emma Newman, Foz Meadows and Kate Heartfield – delve into the world the poet created to weave together a story of courage, transformation and magic.

 WWW.ABADDONBOOKS.COM

Follow us on Twitter! www.twitter.com/rebellionpub

AN ANTHOLOGY OF
HOLMESIAN TALES
ACROSS TIME AND SPACE

Two Hundred And Twenty-One
BAKER STREETS

EDITED BY DAVID THOMAS MOORE

Adrian Tchaikovsky • Emma Newman • Gini Koch • Guy Adams • Ian Edginton
James Lovegrove • Glen Mehn • Jamie Wyman • JE Cohen • Jenni Hill • Joan de la Haye
Kaaron Warren • Kasey Lansdale • Kelly Hale

Two Hundred And Twenty-One
BAKER STREETS

This is Sherlock Holmes as you've never seen him before: as an architect in a sleepy Australian town, as a gentleman in seventeenth-century Worcestershire, as a precocious school girl in a modern British comprehensive. He's dodging his rent in the squalid rooms of the notorious Chelsea Hotel in '68, and preventing a bloody war between the terrible Lords Wizard of a world of fantasy.

Editor David Thomas Moore brings together the finest of celebrated and new talent in SF and Fantasy to create a spectrum of Holmes stories that will confound everything you ever thought you knew about the world's greatest detective.

Featuring fourteen original stories by **Adrian Tchaikovsky, Emma Newman, Gini Koch, Guy Adams, Ian Edginton, James Lovegrove, Glen Mehn, Jamie Wyman, JE Cohen, Jenni Hill, Joan de la Haye, Kaaron Warren, Kasey Lansdale** and **Kelly Hale.**

 WWW.ABADDONBOOKS.COM

Follow us on Twitter! www.twitter.com/rebellionpub

DRACULA
RISE OF THE BEAST
with stories by
Adrian
TCHAIKOVSKY
Milena
BENINI
Bogi
TAKÁCS
Emil
MINCHEV
Caren
GUSSOFF SUMPTION
Edited by
David Thomas
MOORE

DRACULA
RISE OF THE BEAST

Vlad III Dracula. A warleader in a warlike time: brilliant, charismatic, pious. But what became of him? What drove him to become a creature of darkness— Bram Stoker's cruel, ambitious "Un-Dead"—and what use did he make of this power, through the centuries?

More than a hundred years after the monster's death, the descendants of the survivors piece together the story— dusty old manuscripts, court reports from the Holy Roman Empire at its height, stories of the Szgany Roma who once served the monster—trying to understand. Because the nightmare is far from over...

Five incredible fantasy authors come together to reveal a side to literature's greatest monster you've never seen before.

"David Thomas Moore is one of the most interesting editors in genre publishing at the moment."
Starburst Magazine

"Essential reading."
SF Bluestocking on *Monstrous Little Voices*

WWW.ABADDONBOOKS.COM

Follow us on Twitter! www.twitter.com/rebellionpub